DESTINY'S
PATH

More from the same author:

DESTINY'S PATH

1. Rhiannon of the Spring
2. Govannon of the Wood
3. Merion of the Stones

www.allanfrewinjones.com

DESTINY'S PATH

Caradoc of the North Wind

ALLAN FREWIN JONES

Hodder
Children's
Books

A division of Hachette Children's Books

A Catalogue record for this book is available from the British Library

ISBN 978 0 340 99941 7

Typeset in Caslon by Avon DataSet Ltd,
Bidford on Avon, Warwickshire

Printed and bound by CPI Group (UK) Ltd, Croydon, CR0 4YY

The paper and board used in this paperback by Hodder Children's Books
are natural recyclable products made from wood grown in
sustainable forests. The manufacturing processes conform to the
environmental regulations of the country of origin.

Hodder Children's Books
a division of Hachette Children's Books
338 Euston Road, London NW1 3BH
An Hachette UK Company
www.hachette.co.uk

For James, with thanks

CHAPTER ONE

Branwen ap Griffith narrowed her eyes against the glare of the sunlit snow. Through the brittle black branches of a sheltering rowan, she could see that the sky had been swept clean of clouds; for once, winter had loosened its grip on the land and offered some brief respite from its insatiable malice.

It was a winter the like of which Branwen had never known. Relentless. Unendurable. And yet she and her small band of warriors had to endure it, live through it – *fight* through it.

Fain, Branwen's falcon, was circling low in the crystalline air. 'It seems Fain has led us a true course. That's the place we sought, there can be no doubt of it.' Branwen turned her head at Iwan's words. He was at her side now, swathed in a white ermine cloak, the hood drawn down to his eyes, the blade of his sword flaring in the slanting light.

'I see no Saxons,' added Dera, wading up the tree-thick hillside through the deep, powdery snow. 'Have we come too late? Have we failed in our mission?'

Branwen peered up through the branches again at the tall stone tower that lifted its blunt head among the higher ridges. 'No, I don't think so,' she said. She had reason to be hopeful. Blodwedd had translated the falcon's cries: *The doorways and lower windows of the old Roman watchtower are blocked with rubble – the Saxons will be hard-pressed to clear a way through without bringing arrow-fire down upon them.*

'More likely they'll have camped outside the walls,' Branwen said. 'They'll seek to starve their quarry out rather than risk a full-on assault.'

'And so we take them unawares from behind, and bathe the snow red with their blood,' murmured Blodwedd, her inhuman eyes glowing like molten gold. 'A fine plan, and good sport to warm the bones on such a day as this!'

Branwen nodded. While she did not share the owl-girl's joy in slaughter, she understood well enough the necessities that drove this war: kill, or be killed.

The rest of her band had arrived now, plodding up the forested hillside through the pitiless snow. They gathered around her, their faces pinched and pale from the fearsome winter. Aberfa, tall and heavyset, powerful as a bear. Banon with her pale, freckled face and gangling limbs. Little Linette, bright-eyed and delicate, but a fine fighter for all that. And Rhodri, friend of friends, warm-hearted and wise as the hills. White as ghosts they were, wrapped in their heavy hooded cloaks of ermine, their feet clad in tough leather boots lined with the white fur of mountain hares.

Six months fighting a war on two fronts had changed them all. It had worn them down, hardening them like iron blades forged in fire and tempered in ice water. But it had not broken them – rather it had strengthened them, moulding a ragged band into a deadly fighting force.

The *Gwyn Braw*, King Cynon called them: the White Death. And it was always upon the most dangerous missions that he sent them, missions no one else would be allowed to attempt. Far from hearth and home, and always into the very deepest peril. It was a joy and astonishment to Branwen that in all these long months of warfare, she had not lost a single one of her followers.

Branwen turned from surveying the stone tower, a plan of attack already formed in her mind. Now it was time to put it in motion.

'Iwan, Dera, Banon – you three take the left flank,' she told them. 'Rhodri, you, Aberfa and Linette go to the right. Blodwedd and I will take them from the front.'

As always she recited to her followers the litany taught her long ago by her murdered brother, Geraint. 'Be calm, be silent, be swift, be still.'

Rhodri touched hands briefly with Blodwedd before they parted. This was always their ritual when death threatened – one last touch, one final moment of bonding. Just in case.

Branwen drew her sword and tightened her grip on the leather thongs of her shield. Blodwedd stood at her side, as slender as a sapling, but hiding in her slim body a fighting spirit that outmatched even Dera's ferocity and Aberfa's overwhelming strength.

A good companion to have at your side when danger bore down, the messenger of Govannon of the Wood – an owl in human shape, wild and ferocious and merciless to her enemies. Branwen had once thought she could never befriend such a creature – but now she could not imagine going into battle without her.

'*Caw!*' Branwen smiled as Fain came scything through the trees, his wide wings the colour of rain-washed slate, his eyes like black beads, brimming with intelligence. He alighted on a branch above her head, dislodging a steeple of snow.

'Keep watch, my friend, but keep back,' Branwen told him. 'There will be arrows, for sure, and I cannot afford to lose you.' Fain's eyes had led her safe through the deadliest jeopardy, scouting ahead, warning her of coming perils. Without him she would have blundered blind into many a trap set for her by her enemies.

And she had many enemies. As many from within as from without. The traitorous Prince Llew ap Gelert beating upon them from the west, and Herewulf Ironfist's Saxon hordes swarming like rats in the east. And Powys in between, pressed like a trapped limb between two crushing rocks.

But it was not the time to dwell on the tribulations of this double-edged war. It was not even the time to ponder the implications of this latest desperate mission.

This was the time to fight.

'This is most strange,' murmured Blodwedd. 'Where is our enemy?'

Where, indeed? thought Branwen.

The two young warriors had climbed up the snow-shrouded hills, almost to the very feet of the half-ruinous old stone tower. It loomed above them now, surrounded by the winter-scoured forest, ancient and ominous with its head bowed under a heavy cap of snow. As Fain had reported, the lower windows and square entrance way were blocked with rubble. From the little snow on the heaped stones, Branwen guessed they had been crammed there by the defenders, probably gathered from the remnants of some age-gnawed wall within.

They were at the edge of a forest clearing, in a place of boulders and rocks, keeping low behind humps and ridges blurred by snow as thick and soft as silken pillows. As they stared from cover, they saw ahead of them a wide, flat area in front of the tower, where the snow was churned up and tramped down by the passage of many feet. A few arrows lay in the snow, and others stabbed down into the earth.

But a curious silence wrapped the tower, and of the Saxon besiegers Fain had warned them about, there was no sign.

'Gone?' Branwen muttered uncertainly. 'Surely not?'

'They would not have departed, if they knew who was within the tower,' murmured Blodwedd.

'Perhaps they did not know?' mused Branwen. 'Perhaps it was no more than bad fortune that brought them here. If so, they may have thought the siege not worth the effort.' She glanced at her companion. 'That's rare good fortune, if it proves true.'

To gain their prize and return to the king's court at Pengwern without bloodshed would be a rare treat. It would also remove from her mind an ominous shadow – the unshakeable fear that tragedy would accompany this mission.

'Let us pray that the Shining Ones gift us with good

fortune and an easy task,' Branwen said, glancing at Blodwedd. The owl-girl made no comment. It was a long time since the Shining Ones had shown themselves to Branwen, for good or ill – not since she had turned her back on them in the high summer and ridden hard to King Cynon to offer him her fealty in the brewing conflict. It was a promise she had made to a dying man.

Unless, of course, this monster of a winter was Caradoc's doing. Branwen half believed it might be so – some petty but deadly retribution meted out by the god of the North Wind to rebuke her for her temerity. Not that he had cause to be angry with her. She had rescued him from a hundred years of captivity.

All the same, he was a wild and a dangerous elemental; the reasons and actions of the Shining Ones were not easily understood, and defying gods was no small matter, as Branwen knew only too well.

Blodwedd's slender arm jutted forward. 'Look!' she hissed.

Some thirty paces away across the disturbed and trampled snow, Branwen saw movement in the blocked entrance. The plug of rubble burst, spraying outwards, the stones rolling black in all the whiteness.

A figure emerged from the sudden dark hole. A Warrior of Brython, clad in chain-mail and with a red cloak and a face as lined and worn as old leather. There was grey in his heavy moustache, and grizzled hair showed under his helmet. He bore a sword and on his arm was a shield that displayed the red dragon rampant of Powys. He stepped out into the open and several more armed men followed.

Branwen gave a hiss between her clenched teeth.

Captain Angor ap Pellyn of Prince Llew's court in Doeth Palas. Treacherous follower of a treacherous prince; merciless killer, sly tactician and one of the most cunning leaders in Llew ap Gelert's rebellion against the king.

Branwen had often wondered how long it would be before she met this man in battle. Had she known he would be in the party coming over the mountains, she would not have been so quick to agree to King Cynon's orders to bring *all* of the travellers safe to Pengwern. And how would Iwan react to meeting again the man who had threatened to torture him to death in front of his mother and father?

'Be wary, men,' she heard Angor call. 'We must be sure our enemy is gone ere we bring the princesses out.'

So, it seemed that Angor was as puzzled by the disappearance of the Saxons as she was. And what a curious web fate was weaving, that Branwen and her band were here for his succour. A month gone, they would have fought to the death.

Branwen rose to her feet, pulling back the hood of her ermine cloak. She leaped up high on to a boulder, her white shield up, her sword ready in her fist as she revealed herself to the men of Doeth Palas.

'Angor ap Pellyn!' she called. 'Do you know me?'

Angor started at the sight of her, his heavy-lidded eyes growing wide, his knuckles whitening around his sword hilt. 'I know you, indeed,' Angor shouted. 'You are Branwen of the Dead Gods – the shaman witch girl of Garth Milain, a shame to your kin and a blight to this fair land.'

'In the eyes of such as you, for sure,' Branwen laughed. 'But heed me! I have come in search of the daughters of Llew ap Gelert. Are they safe, Angor ap Pellyn?'

His eyes narrowed, glittering like garnets. 'What is that to you?'

'I am here in King Cynon's name,' Branwen said. 'I have been sent to lead Llew's daughters safely to the royal court.' She turned, making a wide gesture to the east with her outstretched arm. 'No way is secure between here and Pengwern,' she said. 'The land hides Saxon raiding parties aplenty. But I will guide you true, Angor, if you will follow my lead.'

'Get you gone!' shouted Angor. 'I was a seasoned warrior two score years before you were born. The princesses are under my protection and want for no other.' Cold contempt came into his voice. 'Most especially not the aid of one who worships ancient demons.'

Branwen smiled grimly. It was a long time since barbed words such as that had caused her any discomfort. 'We are the Gwyn Braw!' she called, 'the king's reavers – and you are surrounded. Do as I command, and all will be well.'

Branwen saw fury transform the old soldier's face, but before he could spit out a response, the sounds of fighting erupted from Branwen's right. All heads turned at the noise; nothing could be seen through the shrouding trees, but there was shouting and howling, the thud of weapons on shields, the clash of iron on iron, the hiss of arrows.

And above all, Branwen could hear Aberfa's roaring voice. 'Gwyn Braw! Gwyn Braw for the king!'

It seemed the Saxons had not departed.

They had been lying in wait, hoping to lure their enemies into the open – and now they had struck.

CHAPTER TWO

An arrow cut a dark path through the air, thudding into the chest of one of Angor's soldiers. And then came another arrow from the hem of trees, chiming as it glanced off the wall of the tower. A third flew, catching a man in the leg.

'Saxons, curse them!' Blodwedd cried. 'I should have known they were close by! I *would* have, if not for this deadly cold numbing my senses!'

More arrows came flashing out of the woods to the right. Several men fell. Some crawled back towards the entrance to the tower, others made no further movement.

'To cover!' bellowed Angor. He ran for the dark entrance, arrows slicing all around him. With a liquid reflex that would have been astonishing in a man a third his age, he swung his sword, striking an arrow in mid-flight and deflecting it into the sky.

'Gwyn Braw to me!' howled Branwen, throwing

herself over the boulders and racing towards the sounds of conflict. She was aware of Blodwedd at her side, and as she ran she heard cries from behind as Banon, Dera and Iwan came charging from the tree-cover.

A Saxon soldier came out of the trees ahead of Branwen, running at the half-turn, slashing behind him as Linette pursued him with her sword whirling. Straight on to Branwen's blade he ran, almost knocking her off her feet as he collapsed with a groan.

A spear sang close by Branwen's head, the sound of its passing fierce in her ears. A spear flung from behind! She turned. A score or more Saxons were swarming from some hiding place behind the tower, streaming out now, brandishing swords and axes and screaming their deadly war cries. '*Ganghere Wotan! Hel! Gastcwalu Hel! Hetende Tiw!*'

They crashed into Dera, Banon and Iwan, driving them back, their feet slipping in the slithering snow.

This new assault trapped Angor and his remaining men in the open, some few Saxons racing along the tower walls to cover the entrance while the others attacked with all the ferocity of their warlike race.

Shouts and screams rang through the frozen air and hot blood sprayed high as iron cut deep into flesh. Yet more Saxons were running from the trees now, cloaks billowing, mouths open like red wounds in their bearded faces.

With a deep howl, Blodwedd flung herself at a tall Saxon warrior wielding a double-headed axe. Her clawed fingers tore at his eyes, her mouth open at his throat.

The man blundered back, snatching at her as she clung to his chest. Blood spurted and he toppled backward. Blodwedd rose like an avenging spirit, gored to the chin, her eyes blazing, seeking new prey.

A man came at Branwen with a spear. She pranced aside, bringing the rim of her shield down on the wooden shaft, cracking it apart before twisting at the hip and thrusting the shield hard into his face. He stumbled sideways, dropping to one knee, spitting blood and teeth.

Her sword rose and fell and his open-eyed head rolled like a boulder in the snow. Even before the severed head came to rest, Branwen was poised on the balls of her feet, shield up, sword ready – eager for her next enemy to come.

As Blodwedd had said: this was good sport to warm the bones on such a day!

Branwen sprinted into the trees. Through the lattice of trunks and branches, she saw Aberfa, tall and solid, like an oak tree herself, a spear in one hand and a sword in the other, while Saxons crowded around her like pack-dogs. Branwen had no fear for Aberfa – she could deal with twice the number that assailed her.

But where was Rhodri? True, he had learned much of the art of war; it was a long time now since Branwen had cause to keep him from harm's way, and his skills with shield and sword had grown with each encounter. But she still worried about him. He did not like shedding blood and he lacked the killer instinct of a natural warrior. She feared that one day he would look into the eyes of the man in front of him, and hesitate one second too long.

Branwen ran forward, and caught sight of Rhodri. He was being beaten back step by slow step by a mighty Saxon with an axe in either hand. Tall and broad-shouldered as Rhodri was, his opponent towered over him, blows ringing down like hammers on an anvil.

But with a fiendish howl, Blodwedd was upon the giant's back, her nails feeling for his eyes, her arms pulling his head back as her sharp teeth sank into the exposed neck. There was a gurgling cry cut short, and then the man came down in a flurry of fine snow, like a felled tree.

A hard-won instinct made Branwen turn the moment before a sword would have taken her in the back. She fended off the blow with her shield and stabbed quick and true. Her enemy fell. His hot blood steamed in the cold air.

New cries erupted among the Saxons.

'*Awyrigende galdere! Awyrigende Waelisc galdere!*'

A fierce smile widened on Branwen's face. She had heard those fearful cries before – many times.

'*It is the accursed shaman! The damned waelisc shaman girl!*'

In their brutal language *waelisc* simply meant foreign. They, the invaders of Brython, referred to its native people as *foreigners* in their overweening arrogance! But there was fear now in the Saxon voices. They had not reckoned on confronting the fearsome waelisc shaman and her followers.

Branwen swung her sword. '*Astyrfan!*' she howled. '*Astyrfan!*' A Saxon word she knew well. *Kill! Kill!*

Her followers took up the war cry till the snowy hills rang with it.

Kill! Kill!

Arrows flew from Rhodri's bow. Dera's sword weaved a net of gleaming fire around her head as she plunged into the fray. Iwan pursued fleeing Saxons and cut them down.

'Do not follow them!' Branwen shouted as the last of the Saxons went pounding away through the trees. 'Let them limp home, if they can, to tell others of the dread of the Gwyn Braw of Powys!'

It had become her custom always to leave someone alive to spread the word about the dreadful shaman girl and her warriors. The more the stories were told, the greater would be their fear. Fear was a greater weapon than any forged of iron. If men fled from her, she would not need to slaughter them, and already she felt the weight of too many deaths upon her head. Not that she flinched when need drove her to aim for throat or heart. But her own blood lust in battle worried her. She dreaded that one day the red mist would fall down over her eyes never to rise again. On that day she truly would become the thing that everyone feared.

She strode from the trees, sheathing her sword and slinging her shield over her back.

Angor was standing close to the tower's entrance, panting a little, his sword bloody and two Saxons dead at his feet. Of his soldiers, five lay dead, three were injured and another two showed no sign of hurt.

Iwan turned from the forest, grinning from ear to ear. 'This Mercian rabble grows more cowardly by the day!' he called.

Banon's voice was raised in response. 'They are like vermin before the broom of the good housekeeper of Brython!'

Aberfa and Linette came out of the trees, Aberfa's weighty arm about Linette's slim shoulders. Rhodri and Blodwedd were not far behind them, the owl-girl wiping the blood off her face with her sleeve.

Iwan came to a halt, staring at Angor with narrowed

eyes. A muscle jerked in his cheek; Branwen knew he was recalling his last encounter with the captain, at the gates of Gwylan Canu. Angor had promised his parents that their son would suffer an agonizing death if they did not open the gates of their citadel to him.

Iwan never took his eyes off Angor. 'You are in our debt, Captain,' he said with a sly smile. 'But you need give us no word of thanks; it is enough to see the gratitude in your kindly eyes.'

Angor scowled but said nothing.

Dera was less insouciant. She confronted Captain Angor, her black hair like a banner down her back as she looked into the old warrior's face. 'Well now, you are saved from your folly by the Gwyn Braw, and yet *I* see no gratitude in your eyes, old man.'

Angor stared her down, his face stern and grim. 'Have you no shame, daughter of Dagonet ap Wadu?' he snarled. 'To take arms with the witch girl of the dead gods? Your father must howl his misery to the stars that ever you were born.'

Dera gave a hiss of rage and half drew her sword. Banon leaped forward and caught her arm, dragging her away from the sneering captain.

'Peace, Dera,' Branwen demanded, standing between her and the captain. 'Remember why we are here.'

'I remember well enough!' spat Dera. 'And it was not

my will that we should play nursemaid to Llew ap Gelert's brats. For all of me, we should leave them to this man's care and see them all dead ere nightfall!'

'That would have no honour in it,' Blodwedd responded, gliding up to Angor and gazing up into his face. 'You believe that Branwen follows dead gods, human?' she hissed, her voice as soft and deadly as snakes. 'The Shining Ones are not dead. Look you, man – their eyes are upon you even now.' Her own eyes widened to golden wheels, and Branwen saw alarm and distaste battle in Angor's face before he tore his gaze from hers and turned to stare fixedly at Branwen.

'Do you have no control over the demons and fools in your charge?' he said, a note of derision entering his voice. 'Do your worst. I do not fear you, Branwen ap Braw!'

Branwen ap Braw – *Branwen, Death's daughter.*

'Branwen ap *Braw*, is it?' Rhodri said mildly. 'I think her mother would take offence at that jibe, Captain Angor.'

'Why waste words on this wretch?' demanded Aberfa. 'Let us fetch the girls from their hiding holes and get away from here as quick as we may. The wind is getting up and I'd be under shelter before the night falls.'

'We shall depart in a moment,' agreed Branwen. She held Angor's eyes. 'Your path is yours to choose,' she said calmly. 'You will release the daughters of Llew ap

Gelert into our custody, but whether you come with us to Pengwern or make your way elsewhere, I care not.' She eyed the three injured men. 'It is a long path that will take you back to Doeth Palas, Captain Angor. For your men's sakes, I'd have you in my party – so long as you will obey my commands.'

Angor's eyes blazed. 'That I shall never do!'

'Then they will likely perish of their wounds,' Iwan said. 'Cursing you for a stubborn fool with their last breaths.'

'I have healing skills, Captain Angor,' added Rhodri. 'I will tend your men whether you come with us or no.'

'He will take the road to Pengwern with you, do not doubt it,' said a new voice from the half-blocked entrance to the tower; a female voice, young but full of authority. 'Captain Angor will follow my commands, or my father will have his head!'

And so saying, Meredith ap Llew, eldest daughter of the prince of Bras Mynydd, stepped out over the rubble and came into the open.

'Greetings to you, Branwen ap Griffith,' she said. 'Far have we both travelled since last we saw one another under my father's roof in Doeth Palas.' She bowed her head. 'My life is in your hands. I know we were never friends, but I hope you will see me safe to my wedding with the king's son.'

CHAPTER THREE

It was so strange for Branwen to encounter the daughter of Llew ap Gelert under such circumstances that for a few moments she could do no more than gaze at her in silence.

They had last seen one another during the long-lost summer before the war had begun. They were of an age, the two girls, but shared nothing else in common. Spoilt and pampered, Branwen had thought Meredith and her younger sister Romney, forever preening themselves, their soft bodies draped in silken gowns, their minds empty and vain.

They in turn thought her quite the barbarian – an unsophisticated ruffian from the eastern wildernesses. And they were not slow to show her their disdain, nor their amusement at her unkempt appearance.

But it seemed the journey across Bras Mynydd and over the mountains had taken their toll on the elder sister.

Meredith's usually immaculate hair was a ruin of half-fallen braids and knots, gleaming here and there with displaced green and yellow jewels. There was grime on her face and her thick woollen cloak was dirtied and frayed about the hem. Her slender face was still beautiful, but there was a new, haggard look to her features, and in her eyes Branwen saw fear and misery.

After the space of maybe five heartbeats, Branwen found her voice. 'Well met, Meredith,' she said in as kindly a tone as she could manage. 'You need have no fear. Where is your sister? I was told she would be travelling with you.'

'She is in an upper room,' said Meredith. 'She is very frightened and she is sick with cold and hunger.' A tear crept down her face. 'Our servants are dead and our carriage and horses taken by the Saxons. How are we to get to Pengwern now?'

Captain Angor dropped to one knee in front of her. 'I gave a promise to your father to deliver you and the Lady Romney safe and well into the king's court,' he said. 'I won't fail you.'

'I will find Princess Romney,' said Rhodri, stepping up on to the rubble that spilled from the entrance way. 'Then we should get away from here. Blodwedd is right – the Saxons may rally in the forest and return.'

'Yes,' agreed Branwen. 'Linette, Banon? Go and fetch

our horses. We shall have to ride double to give everyone a seat, but speed is of the essence.' She looked up into the sky. The sun was gone now, dusk seeping across the pale wintry blue, throwing down long shadows. She turned to Captain Angor. 'Are you with us or not? Choose swiftly.'

'He is with you, Branwen,' said Meredith.

Angor gave a curt nod to the princess and stood up, avoiding Branwen's gaze as he went to check on his wounded men.

A fine foe to have with us on the way back, she thought. *I'll be needing one eye open for Saxons and one eye for Captain Angor on the long road to Pengwern.*

As was usual in the aftermath of a skirmish, Branwen's band moved among the slain Saxons, stripping from the corpses anything that might be of use and was light enough to be carried. Weapons were always of value, as were the thick winter cloaks and any provisions. In this hard winter, every morsel of food was worth more than gold, and as the months dragged by even the storehouses of the king were beginning to look disturbingly lean.

Fain came gliding from the filigree of bare forest branches and alighted on Branwen's shoulder, folding his wings and rubbing his beak against the side of her face in greeting. Branwen walked through the steaming bodies, one hand on her sword hilt, the fingers of her other hand lightly stroking the falcon's soft feathers. In her mind, she was already tracing the journey back down the mountains. They would overnight in the deep cave known as Cêl Crau, then make an early start down into the rough and tumble of lands that led to the king's court at Pengwern. With good luck and no unwelcome interruptions, they would be with King Cynon before nightfall the same day. Another mission accomplished. And all without a drop of Gwyn Braw blood spilled.

She smiled to herself. The Shining Ones may have withdrawn from her over the past months, but she felt sure that Rhiannon and Govannon must still be watching her with kindly intent. How else could such luck have travelled with them?

Not for the first time, she roved the horizon with her eyes, seeking among the barren trees and rocky heights for some sign that she was right. The glimpse of antlers against the sky to show that Govannon of the Wood was at hand. A star-bright jewel among the branches that would reveal that Rhiannon of the Spring was close.

She sighed, seeing nothing, but still convinced of their presence and guardianship. She knew who she was! She was Branwen of the Shining Ones. The Warrior Child whose destiny it was to be the saviour of Brython.

That would never change.

She turned to see Rhodri leading Romney out over the

rubbled entrance and on to the bloodstained snow. The younger princess was short and sturdy, with dark hair and a broad, sullen face. Like her sister, Romney was swathed in a tattered cloak and showed clear signs of her hard journey in the wild, but unlike Meredith, when she saw Branwen there was only cold dislike in her eyes.

She stumbled on a loose stone as she came into the open. Rhodri reached a hand to help her but she glared at him and drew off. 'Get away from me,' she spat. 'Do not presume to touch a princess of Doeth Palas!'

So, her travels had done nothing so far to improve her personality, more was the pity. Branwen shook her head. It was going to be a long trip home, playing nursemaid to Romney and suffering Angor's barbed loathing. A merry jaunt, indeed!

Rhodri bowed to Romney, stepping back to let her make her faltering way to her sister's side. A small smile flickered on his lips. Romney saw it and scowled. She turned to Captain Angor, who was kneeling at the side of a wounded man.

'Fetch a carriage,' she demanded of him. 'I'm cold and hungry. Bring me some food immediately, and then get us away from this place and these *people*.' She said 'people' as though she meant *vermin*.

Angor's voice was clipped and strained. 'Your carriage

was destroyed by the Saxons, my lady,' he said. 'Our horses and all our provisions are lost. What would you have me do?'

Just then, Banon and Linette came into the clearing, leading the eight horses of the Gwyn Braw. Among them was Branwen's great bay destrier, once the steed of Skur the Viking warrior, but now taken by Branwen and named Terrwyn, meaning *The Brave*.

Romney jerked a finger towards the horses. 'We can take those,' she said.

Angor glanced at the horses. 'They belong to others,' he said.

Romney looked at Branwen's followers. 'What of it?' she said. 'Does a princess of Doeth Palas need to ask permission of vagabonds? Take the horses and whatever food they have, and be quick about it, Captain!'

Angor's jaw twitched, as though he was biting back some inappropriate retort.

Aberfa burst out laughing, and even Dera was forced to smile.

'Oh, the audacity of the child!' roared Aberfa, clapping her hands together. 'She's a queen among us peasants to be sure!'

Iwan grinned, shaking his head. 'Angor ap Pellyn does not command here, Romney,' he told her. 'If you seek special treatment, ask Branwen.'

'But I'd keep a civil tongue, if I were you,' added Banon, drawing the horses to a halt.

'How dare you!' Romney exploded, her cheeks red with anger.

Blodwedd gazed at the young girl. 'If not for Branwen and the Gwyn Braw, you would likely be dead in your own blood by now,' she said. 'If you cannot be grateful, then at least be silent.'

The look that Romney gave the owl-girl was of uttermost disgust, but she kept her lips together, letting her expression speak for her.

'Let's not rebuke the child overmuch,' Linette said, looking at Romney with a gentle smile. 'She is cold and tired and far from home.'

'Keep your pity, savage!' said Romney. 'I don't want it.'

'You have it, nonetheless, little one,' Linette said.

Branwen walked up to Romney, gazing deep into the small girl's angry, frightened eyes. 'You are under my protection, Romney, whether you like it or not. You will have food shortly, but we must ride some way first.' She turned, doing a quick head count. 'Eight horses and sixteen riders – it can be done.'

'Fifteen riders,' said Angor, standing up. The man at his feet was staring sightlessly into the evening sky. 'Colwyn ap Arion will not be travelling with us.'

Branwen looked at the other two injured men. One had an arrow wound to the thigh, another a deep cut on his forehead. 'There is no time to bury the dead, and for that I am sorry,' she said. Angor nodded, as though he understood the importance of moving on as quickly as possible. Branwen continued: 'Such men of yours that are unhurt will each ride with an injured man. Linette will ride double with Romney. Meredith will ride with me. Rhodri? Tend the injured men as best you can, but do not delay us. I'd not pick my way down to Cêl Crau in darkness.'

The riders made their long, slow way down through the forested hills as the day gradually ebbed into a deep, silvery gloaming. Fingers of evening cold came creeping through the trees, nipping at toes and ears, turning breath to white fog. The snow-mantled landscape shone with an eerie ghost-light, and even the darkest shadows glowed.

Fain came and went, sometimes flying ahead and at others slowly circling the line of horse-riders, calling out sharply every now and then as if to spur them on. Stars began glittering like frost on the eastern hem of the sky. Their journey was silent, save the rattle and slap of harness and reins, the snorting of horses and the padded crunch of hooves in snow; and the occasional stifled groan from an injured man. But these sharp sounds only made the profound silence of the winter forest all the more unearthly.

Aberfa led the way, Banon riding double with her. Behind her the others rode in single file – Rhodri and Blodwedd, followed by Linette and Romney and then Angor, alone in the saddle. Branwen wasn't quite sure why she had decided to let the captain of Doeth Palas ride solo. Possibly because she knew none of her party would wish to share with him, possibly to isolate him.

Meredith's arms were wrapped tight around Branwen's waist. Both princesses had baulked at the idea of riding astride the horses, and Romney had been forcibly put in the saddle by Aberfa, the enraged child planted on the horse's back like a bag of grain.

Branwen could feel Meredith trembling at her back through many layers of clothing, and when Terrwyn's hoof faltered or slid, the princess's arms tightened so she could hardly breathe. Behind Branwen rode the four soldiers, two to a horse, and behind them, keeping a sharp eye out, were Dera and Iwan.

They came to a gloomy place where a sheer wall of rock reared on one side, and the trees fell away down a steep decline on the other. Icicles as long as Branwen's arm hung from the overhanging ridges.

Fain was ahead of them again, lost in the gathering twilight.

Aberfa halted her steed and turned in the saddle. 'The way ahead is dangerous,' she called, her breath billowing like a cloud. 'Melt-waters have turned to ice on the stones. We should dismount for a little and lead the horses on foot.'

'Can you get down?' Branwen asked Meredith.

'I think so,' came the quavering reply.

'Take my hand, and mind your footing,' said Branwen. Meredith slid awkwardly from the saddle.

All but the injured men dismounted. The ground was slick and treacherous underfoot, and their progress was slow as they made their cautious way down over the shelving icefields. All the same, more than one person slipped and fell as they descended, and the horses were jumpy at the feel of the slithery ice under their hooves.

'What is that noise?' called Iwan from the rear. Branwen had heard it too, a strange grumbling, rumbling sound that seemed to drift down to them from out of the sky.

'The snows are unstable in the high places,' Aberfa replied. 'We should get out from under this cliff as swift as we can.'

'Easier said than done!' panted Rhodri, struggling with his horse. 'I'd rather we got to journey's end with sound limbs, given the choice.'

'Speed and caution!' called Dera. 'In such an exposed

place, an avalanche could sweep us all to our deaths!'

Alarmed by Dera's words, the strung-out party edged forward down the uneven, ice-glazed path, often clutching at one another as their feet slid from under them.

After a brief time, a small, shrill voice sounded. 'No! I cannot do it! I'll fall! Someone must carry me.'

Branwen turned at the sound of Romney's voice. Would the girl never cease with her complaints?

'Come, Romney,' said Linette. 'Don't be afraid. Hold on tight to my hand. I shall not let you fall over.'

'She's terrified,' Meredith murmured to Branwen, watching anxiously as her sister's feet slithered on the ice. 'I should never have agreed to her coming with me. She thought it would be a great adventure.' She rested a cautious hand on Branwen's arm. 'I know you hate us, but Romney is only a child. Don't let her sharp tongue turn you further against her.'

'I do not hate either of you,' said Branwen. 'And it's a long time since Romney's spite might have stung me.' She smiled. 'You will both have my protection till we get to the king's court, even if Romney spits venom at me every step of the way.'

Meredith looked solemnly into Branwen's eyes. 'You have changed, Branwen,' she said quietly. 'You've grown since the days at Doeth Palas. You make me feel like a stupid child.'

'Warfare and a long hard winter will do that,' Branwen said. 'But I don't think you're stupid, Meredith. I'd say . . .' She frowned, looking up in mid-sentence as the low rumbling sounded again.

A horse whinnied in fear. Pale faces stared upwards. The rumbling noise was like thunder now, steady and continuous, and growing ever louder.

'Ware!' howled Dera. 'Find cover or we are lost!'

The rumbling deepened, burgeoning into a roaring, rushing tumult that rocked the world. Spits and spatters of snow began to rain down on them. Among the snowfall, stones and rocks cracked and bounced on the icy path.

There was no time now for caution – no time to guide the horses in safety as the snow came cascading down in thick, stifling curtains, deafening, blinding, blotting out the sky.

'We cannot outrun it!' bellowed Aberfa. 'Get under the cliff!'

Through the raging din of the avalanche, Branwen heard voices shouting and calling. She saw her comrades struggling with their horses, seeking to drag them under the meagre shelter of the cliff as the flood of snow came gushing down. She felt helpless, powerless under nature's fearsome spate.

She saw Romney, a small dark shape in all the chaos,

running the wrong way. Running away from the cliff in her terror. She saw the girl trip and fall. Linette went leaping after her. The snowfall was thick with tumbling rocks, dragged down from the mountain slopes, deadly missiles with the power to break limbs and smash skulls. Linette dragged Romney to her feet and they forged their way to cover, buffeted by the snow. Linette stumbled to her knees, and then the veil of snow thickened between them, and Branwen could see no more.

Linette will save the child. All will be well.

Now Branwen had to concentrate on her own survival. She hauled on Terrwyn's reins as he reared and kicked in the overwhelming deluge. Her face grey with dread, Meredith stayed at her side, snatching at the reins and helping to pull the terrified animal in under the lee of the cliff.

Branwen saw the dark shapes of others close by, huddling together, cowering from the cataclysm that was beating down on them. There were more cries and the frightened scream of horses, but the white spray blinded her. Her instinct was to run from cover and to help her comrades to safety, but even a single step from the cliff foot was impossible. The snow inundated her with a pounding, hammering, stunning force that drove her to her knees and sent her crawling back to safety.

Half blind, she felt Meredith's hand reaching for her.

The rush and torrent of falling snow was all around, clogging her eyes, caking on her body, making it hard to draw breath. She couldn't think for the noise, she couldn't move for the weight of snow piling over her.

She threw her arms around Meredith and the two girls clung desperately to one another as the whole world fell in on them and the howling abyss of Annwn swallowed them up.

CHAPTER FOUR

This is wrong. This is not how I was meant to die. Not like this. Not in this place. Not at this time. No! No! No! I will not allow this! I am the Bright Blade! The Emerald Flame!

Fighting against the weight that bore down on her, Branwen pulled her shield round from her back and pressed upwards with it, forcing the snow away from her head and shoulders. She felt around blindly for Meredith, concerned that the girl had been crushed. But she found her alive and gasping for breath. With her free hand, she clawed the snow out of Meredith's face. Now they had a pocket of clear air to breathe. Meredith coughed and choked, her breath warm on Branwen's cheek. But Branwen could see nothing. They were in a place of utter blackness.

Annwn, surely? She was dead and did not realize it!

'No!' she snarled. '*No!*'

Using every ounce of strength, she heaved up against the burden of snow, teeth gritted, muscles straining until her ears rang.

With a cry of triumph and relief, she felt the pressure lift away from her shield arm. A crack of pale evening light broke through the carapace of snow. She struggled to her knees and then to her feet, pushing upwards, using the shield like a plough, heaving the snow back, widening the hole in which she was standing.

She dreaded to see a dead world all about her – a world of thick, suffocating snow in which nothing had survived.

But by some turn of fortune, the aftermath of the avalanche was not nearly so dire. She and Meredith had sought shelter under a low dip in the cliff face, and it was over them that the snow had fallen most thickly. All along the leaning line of the cliff, she saw horses and people alive and seemingly unhurt.

Even Terrwyn had lived through the onslaught of the mountain. He stood close by, head down, eyes wide, snorting white fog as he shook the snow from his mane.

The dazed survivors of the avalanche rallied themselves, slapping the snow off their clothes, picking possessions out of the ankle-deep drifts, comforting their horses. They were caught in a narrow furrow that hemmed them in between the cliff foot and a high wall of snow. Occasional rocks toppled off the cliff, arcing over their heads and plunging into the dense snow dyke.

Aberfa's warning had saved them all. Had they tried to outpace the avalanche, they would have been swept away. Even the wrath of the winter-clad mountains could not harm them. The guardianship of the Shining Ones made them invincible! Branwen smiled despite the intense chill of the snow. With wet clothes, getting quickly to Cêl Crau was all the more urgent now.

An alarmed voice cut through her thoughts. Iwan's voice.

'Linette? Sweet saints, she's hurt! Rhodri – quick. Come here.'

Her heart in her throat, Branwen heaved herself out of the snowdrift and ran to where Iwan was kneeling over Linette. Romney was nearby, pressed up against the cliff, wide-eyed and shivering.

Linette was half sitting, her back against the cliff. Her long pale hair was thick with snow, her face ashen and wracked with pain. Her hands were clutched to her abdomen.

Rhodri dropped to his knees at her side. 'How were you hurt?' he asked.

'I was hit,' Linette gasped. 'A boulder, I think. My stomach.' She grimaced. 'Help me up. I will be all right in a moment.'

She lifted her arms and Iwan took her hands. She tried to stand, but fell back with a groan.

'Wait!' Rhodri said. 'Let me check the injury first.'

Others were gathering around Linette. Romney began to weep, her hands over her face. Meredith folded her in her arms and held her close.

Branwen heard Dera's voice, giving orders she knew she should have given herself. 'Angor ap Pellyn, stand where you are! Any of your men who would seek to use this as a chance to escape will be cut down.'

Branwen crouched at Linette's side. In her mind she saw again how Romney had run into danger. How Linette had pursued her. How Linette had cried out and dropped to her knees . . .

'Will she be able to ride?' Branwen asked Rhodri. 'Cêl Crau is not far from here. We can carry her if needs be.'

'A moment,' Rhodri said. He looked into Linette's eyes. 'I must test the place where you were hit. Say if I give you pain.'

Linette nodded sharply, her eyes narrowed and her lips pressed tight together.

Rhodri slipped his hand inside her cloak.

'I will be as gentle as I can,' he said.

She winced as his hand moved over her abdomen. Suddenly, she convulsed, her legs thrashing, her mouth opening in a terrible scream of agony.

Rhodri drew his hands back. 'I'm so sorry.' Branwen saw that his face was white, as though Linette's violent reaction to his gentle probing had cut him to the heart. 'I will get you something for the pain. I will be as quick as I can.'

'What do you need?' asked Blodwedd, poised at his back.

'In my saddlebag,' said Rhodri. 'There is some white willow bark, and some dried flowers of feverfew and skullcap.'

Blodwedd went skittering away through the snow.

Branwen reached for Linette's hand. 'All will be well,' she said, but it disturbed her how her own voice cracked as she spoke. 'Rhodri will have you up and hale in no time.'

Linette gave a weak smile and squeezed Branwen's fingers.

Branwen glanced at Rhodri again and was alarmed by the unease in his face. She released Linette's hand and stood up. Iwan was still at Linette's side, smiling into her face as he smoothed the hair out of her eyes.

The handsome young prankster of Doeth Palas had always enjoyed the company of pretty little Linette. Sometimes, when they had ridden together talking and laughing so easily, Branwen had envied Linette her sweet good looks and the light-brown tumble of her hair.

Memories of such petty jealousies stabbed now at Branwen's heart.

Banon and Aberfa were close by, their faces concerned. Angor and his four men were a little way off, the two injured men seated in the snow. Dera watched them closely, her hand on her sword hilt. None of the horses strayed. Fain flew watchfully overhead. All was well – or would be, once Rhodri's herbs and potions worked their magic on Linette.

Above them, the sky was afire with stars, glittering in the cold air. A biting wind came sweeping down the mountain. Branwen narrowed her eyes against its sting.

Rhodri! Work swiftly, my friend. Let's be off this bleak mountainside soon. Once we have Linette in the cover of Cêl Crau and warmed by a roaring fire, all will be well.

I know it!

The fire crackled and spat, the flames quickly eating up the tangled tracery of gorse branches and bracken. Often in this endless winter, Branwen and her followers had been grateful for the shelter and relative comfort of the cave they called Cêl Crau. They used it as a storage place, a stopping-off point for their forays into the mountains. A hidey-hole from which they could issue, alert and refresh, to battle with Prince Llew's incursions.

Hidden away deep in the long, winding tunnels of the

cave, they kept barrels of dried fish and meat, rye grain to make flat stone-cooked loaves, oats for broth, dry straw for fodder, and a plentiful supply of fresh water. Here they stored captured weapons and garments, the spoils of many successful skirmishes with the rebellious Prince's soldiery.

Although the entrance was little wider than a doorway, the cavern opened out into a yawning chamber as large as any Great Hall of a Brythonic chieftain. There was easily enough space for their horses, and the dry, sandy floor made for as good a mattress as any they could wish for.

Not that any were sleeping now, save for Linette. While still on the mountain, Rhodri had urged her to swallow a handful of small purple-blue buds, crushed to a mash between two stones. She had fallen into a deep drowse soon afterwards, and Iwan had carried her in his arms all the way to this place, refusing any offer of help.

Now Linette was lying close to the fire on a thick bed of furs, her slim body covered by three woollen cloaks. Rhodri was at her side, his hand on her brow, muttering softly to himself a low rhythmic healing rhyme.

White willow bark, white willow bark
So blood may not thicken nor eyes become dark
Skullcap, oh, skullcap, wound-healing flower
I sing to you, petals of blossoming power

Feverfew subtle in spirit and soul
Work soft your wyrding to make this girl whole.

Branwen herself was busy pounding another batch of feverfew, white willow bark and skullcap into a sticky paste between two flat stones. Linette had already been given one dose of this medicine before she had been moved, and Rhodri wanted more ready for when she awoke. Fain perched close by, watching Branwen intently, as though to ensure she mixed the healing herbs properly.

Blodwedd knelt beside her, feeding branches of rowan into the fire, tree-limbs that Rhodri had insisted they gather, although they were wet from the snow and sizzled and smoked as the owl-girl threw them into the yellow flames.

Banon, Dera and Iwan stood nearby, their faces anxious in the firelight. A little way from the fire, the men of Doeth Palas were gathered against a stooping wall, seated and gnawing meat and bread while Aberfa guarded them from a boulder, her spear across her knees. Meredith and Romney were with them, Romney huddled in her cloak so that only her dark eyes were visible, Meredith watching the scene at the fireside with an uneasy gaze.

'The wet wood smokes badly,' Iwan commented, flapping a hand at the drifting and coiling fume. He gestured to a large store of pre-cut wood against a wall. 'We have plenty of dry stuff. It'll burn better, and it won't blind us.'

Rhodri broke off his chanting and glanced up at Iwan. 'Rowan wood has especial properties,' he said. 'Trust me. Linette will feel the benefit, even if we do not.'

Iwan shook his head. 'Your ancient Druid remedies will have us all choked to death, Rhodri. Are you entirely sure you know what you're doing?'

'He knows very well!' growled Blodwedd, giving Iwan a cold look.

'Pay no attention, Blodwedd,' said Branwen. 'Iwan is being Iwan. He means nothing by it.' She was glad that she could say that and mean it. Six months ago, Iwan's mockery would have had more bite to it. Six months ago, Iwan refused even to use Rhodri's name, referring to him as 'the half-Saxon' or 'Master Runaway' – when he deigned to speak to him at all. The brotherhood of warfare had put a stop to that, but nothing could quench Iwan's mischievous spirit.

Branwen scraped up the greenish paste with the edge of her knife, kneading it together as the green juice ran over the blade. She passed the knife to Rhodri. He spoke soft words over it then peeled back the layers that covered Linette and squeezed the juices out on to her stomach. Very gently, he smoothed his fingertips over her white skin, spreading the liquid evenly. He frowned, seeming more worried than before.

'What is it?' Branwen asked.

'Her belly grows hard,' Rhodri said. 'I'm afraid there is some damage inside her that I cannot remedy.' He sighed and covered her up again. 'When she wakes I'll feed her as much of the potion as she can take. Then all we can do is to make her as comfortable as possible for the ride to Pengwern.'

'And what then?' asked Banon.

'The hope of better medicines,' said Rhodri. 'Wiser heads, perhaps. A quiet bed and the peace in which to recover.'

Branwen touched his arm. 'Don't worry, Rhodri,' she said. 'You're as skilled as any of the king's healers. Linette will get better. I *know* it. She is under my protection, and I will not let anything happen to her.'

Rhodri gave her a long, thoughtful look.

'All's well, then,' he said at last.

It was deep night. The fire glowed like dragon's breath in the flickering darkness of the cave. Many slept, and those awake nodded in the warmth, their bellies full. Branwen stood sleepless at the cave mouth, gazing out into the sky.

Low cloud had come heaping in from the north – mountains of thick, bronze-coloured cloud moving over the stars like a creeping sickness. And with it had come more snow, falling in great slow swathes as though intent to drown the world.

'At least the wind is still,' said a soft voice at her back. 'Pray that it remain so, Branwen.' Blodwedd stood at her side, gazing up into the snow-laden sky. 'Caradoc is in lazy mood this night. Let us hope he does not wake with spite in his heart.'

Branwen looked at the owl-girl. 'Is it Caradoc, do you think?' she asked. 'Why would one of my guardians act against me? Especially one whose freedom was won by my own hand?'

Blodwedd's eyes glowed amber. 'Do you think this winter was created to hinder and discomfort you alone, Branwen?' she asked, a hint of amusement in her deep voice. 'You are a great soul, my friend, and your destiny is awesome indeed, but not all the world revolves around you.'

'So it's *not* the doing of Caradoc?'

'Oh, his hand it is that draws these snow clouds over us, for sure,' said Blodwedd. 'And it is his breath that drives the blizzards. One hundred years trammelled in a box of sorcerous wood has not changed him, deathless and eternal spirit that he is.'

'I don't understand.'

Blodwedd sighed. 'No, you do not.' She looked at

Branwen. 'The feet of Merion of the Stones stand upon the very foundations of the world. Lord Govannon of the Wood has roots that bind him to the soil. Rhiannon of the Spring may flow and dance and rise at times like mist to the heavens – but she too is weighed down by the burden of the land that demands her stewardship. They are all bound to the earth, Branwen. But Caradoc of the North Wind holds no allegiance to any of these things. He leaps free, dancing his wild dance from mountain-top to moonbeam, from the eagle's back to the very lap of the sun.'

'You mean, Caradoc is . . . *different* from the others?' Branwen asked uncertainly, trying to understand what the owl-girl was telling her. 'More dangerous?'

'I would not say *more* dangerous,' mused Blodwedd. 'Forest, river and rock are each most dangerous in their way. Say instead, Caradoc is less predictable, less constant, less troubled by the passing things that crawl upon the world's face. He will act for his own pleasure, Branwen – for his own diversion and amusement. And a merry trickster he can be; his breath can bring death and mayhem, his whims unleash slaughter and misery.' She gestured up into the ocean of steadily falling snow. 'This is not an attack upon you, Branwen – nor upon any living thing. This is Caradoc at his sport. We endure it or we perish – to him, it is all the same.'

'But what of my destiny?' Branwen asked. 'Does he not care that this winter may hinder me in what the Shining Ones would have me do?'

'He does not care,' Blodwedd replied. 'And during the months of the year's turning, his powers are in the ascendancy. He revels in his freedom and his strength, Branwen. He cares for nought else.'

'And I let him loose,' groaned Branwen. 'Why didn't you warn me of this before I opened the casket that held him?'

Blodwedd looked affronted. 'You were acting upon the wishes of Merion of the Stones,' she said. 'I cannot speak against the will of the Shining Ones.'

'And what of them?' asked Branwen. 'Can't *they* keep Caradoc under control?'

Blodwedd's eyes shone with an eerie, inner light. 'Does the mountain control the wind, Branwen?' she asked. 'Does the forest make demands of the gale that rushes through its branches? Does water tell the gust of air which way to blow?'

Branwen's reply was as soft as the falling snow. 'No,' she murmured. 'They do not.'

'You are not invincible,' Blodwedd intoned solemnly. 'You are not deathless. But he is both these things and more. Beware him, Branwen of the High Destiny. Beware Caradoc!'

CHAPTER FIVE

The day came snowbound and silent. They ate a brief meal by the fading firelight, before gathering such provisions as they would need on the journey to Pengwern.

Linette was awake and in pain. Rhodri crushed some more of the dark berries to make her sleep. She swallowed the narcotic mixture, her face twisting in agony. A little while later, a kind of fragile peace came over her features.

'She cannot ride a horse,' Rhodri said.

'I could carry her,' said Iwan. 'She's as light as thistledown, almost.'

'You'd bear her in your arms all the long leagues to Pengwern?' pondered Dera. 'I think not.'

Rhodri shook his head. 'Lying flat would be best, if it can be contrived.'

'We have wood in plenty,' said Banon. 'Let's fashion a stretcher from straight branches and cloaks. It can be attached by thongs to a saddle and she can be pulled along behind a horse upon it.'

'That's a good idea,' said Branwen. 'The snow will make it less rough for her, and we can always carry her over the more uneven ground.'

So it was agreed, and a cradle of wood and tied cloaks was constructed and Linette was laid sleeping upon it, wrapped all around with furs.

While they were doing their best to make the ailing girl comfortable, Angor came over and looked dispassionately down at her. 'Will she live, do you think?' he asked.

Branwen glared at him. 'She will.'

Angor eyed her with a curling lip. 'Let us hope so,' he said. 'For otherwise she will slow us down when speed is of the essence.' His eyes glittered. 'You say there are many Saxon hordes between here and Pengwern?'

'Raiding parties range far and wide, yes,' said Branwen.

'Then she is a burden that could drag us to our doom,' insisted Angor. 'Some of us should ride ahead with the princesses. Their safety should be uppermost in your mind, Branwen of the Dead Gods.'

'And who would lead this speedy party, old man?' growled Dera. 'You, for instance?'

'Do you not understand how vital it is that Lady Meredith gets safely to Pengwern?' Angor snarled. 'Do you not want to see the king and Prince Llew reconciled by the marriage of their children, thus uniting Powys against the shared enemy?'

Branwen looked into his battle-scarred face. For once, Angor seemed to be speaking from the heart. She knew well enough what was at stake here. It had taken long months of delicate negotiations to come to this point. Even while the fighting between the king's forces and the soldiers of Prince Llew had been at its most ferocious, counsellors and highborn lords on both sides had been working to bring the damaging conflict to an end through the marriage of Llew's daughter Meredith to Drustan, son of King Cynon. Once the vows had been spoken and the two families united, Prince Llew would swear again his allegiance to the king of Powys, and together they would turn to face the Saxon invasion. In time, the children of this marriage would be the rulers of Powys while Brython remained a free land. Messengers had sped to and fro across the mountains with documents to bind the accord. Now all that remained was for Prince Llew to deliver his daughter safe to the king's court in Pengwern and for the wedding ceremony to take place.

All had been well, until a breathless and exhausted rider had come tumbling into Pengwern with the news that the princesses' party had been trapped by Saxons in the mountains. Thus had the Gwyn Braw been dispatched to their rescue.

And so the threads of all these great events had wound down to this point – to Branwen facing Angor across the injured body of a loved comrade, and having to weigh Meredith's safety against Linette's life.

She could see many eyes upon her, waiting for her to speak.

'I will not split my forces in two, Angor ap Pellyn,' she said. 'If we encounter Saxons in the wild and we are united, we'll have more chance of fighting them off. Divided, all may be lost.'

'Then let me ride ahead alone and with all speed,' said Angor, and Branwen could tell from his face and tone that he was testing her. 'I will arrive at Pengwern ahead of you and warn them of your coming. I will ask Cynon to send men to your aid – riders to meet you on the road and see you safe to journey's end.'

She noted that he did not say 'King Cynon'. Still only 'Cynon', as though he did not yet acknowledge the man's overlordship.

She shook her head. 'The clear paths to the east are lost under a cubit of snow. Alone you would never find your way to Pengwern – and I will not sacrifice one of my own to be your guide.' She stared resolutely into his face. 'I have decided. We travel as one, and

Linette ap Cledwyn will travel with us.'

'A fool's decision,' Angor said. 'A weak decision! But often the squalling of an infant shouts down the wise voice of an elder. So be it; I shall have the princesses make ready. Their deaths will be upon your head.' As he turned away from her, she saw a flicker of malice come and go in his eyes, like the flashing blade of a knife. She wondered how far he would go to bring her down. She hoped she would not need to find out.

After the stifling warmth of the fire-lit cave, the outside world was bleak and barren, chilling to the bones. As Branwen had predicted, the world ahead of them was lost beneath the snow, the undulating white landscape broken up here and there by a black thicket or patch of woodland, or by the dark wound of a cliff or crag or bluff too steep for the lightly falling snow to settle upon.

All else was a void, a frozen wasteland that stretched away for ever, trackless, lifeless. The cold gnawed relentlessly, smarting in the eyes, sharp as flint in the throat.

Branwen had organized the party in a similar fashion to the previous evening, save that she now took the lead. Terrwyn was the strongest of the horses, and his task was to forge a way into the high snowdrifts, making a passage through which the others might more easily follow. After her came Banon and Aberfa, followed by Angor, to whom she had now given the charge of Romney. With the child in his care, she hoped he would be less likely to cause problems on the way. Branwen had noticed that the little princess had become subdued and withdrawn since the avalanche. Maybe she was feeling guilty that Linette had been hurt rescuing her. Or maybe she simply lacked the strength to carp and whine. Either way, Branwen was glad of the silence.

Behind Captain Angor came his four soldiers, and keeping a watchful eye on them, riding alone in case she had to take some swift action, was Dera. At Dera's back rode Iwan, the hastily made stretcher tied to his saddle, jutting down at an angle into the snow, its wooden ends jolting a little over the trampled ground. Linette slept deeply now, tied securely to her rough cradle under a heap of warming blankets, her face as bloodless as the snow.

Bringing up the rear of the party were Rhodri and Blodwedd, Rhodri wincing at every jolt and jar of the makeshift carrier ahead of him.

Meredith sat at Branwen's back as before, but she did not cling on so tight now they were on more level ground; instead, Branwen could feel her fists clutching handfuls of her cloak.

'How long will it take us to get to Pengwern?' Meredith

asked as they came down out of the mountains and began to tunnel their way through the featureless snow banks and into the bleak east.

'A single day's ride, even at this slow pace,' said Branwen. 'The further east we travel, the less deep will the snow be. I'll see you safe and warm in King Cynon's court before the sun goes down.'

'You've become very sure of yourself,' Meredith murmured. 'You were so uncertain when you first came to my father's Great Hall. At the welcoming feast, you were tricked into challenging Gavan to combat. Do you remember?'

Branwen remembered it very clearly. Gavan ap Huw had been a formidable warrior of the old wars. He had become her mentor for a brief time, showing her how to fight with sword and shield in the forest outside Doeth Palas. In rescuing Rhodri from Prince Llew's clutches, she had betrayed his trust in her – and worse had come. Much worse. It had been her poor leadership that had taken them into the forest ambush where he had been killed.

And yet perhaps some good had come of it in the end. It had been his dying wish that had driven her to Pengwern while Merion of the Stones and Caradoc of the North Wind had wished her to follow a different path.

Oh, yes – Branwen remembered the grizzled warrior very well.

'And whose mischievous idea was it that I challenge him?' asked Branwen.

'Mine,' Meredith admitted. 'But Iwan was quick enough to egg you on once I had put the idea in his head.' She was silent for a moment. 'Iwan has changed, as well. I mean, he is still sharp-witted and quick of tongue, but I no longer see the frivolous boy I knew from Doeth Palas.' She sighed. 'But I do not understand how he could fight against my father. How he could ally himself with that weak man . . .'

Branwen half turned in the saddle, trying to look into Meredith's face. 'What "weak man"?'

'Cynon of Pengwern,' said Meredith, her voice grown quieter now, as if she preferred not to be overheard saying such things. 'He is not the warrior king we need in such times as these. He should have stepped aside and let my father lead our armies into battle. All this bloodshed, all this death – it was all so unnecessary.'

Branwen was astonished at this. 'Meredith, your father betrayed us to the Saxons,' she said, also keeping her voice low. 'He made a secret pact with Herewulf Ironfist. He plotted against us all.'

'You don't understand,' said Meredith. 'My father is not a traitor. He explained it to me. He never intended to keep faith with the Saxon general – he *pretended* to be his friend in order to lure him to his death. All would have been well if not for your interference at Gwylan Canu. You ruined all my father's carefully laid plans when you brought down those forest-goblins on to the Saxons. Ironfist escaped my father's trap, and lived to fight again. I know you meant no harm, but it was your fault – you and those dreadful demons you worship.'

Branwen hardly knew where to start in response to this. The distortions and lies Meredith's father had been feeding her beggared belief.

'To begin with, Meredith, I do not *worship* the Shining Ones,' Branwen said, keeping her voice calm and low despite her despair at the wrong-headedness of the princess's allegations. 'My allegiances have always been to Brython, and everything I do is aimed at keeping the Saxons at bay. I was at Gwylan Canu, Meredith – I saw what happened. I saw Angor bend the knee to Herewulf Ironfist. I saw the men of Gwylan Canu led off to death in the east. I saw the slaughter and the triumph of the Saxons.' Her eyes narrowed as the memories ignited in her mind. 'And I was there to witness their downfall and defeat at the hands of those so-called "dreadful demons". Strange and unknowable the Shining Ones may be, Meredith, but they are part of our homeland and they work only to protect it – and us.'

'Poor Branwen,' sighed Meredith, her tone condescending and sympathetic. 'I wish there was something I could say to break the old demons' hold over your mind, but I don't have the learning or the skill to do that for you.'

Branwen bit down the urge to slap some sense into the girl's head. The princess of Doeth Palas knew nothing, and the things she did know were entirely false. But what purpose would it serve to try and turn a daughter from her father? Words alone could hardly do it, not when Prince Llew had been whispering his poisoned lies into her ear for all her life.

They rode on in heavy silence for a while, forging their way through the deep snow while the cold bit at their hands and the cruel north wind threw spiteful ice into their eyes. Fain was ahead of them for much of the time, a black dot low in the eastern sky, seeking out landmarks in the white desolation and then returning to Branwen's shoulder for respite.

After a while, Branwen fetched a hunk of stale bread from her saddlebag and handed it to Meredith. Looking back past the other riders, she was surprised and pleased to see how far away the mountains now seemed. They were making good progress under the circumstances and already the snow lay less deep.

On and on they plodded, the long and weary line of

horses and riders. Every now and then they would find themselves in a valley where the snow was too deep to push their way through. Then they would need to make the difficult scramble up the hillsides, their cloaks clawed by gorse, their faces slapped raw by lithe branches. At these times, they detached Linette's stretcher from the saddle and carried it up between them, fearful that they might slip and fall and cause her more harm. Fortunately, Rhodri's medicines kept her in a deep sleep, although Branwen was concerned by the bluish tint that coloured her lips.

Then the land would open out and Branwen would look up to see the steadily falling snow turned black against the jaundiced sky, and her eyes would swim and the blood would pound in her head until all she wanted to do was slip from the saddle and curl up in the soft whiteness and fall asleep.

Sleep. That would be good. All work finished, all duties done. A sleep resonant with happy memories of better winters. Yuletide adventures with her father and mother and her brother Geraint. Jaunts into the snows that ended with good food and blazing fires and tales and songs and laughter in the Great Hall of Garth Milain.

'Do you know Prince Drustan?' Meredith's question broke Branwen from her giddying daydreams. She blinked herself back into grievous reality.

'I do,' she replied thickly, disturbed by how her mind had wandered.

'What's he like?'

Branwen paused for a moment, gathering her wits. 'Have you never met him?'

'Never.'

'I think you will like him,' Branwen said slowly, conjuring an image of the nineteen-year-old heir to the throne of Powys in her mind's eye. 'He is tall and dark, like his father. Not overly sturdy, but no weakling. Well-knit, I'd call him. He has some skills with a sword and a bow and he has a sharp mind, I think.'

She omitted speaking aloud her other impressions. *The boy is more open and frank than his father, I'd say. There is something about King Cynon that always makes me feel he's keeping his true thoughts and desires secret. The king never laughs, but Drustan is often merry. Perhaps the burdens of kingship weigh too heavy for mirth. But, given all for all, I'd say Drustan has a kindlier and more generous heart than his father.*

'Do you think he will like me?'

The question took Branwen aback a little. 'Why would he not? You have a comely face, and you know how to behave in highborn company. When I left Pengwern he was away on some urgent errand, meeting with the lords of the southern citadels. But I am sure he will hurry back to meet his intended bride.' She wrinkled her brow as a sudden thought struck her. 'How do you feel about being sent to marry a boy you have never met?'

'It is my bounden duty to Powys, and to the house of my father,' Meredith said quickly, as though repeating a carefully learned lesson. 'I will be the mother to a long line of kings. It is an honour to do this. A great joy.'

'Really?' Branwen twisted to look into Meredith's face. 'Do you feel a great joy inside you then, Meredith?'

'I must,' said the girl, shifting her eyes away from Branwen's face.

'I certainly had no feelings of joy when I set off on the journey that was to end with me becoming the bride of Hywel ap Murig of the house of Eirion in Gwent,' Branwen replied. 'In fact, I resented it, if I am honest with you. But then, I had already met Hywel and knew him to be a spiteful little wretch with the face of a sickly, bloated toad.'

How curious that seemed, now she thought of it. It would not have occurred to Branwen to think for a moment that she had anything in common with the princess – and yet both of them had been sent from home to marry a stranger for the greater good of Powys. That was a bond of sorts, to be sure.

Meredith smiled a little. 'Is Drustan handsome, then?'

'I suppose he is, all in all.'

59

A spark came into Meredith's eyes. 'As handsome as Iwan, for instance?' she asked pointedly. 'I seem to recall he had eyes for you in Doeth Palas – and you liked him, too, I think.'

Branwen turned away from the princess, feeling her cheeks redden. 'Where has Fain got to? I don't like it when he's away too long.'

At her back, Meredith sang softly a snatch of a song that Branwen had never heard before.

> *. . . and the maiden she cried, I will not be your bride,*
> *For your looks and your antics I cannot abide.*
> *But the plain truth was this, that for heart's ease and bliss*
> *She would give all she owned for a single sweet kiss . . .*

And now Branwen was very glad indeed that she was facing away from the princess of Doeth Palas, as she felt her cheeks begin to burn like a raging fire.

On and on through the snow. Horses struggling where the drifts were high, moving more easily when the snow was only fetlock deep. But all the time, the unending whiteness of the world seeping into Branwen's brain so that her thoughts were deadened and senses numbed.

'*Caw!*'

Branwen was jerked out of a waking stupor by

Fain's harsh cries. The light had changed since last she had been paying attention. The day had grown more grey, the distances more indistinct. Was it late afternoon or early evening?

'*Caw! Caw!*'

These were not Fain's usual cries. He was agitated – alarmed.

'Enemies approach from the north!' shouted Blodwedd from the end of the line. 'Many Saxons on horseback!'

Branwen was alert now, all drowsiness banished. She stared into the dim and grainy north. Across the grey blanket of snow, she thought she could see a moving darkness. An oncoming clot of night, pulsating with danger.

'How many riders?' shouted Dera.

'*Caw! Caw! Caw!*'

'A score counted twice,' called Blodwedd. 'They are at the gallop.'

'A scout must have espied us,' shouted Captain Angor. 'How far is it to Pengwern? Can we outrun them?'

Branwen stared out ahead, trying to orient herself. The land rose before them in a long-backed hill. Patches of dark woodland stood atop, the trees huddled together as though in some strange tryst. She knew this place!

She pointed. 'Pengwern lies half a league beyond the hill!' she called.

'Then we must make all speed!' retorted Angor. 'The dying girl will hold us back no longer! We must race for the hill – for the safety beyond! By all the saints, this cannot be countermanded!'

There was consternation among the riders. Branwen heard the scrape of swords being drawn. Meredith gave a sob of fear. Dera's horse reared and neighed as she struggled to bring it out of line, pushing through the snow to get to Branwen.

'Take the princesses away from here at all speed,' Dera said fiercely. 'I'll stay behind with Linette and Iwan. We will hold the Saxons back for as long as we can.'

'I'll not desert Linette!' boomed Aberfa.

'Nor I!' added Banon.

Branwen hesitated, torn by indecision.

'By Saint Cadog!' howled Angor. 'Would you have us all slaughtered, fool?'

His hard words cut through Branwen's moment of doubt. 'Dera – come closer,' she called. 'You must take Meredith from me!'

'No!'

'Do as I say!' Branwen commanded. Her eyes burning, Dera urged her horse to come alongside Branwen's. 'Meredith – go with Dera. She will see you safe to Pengwern.'

Awkwardly, the girl clambered from Branwen's horse on to the other.

'Angor? Go now with Dera! Your men may go with you if they wish. We will follow as we may!'

Angor stared at her. 'Yours will be a pointless death!' he said.

Branwen returned his gaze. 'Just be sure the king leaves the gates of Pengwern open for us,' she replied.

Angor gave her a final look then slapped the reins upon his horse's neck. 'On!' he roared.

The horse broke into a canter, and then to a gallop. Dera was close beside him, and the four men of Doeth Palas not far behind, their horses slowed by the double weight of men they had to bear as they made for the long hill.

Branwen saw Meredith look back as they came to the rise, but she was too far away for the princess's expression to be guessed at.

'Do we stand and fight or do we flee?' called Iwan.

Branwen turned her eyes to the approaching Saxon riders. Their galloping horses had already eaten up half the ground between them. She could see axes and swords being brandished, cloaks cracking, bearded faces fierce and wild under iron helmets.

To stand or to run?

A dismal choice, and either could mean Linette's death.

CHAPTER SIX

'We run while we can!' Branwen called, urging Terrwyn back down the broken line of horses. She leaped from the saddle, her sword in her hand. 'Help me with Linette – cut the stretcher loose. She must ride now, no matter what the cost!'

In an instant, Aberfa and Blodwedd were with her in the snow. The thongs were cut and the stretcher lowered to the ground. Branwen tore the blankets away and sliced through the bonds that held Linette safe on the stretched cloaks.

'Iwan shall bear her before him,' shouted Branwen. 'Iwan, take these thongs – tie her to you so that you can fight if needs be.'

Aberfa helped Branwen raise the limp girl up into the saddle. Iwan threw the leather thongs around himself and tied them tight under Linette's armpits. He looked down at Branwen, his sword in his fist. 'While I live, so shall she!' he said, his eyes afire.

'Banon! Use your bow as you may,' howled Branwen, leaping back on to Terrwyn. She raised her sword to the sky. 'To Pengwern! None of us shall die this day! Branwen of the Shining Ones swears it!'

A moment later, all were mounted again and so the mad race began. Branwen knew that her great bay destrier could have gone like the wind had she given the noble beast its head. But she had no intention of outriding her comrades. To arrive safe at Pengwern and leave her friends as corpses in her wake? It wasn't to be thought of. So she held back a little, letting Iwan take the lead, Banon and Aberfa half an ell behind, Rhodri and Blodwedd riding apace with Branwen. Fain flew with them, skimming on the wind above Branwen's head, shrieking encouragement.

The Saxons were no more than three furlongs away now, and their voices could be heard, carried on the north wind.

'*Wotan! Gehata Wotan!*'

Branwen leaned forward, gripping Terrwyn's sides with her thighs, the reins gathered in one fist as the clots of snow rose like startled doves about her ears and the breath was like knives in her chest.

Iwan was riding magnificently, encumbered as he was. His sword arm was about Linette's waist, his other hand holding the knotted reins, his hood ripped back by the wind so that his long light-brown hair was plastered to his skull.

Aberfa held the reins while Banon sat behind her, twisted to one side, gripping the horse with her knees while she aimed with bow and arrow. She would not shoot unless a target was in her eye-line. Banon was too canny a warrior to waste arrows uselessly. Rhodri's face was clenched with determination as he urged his steed onwards. Six months ago it had been all he could do to remain upright in the saddle, but dire necessity had made a good horseman of him. Blodwedd sat behind him, her hands gripping his shoulders, her face filled with fury. Had she been able, Branwen was certain the owl-girl would have leaped into the air to get at the Saxons.

Even in the rush and confusion of their flight, Branwen gave a hard, glad grin to see that they were outrunning the Saxons. At one point she had feared that their enemies would come between them and the hill, but now they were edging away from the pounding mass of the enemy riders.

An arrow flew, skimming close behind Banon before arching down and stabbing into the snow. Now Banon let an arrow loose. There was a cry of triumph from Aberfa as one of the Saxon horses stumbled and fell, sending its rider crashing to the ground.

They came to the foot of the hill and began to pound their way up the long slope. Branwen saw the swathe that had been swept through the snow by Angor and the others – but of those leading horses there was no sign. They must have crested the hill. They would be within sight of Pengwern now. If the king were keeping close watch, as he ought, then the gates would be flung open – a sortie would ride out. The princesses would be safe, the mission accomplished.

The hill was not as smooth as the snow made it seem, and it was hard to move at speed up the steady slope for fear of a hoof plunging into a sudden hole or dip and horse and riders being felled. Branwen drew back a little, needing to have her comrades in her sight. If the Saxons were to fall upon the Gwyn Braw, then it would be over the body of Branwen ap Griffith.

Trusting in Terrwyn to guide her true, she swivelled at the waist, sword ready, shield still over her back. At a slower pace, she might have let go the reins and used her strong legs to keep in the saddle, but over such uneven rising ground and at such speed, she knew that would be impossible.

Arrows whipped through the air. One struck off her shield and snapped. Another almost struck Terrwyn.

Fain had not been far wrong in his reckoning – there were at least forty horsemen pounding up the slope at her back. Branwen could see their chieftain, clad in a leather jerkin, his arms encased in chain-mail, a round iron helmet on his head, his face hidden under a sinister iron mask. There was a round shield on his arm, stained red but bearing the design of the white Saxon dragon. He brandished a spear. The eyes of his thundering horse were rolling wild and there was foam at its lips.

A sudden thought came into the flurry and chaos of Branwen's mind. Working to keep her balance, she sheathed her sword and fumbled for a familiar object at her waist. A long, supple strip of leather. She slipped it out of her belt and felt for her pouch of stones.

An arrow came at her and she lifted a shoulder, so that her shield fended it off. The galloping Saxons were so close behind her now that she could see the glaring eyes of those who were not wearing war-masks. Their shouting filled her ears, louder almost than the hammering of her horse's hooves and the beating of the blood in her temples.

With the skill of long practice, she managed to load the stone into her slingshot. She raised her arm, sucked in a deep breath and held it. She swung the slingshot twice around her head and with a deft flick of her fingers let the stone fly.

She couldn't see the stone's trajectory, but she knew she had aimed well. The chieftain jerked back in the

68

saddle, his spear falling from his grip as his hand came up to his throat. She saw a spatter of red between his fingers before he went cartwheeling over his horse's rump. Other riders jerked this way and that, to try and avoid trampling their fallen leader. Several fell in the mêlée. Horses screamed, iron rang on the frozen earth, men cried out in pain.

Branwen turned again to the rising hill. With a single shot she had brought down a Saxon – fortune was on their side! How could they not prevail?

Iwan was upon the very brow of the hill, Aberfa and Banon close behind. Rhodri's horse was high on the ridge, moving fast. Blodwedd was turned towards her, the huge amber eyes blazing with furious intent.

Iwan and Linette vanished over the hill. The Saxons howled their rage. Swords and spears drummed on shields. Arrows stabbed the ground. The Saxon archers focused their arrows on Branwen, but the shield's uncanny powers sent them all glancing away from her. There was no arrowhead forged that could pierce that mystic shield. A gift it had been, a promise of wonders to come. Made from the wood of a sacred tree, overlaid with the hide of the White Bull of Ynis Môn. An ancient thing of power and portent. While she bore it, she would know only good fortune. That was what Blodwedd had told her in the long-ago summer when she had dreamed the shield and then found it in the real world, hanging in the branches of a rowan tree.

Branwen turned to face her enemy again, and defiant words came roaring from her throat.

'Fear me, carrion!' she howled. 'None that live can stand against my wrath! Do you not know me, filth of the enfeebled east? I am Branwen ap Griffith! The witch girl of Powys! Turn back or you will all perish!'

She felt a sudden wind in her hair. She turned. She was upon the breast of the hill. Her companions were riding pell-mell down the far slope. Not far away now, she saw the black line of the tall palisade of Pengwern, and beyond, the thatched and shingled roofs of the royal court.

Out on that flat, she could see four horses moving fast towards the tall gates of timber that stood closed fast beyond the deep encircling ditch. A wild elation filled her and she began to laugh as she dug her heels into her horse's flanks and went dashing down the hill in pursuit of her comrades.

The horses bearing the two princesses were on the narrow causeway now. Branwen let Terrwyn stride out, catching up quickly with Rhodri and Blodwedd.

Now the four horses of the Gwyn Braw were galloping together on the plain that lay before the high palisade of the king's court. Branwen flicked a glance over her shoulder. The Saxons were close behind, riding like fury, slowly gaining ground.

'The gates!' howled Aberfa. 'The gates are opening!'

Yes! Branwen could see it, too. Beyond the causeway, the strong gates of Pengwern were being drawn open. Just a few furlongs more and they would be upon the narrow strip of beaten earth that spanned the deep protective ditch.

And none lost! Branwen thought. *None dead!*

The horses bearing the princesses and the men of Doeth Palas passed between the gates. Branwen's blood roared in her ears. So close now! Every muscle strained as she drove Terrwyn on to even greater efforts. The noise of hooves and harness reverberated in her head. She could feel Terrwyn's huge muscles and sinews working beneath her, his head rising and falling as he strove onwards. And on either side, she could see Iwan and Aberfa and Rhodri, their eyes on the blessed gap that had widened in the wooden fortifications of Pengwern.

Branwen gasped, staring ahead, thinking her eyes must be deceiving her. The gates were closing again. No! It couldn't be.

So close now – less than a furlong from safety. And yet the gates were swinging shut in their faces. Branwen could see men on the high walls – soldiers watching them from above.

'Keep the gates open!' she shouted, but her words were lost in the clamour of their frantic ride.

'They shut us out!' howled Aberfa. 'We are abandoned!'

They were on the causeway now, the plunging ditch falling away on either side. The earthen bridge was no wider than would allow six horsemen to ride abreast, and there were twin towers on either side of the gates, from which defenders could shoot arrows and hurl rocks upon any attacking force.

The gates thudded shut. Branwen heard the boom of the timber bars being thrown across.

She brought Terrwyn up sharp, heaving back on the reins, feeling him buck and shy beneath her. Around her, the other horses were brought to a chaotic halt under the looming gates of Pengwern.

Branwen turned Terrwyn to face the oncoming enemy. She drew her sword and pulled her shield around on to her arm as the Saxon riders galloped on.

Aberfa was right. They had been abandoned. They would have to fight alone – six against forty.

'Gwyn Braw!' Branwen shouted. 'Gwyn Braw to the death!'

And around her she heard the voices of her comrades raised in the same wild cry.

'Gwyn Braw to the death!'

CHAPTER SEVEN

Had Branwen been given time to despair, she might have despaired.

Had she been given time to wonder why the gates of Pengwern had been thrown shut in their faces, she might have wondered.

But she was not given the time.

She had time only to act on instinct.

'Iwan, keep Linette safe!' she shouted, kicking her heels in Terrwyn's sweating flanks and cantering back along the causeway towards the ranks of the Saxon horsemen. 'All others – follow!'

The Saxons had slowed, gathering at the end of the causeway, spears ready to strike, swords and shields up, their exhausted horses blowing smoke about them so that they seemed wreathed in the fumes and steams of Annwn.

Branwen came in among them like a thunderbolt, her

73

sword whirling like striking lightning, her shield beating back their blows. They roared and hacked at her, taken off guard by the ferocity of her assault. And before they had time to regroup to surround and destroy her, Aberfa and Banon and Rhodri and Blodwedd came hammering down on them like the Furies of the Underworld.

For a time of madness and chaos, all Branwen could do was stab and parry, lunge and duck, as spears grazed her and swords rang on her shield. There was a noise like a raging ocean in her head, and over her vision came a veil of red fire. An axe scythed past her shoulder. She turned and stabbed for a throat. Blood sprayed.

Horses crowded together, barging and bumping, turning and wheeling as they neighed and struggled in the mêlée. She heard Aberfa shouting. She saw Banon rip a Saxon from his saddle and leap into his place, snatching up the reins as her sword sang. Blodwedd was on the ground, tumbling over and over as she fought a Saxon soldier, teeth and claws against a stabbing seax knife.

A heavy blow hammered down hard on Branwen's shield, numbing her arm and throwing her from the saddle. She crashed on to her back, pounding hooves all around her. She was on her feet in an instant, the taste of blood in her mouth where she had bitten her lip.

The horses crowded her, buffeting her, making it hard for her to keep to her feet.

She slashed at a man's thigh and stabbed up into an unguarded stomach, sick with the pain of her fall, spinning and turning with her shield as blows rained down on her from all sides.

She saw Rhodri tumble from his horse. She saw Aberfa tall in the saddle like a mighty bear, a spear thrusting in one hand and a sword hacking in the other.

And then she felt the ground trembling under her feet and she heard war cries in the distance, growing rapidly louder.

Half blinded by the red veil of her wrath, it was a moment before Branwen realized that the Saxons were drawing off. She stood gasping, staring after them as they galloped away – those who still could. Some of the Saxon horses ran riderless, their reins flying. And even as Branwen watched, she was aware of horses streaming by on either side of her. Horses bearing soldiers who wore the king's standard – the red dragon of Powys on a field of white.

One horse came to a rearing halt at her side. 'Are you hurt, Branwen?'

Branwen stared dizzily up into Dera's face.

'No,' she gasped, amazed to find herself alive. She stared around. One Saxon horse lay dead in the bloody snow, and several Saxons were sprawled motionless on the battlefield. But of the Gwyn Braw, none seemed to have been injured.

'Why were the gates closed?' shouted Rhodri.

'They were closed on Angor's orders,' said Dera, her face angry. 'Only by threatening death to any who disobeyed me was I able to force the gate guards to raise the bars and come to your aid.'

'Treacherous lickspittle of a treacherous lord!' snarled Branwen. 'He would have seen us cut to collops before the gates and not raised a finger in our aid.'

'It was in good time that you came, Dera,' growled Aberfa. 'Much longer and we may have been overborne.'

Branwen hunkered down, wiping her sword on the cloak of a dead Saxon. Now that the immediate danger was past, she began to feel a new, sharp anger building in her. She stood up, sheathing her sword and striding over to where Terrwyn stood snorting and sweating, the steam rising from him in clouds.

'I will speak with Angor ap Pellyn,' she said, climbing into the saddle. 'I will have a reckoning with him, even if it comes to death blows.'

She twitched the reins and rode Terrwyn back across the causeway. She passed Iwan, who watched her with shining eyes. One of his arms was about Linette's waist, the other hand held her forehead so that her head was resting on his shoulder. Her eyes were blearily half open. She smiled weakly and Branwen nodded in response. Old Gods be praised! The injured girl had survived the journey.

Despite the best efforts of Captain Angor of Doeth Palas, they had all survived the journey.

The king's court at Pengwern stood in a bend of the wide River Hefren, guarded from the east by the deep, fast-flowing waters and by a high dyke that had been thrown up in ages past on the river's western bank. Only by crossing the river and climbing the steep dyke could an enemy come to the citadel of the kings of Powys from that side, and then they would find themselves trapped under a timber palisade that reared up to the height of five grown men.

To the west, a deep ditch and the continuation of the solid wall of tree trunks guarded the citadel. A narrow earthen bridge led to the gateway, upon either side of which stood defensive towers of square-trimmed timbers. Even if an enemy stormed the wooden wall and broke through the gates, they would only have gained access to an empty bailey, and would be confronted by a high rampart of packed stone.

A path wound up the side of the rampart to another gateway that could be closed against invaders and defended to the last. Only if that second gate were burst open would the enemy have reached the heart of the citadel, where over five hundred peasants, merchants, lords and soldiers had their homes.

Some said that the king was unwise to keep court in such an exposed place, hardly a day's hard ride from the Saxon stronghold of Chester, but never in all the wars that had raged over the wide, wild lands east of the Clwydian Mountains had an armed Saxon ever set foot within its walls.

And while Branwen had breath in her body and a sword in her hand, none ever would! She rode through the wide-thrown gates and into the circular bailey that ringed the inner ramparts of the citadel. A few soldiers watched her from the walls, shrouded in their cloaks, stamping their feet for warmth.

She had led the warrior band that had brought the daughters of Prince Llew of Bras Mynydd safe to Pengwern, and yet there was no cheering for her return, no glad faces, no hands reached up in friendship as she passed.

Branwen of the Old Gods, she was, a useful tool in the wars, but trusted no more than a snake whose venom might be used to poison the enemy.

She urged Terrwyn on to the slithery earthen slope that wound up to the second gateway. The path had been cleared and the snow lay in heaps on either side. There was no sign of Meredith or her sister. Captain Angor waited for her astride his horse, alone in the open gateway, his sword sheathed, his manner unconcerned, watching her with cold eyes.

Branwen brought Terrwyn up sharp, a few paces from Angor. Beyond him she could see the crowded thoroughfares of Pengwern, the granaries upon their thick timber stilts, the long houses with walls of yellow and tan daub, the paddocks and pens for animals, and the smaller huts and shanties and workshops that gathered around the lofty walls of King Cynon's two Great Halls. Gate guards stood nearby, wrapped in winter cloaks, leaning on their spears, watching them closely, their white breath gusting. Other people went about their everyday tasks, some intrigued by the two riders, others indifferent, busy with their own affairs and wanting only to be out of the piercing cold.

'You ordered the gates shut in our faces, Angor ap Pellyn,' Branwen said, her voice trembling with suppressed fury. 'To have us killed, in the name of revenge for whatever slight you feel I have done you.'

'Is that so?' Angor retorted. 'And are you not protected by the Old Gods, Branwen ap Braw? Were I to wish you dead, would not your guardians save you?'

Branwen shook with pent-up rage, fighting the urge

to fling herself at the scornful old warrior and answer him with cold iron.

Angor leaned forward, as though to share secrets. 'But know this, shaman girl, I *would* have you dead if I could, because you are more dangerous to the heart and the soul of Powys than ten times ten thousand Saxons. You would drag us back to the old ways, the *dead* ways.' His eyes flashed. 'I would rather see Oswald of Northumbria seated upon the throne of Powys than allow you to unleash the terrors of the Shining Ones upon our people.' He thumped his chest. 'We are *men*, and we will not be ruled by wood demons and water sprites!'

And with that, Angor flicked the reins, turned his horse round and rode away from her into the bustle of people. Branwen swallowed her anger. He hated her and feared her in equal measure, that much she saw. Was it always going to be like that? Would her own people never accept her while she held her faith in the Shining Ones?

A soldier of the king's guard stood on the ramparts above her, his booted feet rising and falling rhythmically as he struggled to keep the chill from his bones. From his expression, Branwen could tell that his thoughts ran in agreement with those of Captain Angor. She caught his eye for a moment, but he looked quickly away.

'They say that the heralds of great change are never

loved by their kinsfolk.' Branwen turned at Blodwedd's voice. She and Rhodri had climbed the path unheard by her, Rhodri leading his sweating horse.

'I don't need their love,' snapped Branwen. She turned and looked down beyond her two friends to where Iwan was approaching on foot, carrying Linette in his arms. Banon and Aberfa were at his back, leading their exhausted horses. Dera was by the gates, speaking with the king's riders, who had turned back from their pursuit of the fleeing Saxons and seemed in fine spirits. Others were pulling the gates together and hefting the two great timber beams into place.

Branwen slid down from the saddle and strode to meet Iwan.

'How is she?' Branwen asked gently.

Linette's eyes opened, but the usual brightness was not in them. 'I am alive, at least,' she whispered. 'It was a foolish thing you did, Branwen – risking all our lives to bring me here.'

'Hush now!' Branwen chided gently. 'Rest. Sleep. I'll see you safe abed before I do anything else.' Linette's eyes closed, but her pretty face was shadowed and corroded with pain. Branwen touched her cheek. It was as cold as death. 'You will be well again, my friend,' she said, leaning in to kiss the ashen forehead. 'I promise.'

Even before she went to speak with the king, Branwen was determined to see that Linette was made comfortable. She had fallen into a deep slumber as they laid her with utmost care on a low straw palette in a clean and spacious hut close to the western ramparts. There were no windows under the deep-stooping thatch, but the doorway looked out towards the mountains and the fire-pit in the middle of the floor gave out a fierce, welcome heat.

All of the Gwyn Braw crowded into the hut as Rhodri knelt at Linette's side, bathing her forehead with warmed water infused with herbs.

Branwen looked at her companions. They were tired and worn down by their efforts, bone-cold and wet through. But the emotion that burned most brightly in their faces was anxiety for their wounded comrade.

'Can we do anything for her?' asked Banon.

'More than anything else, she needs rest and quiet,' said Rhodri. 'Branwen? Could you send for Pendefig ap Dyfed?'

'The king's physician?' said Branwen. 'Of course – but his skills are no greater than yours.'

'But he will have remedies and herbs that I do not.' Rhodri looked up at the worried faces. 'Blodwedd will stay with me, the rest of you should leave us now.'

'Use all your skills, Druid,' said Iwan. 'Call me if she

awakes. Seeing a handsome face when first she opens her eyes may hasten her recovery.'

Druid. That was a new nickname Iwan had given Rhodri, half in jest, half seriously. Branwen had no idea whether it was true or not, but Rhodri had told her he believed he came of the ancient Druid stock – that hundreds of years ago the last of the Druid priesthood had fled their final stronghold of Ynis Môn and had hidden themselves away in the lands where his father had been born.

She hoped it was true – the Druids were said to have had formidable powers of healing and prophecy. So far, Rhodri had not shown any ability in foreseeing the future, but when it came to wounds and ailments, his skills were second to none.

'Hot food, dry clothes and a warming hearth for all,' Branwen said, looking at her companions. 'We have earned it today!' She rested her hand on Rhodri's shoulder. 'Call me if I am needed,' she said, giving Linette a final worried glance. 'I must go and speak with the king.'

CHAPTER EIGHT

The two Great Halls of King Cynon towered up side by side at the highest point of the ancient citadel of Pengwern. The Halls of Arlwy and Araith, they were named, the Halls of Feasting and of Debate. They were roofed with wooden shingles, their outer walls painted a vibrant yellow, making them shine like gold in the sun. Not that the Great Halls had seen much of the sun in recent weeks; the roofs were white with snow as Branwen strode up the slushy hill towards them.

It still rankled a little that the people of Pengwern moved away when she approached, as though they feared contagion. They were happy enough for the Gwyn Braw to risk their lives by riding out on one of the king's lethal missions, but few would meet her eye as she walked among them, and fewer still had kind words for her.

Branwen and her followers were housed in a modest long house a little behind the Great Halls – out of sight.

Branwen didn't care overmuch; they had warm beds, food, and stabling for their horses when they were not out in the winter-choked wildernesses. And as much as she felt like the outsider – always treated with suspicion and doubt by Cynon's counsellors – she at least had access to the king when she needed it. She had that much power!

The Great Hall of Arlwy was a meeting place and a feasting place, its high roof rising above a single long room lit by torches and braziers, a stone fire-pit in the middle of the hard-packed earthen floor, its walls draped with banners and hung with shields, swords and spears.

The other hall, the Hall of Araith, was divided into several smaller chambers: separate apartments where the king's family lived and slept, bowers to accommodate his most trusted counsellors and guests, alcoves and antechambers where the business of the two-edged war was considered, plans and tactics decided.

Branwen had been privy to some of these debates, called in when she and her people were needed for some especially dangerous task. A sortie across the river to snatch Saxon prisoners for interrogation. A hard ride north to learn where Prince Llew's forces were gathering. An assault from cover upon a supply line, charged with capturing the enemy's wagons and bringing much-needed food back to Pengwern.

And most recently, of course, the mission into the mountains to find and rescue the daughters of Llew ap Gelert. Branwen found it hard to reconcile her hatred of the traitorous prince with the plan for his daughter to marry the king's son. It felt to her that the king was offering Prince Llew everything that he wanted – power, influence, the expectation of his own grandsons upon the throne of Powys. And what had he done to earn these rewards? He had risen up in arms against King Cynon and thrown Powys into utter turmoil when they most needed to unite against the Saxons.

'It's sheer madness to reward him so,' she had said to Iwan, when the truce had first been mooted. 'He deserves to have his head struck from his neck – no more, no less!'

Iwan had smiled wryly at her. 'It is not madness, barbarian princess,' he had replied. 'It is diplomacy. Would you have this war go on for ever?'

'Of course not! But I'd see Llew defeated and humiliated, as he deserves.'

Again there had been the crooked smile. 'Were the king able to crush Prince Llew by force of arms, he would have done so by now,' Iwan had said. 'The civil war is at an impasse. And while we fight, we lose precious lifeblood that we will need to keep the Saxons at bay.'

Branwen had pondered this. Iwan was right, of course. The war had to be brought to an end somehow

– but it still seemed wrong. 'I do not understand why the Saxons hold off,' she had added. 'Were I in Ironfist's place, I'd use this fight of brother against brother to attack.'

'He's a more cunning tactician than that,' Iwan had told her. 'He knows that if he launches an assault, the king and the prince will unite to keep him at bay. He'd prefer to wait while we spill our own blood.'

Branwen nodded. 'To hold back till he can attack us in our deepest weakness.' She had sighed and sullenly kicked at the ground. 'You're right. There must be a truce before it's too late. Princess Meredith must marry Drustan.' She had given a curt laugh. 'And may he have as much joy in her company as I did in Doeth Palas!'

But that had been said before Branwen had met Meredith for the second time. Now she thought the princess might make Drustan a good wife after all, despite all the damage that her father had done with his whispered deceits. Not that Drustan was at Pengwern to greet his bride; Branwen had already heard word that Cynon's son had not yet returned from his tour of the southern cantrefs, although he was expected imminently.

Guards stood at the doors of the Great Hall of Araith, drawing aside to allow Branwen access. There was a main chamber, narrow and lofty, bestridden by heavy timber columns, the high vaulted roof bridged

87

by beams. At the end of this chamber stood the king's throne draped with banners and standards and backed with long silken curtains emblazoned with the red dragon of Powys, depicted with its foot upon the throat of the defeated dragon of the Saxons, corpse-white and vile.

As if wishing would make it so!

The king was upon the throne, his chief counsellors around and behind him. Sprawling or sitting at his feet were six muscular, long-limbed, liver-coloured dogs – the king's hunting hounds.

Captain Angor was bowed before the king, Meredith on one side, Romney on the other. The sight of the throne and the man who sat upon it twisted a knife in Branwen's heart. In her mind she saw again the double thrones of Garth Milain, where her mother and father had sat. Burned now in the flames that had engulfed the citadel of her home. Burned and gone, and her father dead.

In Branwen's mind, King Cynon did not measure up to her father. He was tall enough, and wide-shouldered, his forehead high, his eyes dark and sharp, his face showing both wisdom and intelligence. But there was a thinness in his lips that worried her a little, a sense that this was a mouth as apt to the cunning lie as to the generous truth. Not that she had any reason to think the king unworthy of his throne; she had been brought up to believe that all the peoples of Powys owed Cynon their allegiance. If she didn't still believe that, she would never have come here. All the same, she did wonder sometimes when she looked into his deep, dark eyes what subtle thoughts were winding through his mind.

Branwen made her way down the chamber, stopping in the shadow of one of the pillars. She could clearly hear Angor's voice reverberating between the walls.

'Most puissant and mighty King of the Western Lands, I bring greetings and fealty from the prince of Bras Mynydd,' he was saying. 'Through me, his loyal messenger and captain, he kisses your ring and bends the knee.'

'You are most welcome, Captain Angor,' replied the king, his voice smooth and deep. A voice that gave nothing away. 'We receive the greetings of our brother Llew ap Gelert, and acknowledge his fealty as is our due as his king.'

Court manners! Branwen thought irritably, hating the convoluted mode of speech used in these formal situations. *They're no brothers. They'd see one another dead in a ditch if it could be contrived.*

The king stood up now, his yellow robes hissing and swishing as he stepped down from the throne, his arms outstretched, his fingers bejewelled with golden rings. The six hounds all rose to their feet, their eyes filled with a watchful loyalty. The king had no more loyal bodyguards than them. A wrong move from any in that room, and the dogs would be upon them in an instant.

'And the most welcome of all are these two gifts that you bring with you, Captain,' the king said, extending a hand to the princesses. 'Two pearls of the west, offered into my safekeeping.' Meredith and Romney lifted their hands to his, their heads bowed. 'My court welcomes you,' the king continued. 'I hope the hardships you have suffered will be washed away by our hospitality.'

'We have suffered no hurt, my lord,' Meredith replied, and Branwen was impressed by the clear tones in her voice – after all, she must be feeling overawed to be here. 'Our father sent many gifts with us, but they were lost on the mountain, so we offer only ourselves and the gowns we stand in as proof of our undying loyalty.'

'Proofs that I readily accept,' smiled the king, looking from one to the other. 'Would that my dear son were here to welcome you, but alas, Drustan was needed in the south to give encouragement to our lesser lords so that the bulwark of Powys should have no weak links. But this is no time for talk of warfare – this is a time of merriment. Drustan will return shortly and you shall meet him and be glad!' The king released their hands and turned to the lords and warriors at his back, gesturing towards the two princesses. 'No greater gifts could the citadel of Doeth Palas have sent me, not if they had plundered the gold mines of Dolaucothi.'

'We did have gold,' replied Romney, her voice a little shrill and wavery. 'We had gold, jewels and the finest cloth you would ever have seen – but the Saxons took it all. Even my own casket.' Her voice caught in her throat. 'Someone should be sent to find the Saxons and get our things back. It's not fair.'

The king released their hands and gestured to one side, almost as if he hadn't heard Romney's petulant request.

Servants appeared from some nook.

'Go now, daughters of Prince Llew,' the king said. 'Bathe and be refreshed. We shall see you anon – tonight, there is to be a Feast of Welcoming.'

The two girls were led away to some antechamber, two or three of the dogs snuffing at their clothes as they went.

Now Branwen made her presence known, stepping out and bowing to the king. 'The Gwyn Braw have done as you commanded, my lord,' she said. 'We await your further pleasure.' If she was honest with herself, Branwen preferred to be out on perilous missions than stuck brooding in this place. Even the cruellest of winter winds was less chilling than the cold contempt of the people of Pengwern.

The king reached out his arms to her. 'Branwen ap Griffith,' he declared, his voice slightly *too* cordial. 'We are glad to see you return in safety. Are all your folk in good health?'

'Linette ap Cledwyn was hurt, but she will be well anon,' said Branwen. 'What news from the north, my lord? Will the prince come?'

This was yet another strand of the treaty to end the war – the arrival at the court of Prince Llew himself. For several months now he and his army had been laying siege to Gwylan Canu, the great fortress that held the paths between the mountains and the north sea. As proof of good faith, he had raised the siege and the gates had been thrown open to him. What Madoc ap Rhain must have thought of allowing the prince into his citadel, Branwen could only guess. Six months ago, on the prince's orders, the citadel had been given over to Herewulf Ironfist. But as Madoc's son Iwan had said, 'There is bitter medicine to be swallowed if this war is to end – my father knows that. He will drink to the dregs for the good of Powys, as great leaders must always do.'

And once the prince had been welcomed into Gwylan Canu, he would ride down the Great South Way and be in Pengwern in time for the wedding of his daughter and the king's son.

'Messengers arrived this morning,' the king replied to

Branwen's question. 'Prince Llew will arrive on the morrow.'

'Glad tidings indeed,' said Angor. 'And does his army accompany him, my lord?'

'Madoc ap Rhain will hold a strong force at Gwylan Canu,' said the king. 'Lest the Saxons seek to enter our heartlands along the Northern Way. The rest of the army will travel south with the prince to strengthen Pengwern's defences.'

One of the king's counsellors stepped forward now. 'With regard to our defences against General Ironfist, would it not be prudent now, my lord, to speak with Captain Angor so that we may learn what forces the prince can put under your command? I believe he has such knowledge.'

'I do,' said Angor. 'That and many other pressing matters are ripe for discussion, my lord.' He threw a hostile glance towards Branwen. 'In some private place, where improper ears cannot intrude.'

Branwen gave him a calm, cold look then turned to the king again. 'I am at your command, my lord,' she said.

'Go now, rest you and your folk,' said the king, one hand idly fondling the head of one of his dogs. 'We shall meet again at this evening's feast.'

'I beg leave to be absent from the feast, my lord,'

said Branwen. 'I should rather be with my injured companion.'

'We would have you at our side,' replied the king simply.

'Yes, my lord,' said Branwen, hiding her annoyance at this. The last thing she wanted was to have to sit through one of the king's feasts.

The king made a slightly dismissive gesture. 'You may leave us, Branwen ap Griffith. I shall summon you if you are needed.'

Branwen bowed low, then turned and strode quickly down the hall. Glancing back as she passed out through the gates, she saw the king's hand on Angor's shoulder as they and the gaggle of counsellors made their way into a side-chamber to talk their secrets.

Branwen went to the long house set aside for the Gwyn Braw. A grey, bleak dusk was falling over Pengwern and the wet mud was turning brittle underfoot as the temperature dropped. Torches lit up the ramparts, and here and there bonfires burned with thick black smoke, surrounded by soldiers warming themselves at the snapping flames. Lights glowed in the doorways of the houses and huts; the ordinary people of Pengwern were tucking themselves away for another frozen night. But the torches burned brightly at the entrance to the

Hall of Arlwy, and Branwen could smell meat being roasted in preparation for the feast.

In the long house, she found Aberfa, Banon and Iwan basking in the heat of the fire-pit. Aberfa was sharpening a spear point on a whetting stone. Banon was changing out of her wet clothes, having seen that their horses were fed and watered and secure in the stable barn close by. Iwan lay on his back by the fire, his hands behind his head, chewing a stalk of straw.

One wall of the long house was divided by wicker screens into individual sleeping places. Branwen went to her private alcove and changed into dry clothing before spreading her wet garments on the hearthstones and then squatting at Iwan's side to tell him of the things she had heard in the Hall of Araith.

'Doesn't it rankle with you that Prince Llew was allowed into Gwylan Canu?' Branwen asked him at last. 'Angor threatened to torture you to death outside its walls not six months ago, and yet, since our meeting in the mountains, not once have you seemed angered by his past deeds.'

Iwan opened an eye. 'What purpose would anger serve?' he asked. He made a gesture in a vaguely eastward direction. 'We have greater concerns, Branwen. Ironfist is ready to unleash his army as soon as the weather clears. Do you remember the size of the camp outside

Chester when last we looked?'

Very well, Branwen remembered it. The Gwyn Braw had been sent on a scouting mission across the frozen River Hefren to assess the strength of Ironfist's army. They had found it greatly engorged with new soldiery since they had been there in the summer. At that time there had been maybe two thousand men encamped outside Chester – but now they guessed the number must be at least double that as Ironfist drew armies from north, south and east to bolster his forces.

Branwen looked pensively into the fire.

'A kiss for your thoughts.'

She turned to stare at Iwan, only half hearing his comment. 'What was that?'

He smiled. 'You were frowning,' he said, sitting up. 'I wondered what you were thinking about.'

'I was wondering what would happen when Prince Llew arrives and Meredith is married to Drustan,' she said.

'There will be feasting and merrymaking, and many will wake the next morning with heads as thick and heavy as holm oak logs,' Iwan said.

Branwen shook her head. 'I meant what would happen to *us*.'

'The Gwyn Braw will continue the fight against Ironfist,' Iwan said.

Banon came and sat with them while Aberfa listened from close by, rhythmically drawing the spearhead across the stone.

'And are we strong enough to hold back the Saxon tide?' Banon asked.

Iwan raised an eyebrow. 'We eight warriors alone? Ha! Of course we are. We need do no more than have Branwen call Ironfist out to single combat. The last time they fought, he lost an eye. Perhaps on a second tournament he will return to his folk minus his swollen head.'

'Fain took out his eye,' Branwen reminded him. 'But I wonder more at the moment what sweet words Angor is pouring into the king's ears about us. He hates us with a vengeance, and he is nothing more than the mouthpiece of Prince Llew.'

'No matter what Llew and his trained fighting-dog may think of us, they cannot afford to lose us yet,' Iwan reassured her. 'The king will be true to us, have no fear. He also needs us while the Saxon threat looms.'

'I trust the king,' Branwen muttered, staring into the flames. 'But I do not trust the prince. I have a bad feeling about this truce.'

'Then let's be the king's eyes and ears,' said Iwan. 'If Llew ap Gelert proves false, let us be the ones who reveal it.'

Branwen nodded. 'A good plan,' she said. 'We shall watch his every move.'

Aberfa's deep voice broke the silence that followed Branwen's words. 'Will the Shining Ones aid us when the great battle comes?' she asked.

Branwen turned to her, oddly surprised by the question, although she supposed she should not have been. 'I don't know,' she said. 'Blodwedd has always told me that the Shining Ones only hold power within Brython.'

'Meaning that even if they are still friendly towards us, they may be unable to help if we are fighting on Saxon ground?' murmured Iwan.

'*If* they are still friendly,' added Banon. 'We turned away from them to come here. Will they have forgiven that?'

'I think they have,' said Branwen. 'They do not show themselves to me, but I know they are close by. How else have we done such things these past months and come to so little harm?'

'What of Linette?' Iwan asked mildly.

'She will recover,' said Branwen. 'The Shining Ones won't let any of us die.' She stood up. 'Have any of you seen Fain?'

Aberfa pointed with the spearhead to a high beam in the roof. Branwen saw the falcon perched up there, warm and snug in the rising heat of the fire.

'Good. Let him rest, he has deserved it,' said Branwen. 'I will go now and see how Linette is doing. Oh, and the king wants us all to attend the feast tonight.'

'Then we shall,' said Iwan, springing up. 'With a light heart and a ready wit.'

Branwen eyed him. 'With neither, for my part,' she said. 'But we shall obey.'

Branwen arrived at Linette's hut to find the girl asleep in the firelight while Blodwedd and Rhodri sorted herbs from a large basket and used a mortar and pestle to mash the half-Saxon healer's miraculous pastes and unguents.

'Pendefig has been here,' Rhodri told Branwen. 'He has given me herbs and roots from his own store. I think they will help.'

'He gave us a charm of nine herbs that he believes will make a great difference,' added Blodwedd, gesturing towards where small bundles of herbs lay ready on the ground. 'Mugwort, waybread, lamb's cress, cockspur grass, camomile, nettle, chervil, fennel, crab apple – we have them all.'

'And a rhyme that addresses each of them,' said Rhodri. 'Pendefig says to speak the charms into Linette's mouth and into both her ears and also recite it over her injury.'

'All the herbs were picked at judicious times and with the appropriate rituals,' said Blodwedd, floating her hand over them. 'I can feel their power.'

'That's all to the good.' Branwen crouched at Linette's side. 'How is she?'

'No better, no worse,' said Blodwedd, her eyes burning like two setting suns in the light of the flames. 'You humans heal so slowly!'

With a single extended finger, Branwen stroked a stray curl from Linette's pale forehead. 'I will tell the king we will not venture out again until she is able to join us,' she said. She smiled down at Linette's peaceful, slumbering face. 'Be well! That is an order.'

The braying of horns sounded.

'That is the call to the feast,' said Branwen, getting up. 'I must go – but I need you to stay with Linette, if you're willing.' Her comment was addressed to Rhodri – Blodwedd never came to the Hall of Arlwy. She had done so once, upon their arrival at Pengwern – but the people had shrunk away as though she carried the plague, and the king's dogs had set up such a barking and howling that the rafters had rung with it. From that time on, the owl-girl had kept out of sight as much as possible.

'Of course,' said Rhodri. 'We'll watch Linette through the night. Perhaps a new dawn will show some improvement in her.'

Branwen walked to the doorway. 'Come for me if there is any change,' she said.

'For better or worse, we will,' said Blodwedd.

'It will not be for the worse,' said Branwen.

'Pray the Old Ones it is so,' murmured Blodwedd, glancing at Rhodri.

'I have,' said Branwen, dipping her head as she came under the low lintel and stepped into the cold night. 'I have prayed and they have heard me.'

CHAPTER NINE

The hall of the great King Cynon is bright tonight
Cold is banished, and the fires leap high
Oxen roast on the bone
and mead fills the cups of horn and gold
The warriors sing of victory,
the women listen with shining eyes.
The retinue of the king have hastened forth
Armed and well shod into the bitter winter
Saxons to pursue and victories to win.
But now they feed together around the wine-vessel
Oh, my heart is full with the telling of it,
My heart swells with pride in the tale of fell deeds
But grief mingles with joy;
too many of my true kinsmen are gone
Out of three hundred that rode
forth wearing the golden torques,
Fully one hundred never returned from the battles in the east

The exalted men went from us;
they ate a final meal of wine and mead.
I am sorrowful for the loss of them in this harsh winter
May our shields resound like thunder as we remember them!
May the Three Saints lead them to their long home
And we who remain, to sweet victory!

The bard finished his song and the chime of his harp strings faded. A moment later, the quiet of the Hall of Arlwy was overturned by raucous cheering as the audience erupted into roaring approval.

The tall, grey-haired singer bowed low and then stepped away from the firelight with his ash-wood harp cradled lovingly in his arms.

Branwen and her band clapped along with all the other men and women of King Cynon's court. Gorsedd ap Gruffud was a fine singer and Aberfa stamped her feet and Iwan whistled shrilly between his teeth to show their appreciation of his skills. Branwen knew how easy it was to get caught up in the excitement and the drama of such battle songs even though the 'victories' spoken of were nothing more than passing skirmishes, as akin to the war that was coming as spring breezes were to the worst of Caradoc's blizzards.

The feast to welcome the two princesses of Doeth Palas was at its height. Meredith and Romney sat in a gaggle of court ladies at the far end of the chamber, close to the king. Branwen and her band were gathered in a little knot near the doors. Peering down the crowded hall, Branwen could see that the princesses were dressed now in fine gowns and had their hair braided and bejewelled. They were clearly glad to be at their journey's end. They hadn't been brought up to endure the hardships of the wild. She smiled to herself, quietly proud of her lean, strong body and of the skills that had kept her and her folk alive all these long months. To be soft and spoiled like them? It would be unendurable.

The warriors and merchants and ladies of Pengwern sat at their ease all around the hall, eating heartily from bowls carried to them by servants, and drinking from earthenware vessels brimming with wine or spicy, honey-flavoured mead. Branwen and her folk were glad of the hot meat and cheese and bread, but they drank only watered wine, and avoided the mead altogether. It was a sweet but dangerous brew, and one night's unguarded drinking could dull the senses for two entire days.

The king and his closest advisers sat at the far end of the hall, amid draperies of purple silk. Captain Angor was with them, and Branwen noticed that often his head and the head of the king were together as though they were exchanging private words.

Among Cynon's counsellors sat representatives of

the courts of the other three kingdoms of Brython, stern and powerful men who had journeyed far to be here. They had gathered from the court of King Maelgwn Hir, ruler of Gwynedd, from King Dinefwr of Dyfed and from King Tewdrig of Gwent. They were here to witness the marriage between Princess Meredith and Prince Drustan, to take back to their masters assurances that the civil conflict that had shaken the kingdom of Powys was truly ended.

When the Gwyn Braw had set out to rescue the princesses, the representatives of Gwent had not yet arrived, but Branwen saw them now, three grizzled warriors and one younger lad with bright, sharp eyes and a pleasant, open face. The son and heir of some powerful lord of Gwent, she assumed the boy must be. She wondered whether any of the three older men were from the house of Eirion. Half a year ago she had been sent out from her home to marry into that family. Oh, but what a strange and astonishing path her destiny had led her down since those simple times!

'I like songs of victory and triumph!' boomed Aberfa, slapping Branwen on the back. 'They warm my blood better than the hottest fire!'

'It would be a fine thing if we could defeat the Saxons by singing alone,' remarked Banon, her milk-white skin glowing in the firelight, her freckles like flecks of gold on her cheeks and arms. 'That's a contest we'd easily win.'

'Two famous bards facing one another on the battlefield to decide the fate of nations in a bloodless tournament!' added Iwan. 'I like the way you think, Banon!'

'All the same,' remarked Dera. 'The wine of victory tastes the sweeter when mingled with the blood of an enemy slain.' She looked at her companions with her deep black eyes. 'What are we, old women to wish an easy victory? Ha! I'd sooner slay the Saxons with bright iron that have them slink away untested!' She frowned, as though a sudden thought had struck her. 'And these old songs – they sound well enough, I grant – but where are recalled the deeds of warrior women such as ourselves?'

'*Men* write the songs,' Banon said with a wry smile.

'We need a song to the Gwyn Braw!' agreed Aberfa, her mouth half full of juicy meat. 'That would be a fine thing.'

'Rhodri the Druid has a way with a rhyme,' said Iwan. 'I shall speak to him about it.' He brandished his knife, running with meat juices. 'A song of Iwan ap Madoc, the fount of all that is brave and noble and comely!'

Aberfa almost spat her meat out. 'The wellspring of all that is conceited, arrogant and swollen-headed, rather!' she cackled. 'It's we women who deserve the praise!'

Iwan laughed. 'It's true that you're good enough warriors . . . for a bunch of weak little girls.'

'"Weak"? "Little"?' growled Aberfa, her eyes shining. 'Would you care to arm-wrestle me, man-child?'

'Not me,' said Iwan in mock horror. 'I'd as soon play tag with the Brown Bull of Cwley. He probably weighs less than you, for a start!'

With an affronted howl, Aberfa snatched at Iwan and he only just managed to scramble out of her way in time.

'Teach him some manners, Aberfa!' chuckled Dera.

Branwen smiled. It was heartening to see her friends at play like this – a pleasant reward for their perilous labours out in the wild.

A man came up behind the laughing band, his arrival unheard in the clamour of the feasting. The first Branwen knew of his presence was a heavy hand coming down on her shoulder.

She turned and looked into the grim, fierce face of Dagonet ap Wadu, a high captain of the king's army and the father of dark-haired Dera.

Seeing him, Dera scrambled to her feet and stood with her head bowed. 'My lord,' she said meekly. 'My greetings and duty to you, as always.'

Dagonet didn't even glance at his daughter, his eyes fixed instead on Branwen. 'The king would have you attend him,' he said.

'I am at the king's command,' Branwen said, standing up.

Dagonet nodded and walked back the way he had come. Following him, Branwen cast a sympathetic look towards Dera, who had sat down again, biting her lip and staring into the fire. As resolute and deadly as any man in combat, the raven-haired warrior girl was forever cowed in the presence of her father.

Branwen felt a stab of heartsickness as she thought of her own dear, lost father. Unlike Dagonet ap Wadu, he had been a man of infinite love and compassion.

'A word with you, sir,' said Branwen, walking quickly to catch up with Dagonet.

He looked at her without interest.

'Why do you treat your daughter so?' Branwen asked. 'She loves you dearly, and seeks only to please you.'

'Dera knows what she must do to earn my forgiveness,' said Dagonet. 'She alone chose the path she is on.'

'You'd have her part with the Gwyn Braw?' asked Branwen.

'I would.'

A response to this screamed in Branwen's head. *Why do you hate me? What have I ever done but strive ceaselessly for the good fortune of Powys?*

But what would be the purpose of such questions? She already knew the answers. She was the shaman girl of the Shining Ones. The cat's-paw of ancient forces feared by everyone.

As she walked with Dagonet to the far end of the hall, she saw that Cynon's queen was seated with Meredith and Romney. She was a pale, thin woman with anxious, nervous eyes and a look about her of a dog that was used to unkind treatment. She spoke little, and Branwen had the impression that she was scared of her husband, although she had never seen him do anything to make her afraid. In fact, Cynon hardly even acknowledged her existence.

How different from the loving and respectful partnership that had thrived between Branwen's mother and father.

She shook her head, pushing away thoughts of her dear mother. It was still too painful for her to dwell on Alis ap Owain – the warrior maiden of Brych Einiog; too hard to endure the thought of the long leagues of warfare and the long months of despair that separated them. Would she ever return to her homeland? And what if she did? What if even her own mother now feared and hated her? No! It was too much to bear.

Don't think of such things! My mother would never

turn away from me.

Branwen stepped over one of the king's dogs, sprawling among the reeds, its belly full of treats and titbits, its long tongue lolling.

The king beckoned her and she moved through his counsellors to kneel respectfully at his side. 'You wished to see me, my lord?'

'Not I,' said the king, his lips greasy from roasted pork and his eyes gleaming with private amusement. 'But someone from Gwent asked after you.' He turned and gestured to the boy that Branwen had noticed from before. 'Hywel ap Murig – come, here's the answer to your question. Here is the daughter of Prince Griffith ap Rhys.'

The boy turned and looked appraisingly at Branwen.

She stared back at him, dumbstruck.

This handsome young man was Hywel ap Murig – the fat-faced toad-boy to whom she had been betrothed as a small child?

'What do you make of her, Hywel?' asked the king, clearly revelling in Branwen's discomfort. 'Would she have made a worthy bride?' He chuckled. 'An ornament to the house of Eirion? The mother of future kings of Gwent?'

A spasm of something close to distaste crossed Hywel's face as he looked at her, but it was gone in an instant and he fixed his expression into one of polite interest as he bowed.

'Greetings, Branwen ap Griffith,' he said, his voice clear and strong. 'We meet again under curious circumstances.' He smiled uneasily. Branwen supposed he had never encountered a warrior girl like her before. 'It has been a long time. Do you remember me at all?'

'A little,' Branwen answered. 'I was very young.'

Hywel nodded. 'We both were.' He paused, as if searching for something more to say. 'I hear you are a . . . great warrior now.'

'I do what I can . . .'

Hywel looked awkwardly at her. 'You need have no fear that I am come to carry you off to a wedding bed. The tryst between our families is quite broken. Indeed, I am betrothed to Lowri ap Garan, of the House of Morfudd in Gwynedd. A fine match, so they say.'

'Oh.' Branwen could see the relief on his face as he told her this. As though he had been dreading the thought of having her as his wife! Not that she should be surprised at that. He must have heard many tales of her exploits over the past few months; and what boy in his right wits would want to be tied to a half-crazed shaman girl who worshipped demons?

All the same, it was a shock to see Hywel again like this, and to be made so acutely aware that he wanted their marriage even less than she did. And to think that he had grown up so courteous and handsome, too!

The tricks that fate plays! If not for her encounter with Rhiannon of the Spring in the high passes of the mountains, she might by now be wed to Hywel ap Murig.

How different her life could have been.

She could be far from here, safe and secure in the deep south, protected by fortified walls and by the loving kindness of her new family. Wandering the halls of her new home, dressed in fine silk, her hair styled into intricate loops and coils, woven with jewels.

She smiled, knowing herself – knowing how she would have chafed and railed at such a life. She knew who she was! Branwen of the Shining Ones – Destiny's Sword! The Emerald Flame! The Bright Blade of Powys!

She thrust out her hand to Hywel and he gripped it in some surprise.

'I'm glad you've found a more suitable wife,' she said. 'My blessings on your union, Hywel ap Murig! All happiness be with you.' She looked at the king. The smile was gone from Cynon's face. Branwen guessed he had been looking forward to watching her squirm. In that at least, she was pleased to disappoint him. 'Is there anything else you would wish of me, my lord?' she asked. 'I am yours to command, but my folk are weary from our travels in your service, and I'd have them retire for the night, if it please you.'

'It pleases me,' the king said with a casual wave of his hand, and he turned to Captain Angor, seated at his side, as though continuing a conversation that her arrival had interrupted.

As she turned to leave, she saw Angor look at her with hard, amused eyes and with a sardonic smile on his lips.

Like that cat that's had the cream, she thought as she walked back down the hall to be with her companions. *That cannot bode well for me and mine. All the same, if he has ill plans for us, we'll doubtless learn of it in good time. Or bad time, more likely!*

CHAPTER TEN

Astrange dream. Not terrible or daunting – but somehow full of a significance that Branwen could not quite grasp.

She was alone in a wide field of deep, untrodden snow. It was daytime, although the clouded sky was the colour of beaten iron and the air was brittle and grainy. She turned round, hoping to see something to show her where she was. But there was nothing. Not even a trail of footsteps in the snow to reveal how she had come to this place.

A distant sound made her start. A dark shape was moving towards her across the snow. It had come out of nowhere, kicking up great spouts and jets of whiteness as it ambled forwards.

A bear!

Some twenty paces from her, the bear came to a halt, its dark eyes staring straight into hers, wild and dangerous and brimming with an unknowable intelligence. Branwen found herself calling out to the great silent creature.

'What do you want?' Her voice sounded shrill. 'Are you going to eat me?'

The bear reared up on its thick back legs and let out a shivering roar.

Branwen fell to her knees in the crisp snow, her ears full of the noise, her eyes fixed on the mighty animal.

And then, the bear began to shrink and dwindle, like tallow in a fire. Its contours melted and changed and suddenly it wasn't a bear at all – it was the goraig-creature that Branwen had met in a previous dream.

'Nixie?' she called, scrambling to her feet.

The slender silvery creature danced across the snow, leaving no trace of her passing on the surface. Her dress floated about her delicate limbs like water spray, her hair as white as moonlight.

'I am she,' called the goraig in her high, clear voice. 'And I am come again to tell you two things of great import.'

When last she had dreamed of the goraig, Branwen had been gifted her white shield. Shortly afterwards, Blodwedd had told her of a sword that went with the shield.

'What things?' Branwen called, her breath billowing.

'Are you going to tell me more about the sword now?'

'Ahh, the sword,' called Nixie. 'In good time and if all goes well for you, then you shall hold the sword in your hand. But you shall grasp it for but a short time, before passing it to the other.'

'"The other"?' Branwen remembered that Blodwedd had spoken of another champion – a boy, chosen like she was. A child of great destiny. 'Will I meet him? Will he help me in the wars?'

Nixie ignored the question. 'The first thing of great import is this,' she sang. 'Beware the eyes like two black moons. Death lies behind those eyes!'

'Eyes like black moons?' Branwen stammered. 'I don't know what that means. Is it a person or a demon or what?'

'Secondly,' continued the graceful goraig-girl, as though Branwen hadn't spoken. 'When all is done for good or ill, and if you survive the ordeal that is coming to you, your destiny lies at the end of the young bear's path.'

And with that, the goraig began to spin ever more rapidly. Snow came flying from her like darts of ice and Branwen threw her arms up over her face and yelled out in alarm.

'Branwen?' Iwan's voice was urgent in the darkness beyond her closed eyelids. 'What's the matter?'

Branwen sat up, gasping, clutching at his offered arm. She stared at the pale blur of his face, only faintly recognizable in the grey of an early dawn.

'A dream!' she panted. 'Only a dream.'

'A dream?' echoed Banon, standing at the foot of her mattress. 'It sounded deadly!'

'Is all well?' called Dera's voice.

'Yes – Branwen had a bad dream is all,' Iwan called back.

From a little way off, Aberfa's snores rang out like ten men sawing ten logs.

'Get back to bed, both of you,' said Branwen. 'It was night fears. Nothing more.'

Banon nodded and slipped back to her bed. Iwan was hunkered down at Branwen's side, looking keenly into her face.

'Will you tell me your dream?' he asked gently.

'It had no sense to it,' Branwen said lightly. 'Hobgoblins dancing in my head, that's all.'

He frowned.

'What?' she asked, puzzled by his expression.

'I wish you would confide in me more,' he said.

She lifted her eyebrows. 'I have no secrets from you, Iwan. What do you mean?'

'Are we friends, Branwen?' he asked.

'Of course.'

There was a strange pause.

'And is that enough for you?' he asked in a voice barely above a whisper.

She narrowed her eyes. 'What do you want from me, Iwan?' she asked, surprised to hear a tremor in her voice.

'What would you *give* me, barbarian princess?' he whispered. 'If we were—'

'Ho!' called a loud voice in the gloom, cutting Iwan's words dead. 'Enemies at the gates! The Saxons are upon us!'

For a moment, alarm flared in Branwen's heart. But then she heard an answering call.

'Hoy, Aberfa!' shouted Banon. 'You're dreaming, girl! A little peace, for pity's sake!'

And as the echo of her voice faded, so Iwan slipped quietly away, leaving Branwen to lie back in the darkness and ponder sleeplessly over what he had left unsaid.

It was a raw, gnawing dawn with a wind that bit to the bone and a sky the colour of dead flesh. Branwen wrapped herself tight in her ermine cloak as she made her way across the deserted courtyards of Pengwern towards Linette's little hut. The churned-up, muddy slush was as hard as knives under her feet, and so slippery that she had to lift her legs high and stamp down hard to keep from falling.

A thin white mist wreathed the palisades, the patrolling guards looking like ghosts as they kept their bitter watches.

By the time Branwen came to the hut, her cheeks were burning and the air was in her chest like frozen stone.

The fire was burning strongly within, and the small round room was full of its rosy light. Linette lay sleeping. Rhodri was alone, grinding herbs in the granite mortar. Branwen glanced at the disturbed cloaks of his bed and the depression in the straw mattress where two bodies had lain together.

'How is she?' Branwen whispered, leaning over Linette and gazing down into the pale, peaceful face.

'She had a quiet night,' said Rhodri, looking up from his work. 'The lavender buds help her sleep, and Pendefig's charmed herbs must do the rest.'

'How long will it be before she shows signs of healing?' she asked.

'It may be several days,' Rhodri replied.

'You are concerned for her?'

He shook his head. 'She has a good chance to be well, I think. Pendefig's charms were wonderfully potent.' He lifted a hand, waggling the fingers. 'I can feel the power tingling in the tips of my fingers when I speak them. The hair stands up on the back of my neck. It's good medicine, Branwen.'

'Then what's wrong?'

Rhodri's brow creased. 'Blodwedd had a bad dream,' he said. 'She woke up wailing and crying. I've never seen her so upset. It was like trying to comfort a wounded animal.'

'She is still an owl, Rhodri,' Branwen reminded him gently.

'I have never forgotten that,' said Rhodri.

'You love her, though, don't you?'

'I do.'

'And she you?'

'In her way, I think,' he said, looking into her eyes. 'It's not a love such as grows and flourishes between a man and a woman, but in so far as an owl can love, yes, I believe she loves me.'

When she had first noticed the affection growing between Rhodri and Blodwedd, Branwen had found it perverse and a little disgusting. But she had come to accept it over the months, and now the sight of them together made her glad. It had taken Blodwedd a while to get used to sleeping as a human sleeps – lying down, curled up under furs with her head on a pillow. But now she could not sleep at all unless Rhodri was with her, his arm protectively across her body, his warmth making up for the feathers that she missed so much. But still a question burned on Branwen's lips. An intimate question she had never felt able to ask. For the hundredth time she bit it back unspoken. 'Where is she now?' she asked instead.

'I don't know,' said Rhodri. 'She ran out without even a cloak to her back. I could not leave Linette.' His eyes pleaded. 'Will you find her for me – try to learn from her what was in the dream that frightened her so much?'

Branwen straightened up. 'I will.' She picked up Blodwedd's cloak and stepped out into the icy dawn. 'And I'll bring her back if I can.'

She found Blodwedd on the northern ramparts, squatting in the crusted snow, her arms wrapped around herself, her breath gusting. She shivered, staring into the mist.

Branwen crouched at her side, throwing the cloak over her. Blodwedd's head turned. There were tears frozen on her cheeks and desolation in her huge amber eyes.

'Come back into the warm,' said Branwen, tightening the cloak around the thin owl-girl, chaffing her arms with her hands.

'I . . . am . . . a . . . coward . . .' The voice seemed to issue from a broken and ice-bound heart. '. . . such . . . a . . coward...'

'That's not true. Why do you say that?'

Blodwedd shook her head. 'I came here to do something that I find I cannot do,' she gasped. She gazed into Branwen's face with haunted, harrowed eyes. 'Did you dream the dream?'

'I dreamed of a bear that turned into a goraig,' said Branwen.

'"Two things of great import",' breathed Blodwedd. So! She had dreamed Branwen's dream. But it had affected her far worse than it had Branwen. A thin, hooked hand darted from under Blodwedd's cloak and caught Branwen's wrist. 'When you encounter the creature with the eyes like two black moons you must strike swift and hard, do you understand me?' she hissed. 'You must kill it. Let nothing stop you.'

'Do you know what this creature is?'

Blodwedd shuddered. 'I know,' she said heavily, her voice quivering.

'Is it human or otherwise?'

'It has not one shred of humanity in it,' said Blodwedd. 'It is a foul and corrupt demon. It will betray you to your death, Branwen. Kill it before it kills you.' Blodwedd's curved nails dug into Branwen's flesh, making her wince. 'When you see the eyes like two black moons, do not hesitate – not for love, nor honour, nor compassion nor friendship.'

'What does it look like?' asked Branwen, frightened to the very soul by Blodwedd's dread. 'Apart from the eyes, I mean.'

'You will know it when you see it,' said Blodwedd.

'Can't you tell me more?'

Blodwedd shook her head.

Branwen gave her a bleak smile. 'Then I'll do as you say – I'll watch for the black moon eyes, and the moment I see them, I'll cut the demon's heart out.' She thumped again at Blodwedd's narrow shoulders, trying to beat some warmth into her fragile frame. 'There. All's well. I have been warned. No Saxon fiend will get the better of me, Blodwedd. Now! Will you return willingly to the hut, or must I carry you?'

Blodwedd stood up, her eyes turning into the misty north. 'The traitor prince approaches,' she said softly. 'He has two hundred warriors at his back, riding upon two hundred war-horses. There are five wagons, also – laden with food and with gear for the war.'

'Prince Llew,' murmured Branwen, 'come at last to fill his hands with his ill-gotten treasures!' She shivered. 'I hope the king does not regret this truce.'

'I do not fear for this king of men,' said Blodwedd. 'I fear for you, Branwen of the Shining Ones.'

Branwen gazed northwards again, thinking that maybe now she too could just make out a heart of moving greyness in the white blur of the fog.

'Llew ap Gelert can do me no harm,' said Branwen, putting an arm around the owl-girl's shoulders and turning her, leading her back to the hut where Rhodri was waiting.

'What did you make of the goraig's other thing of import?' Branwen asked as they crunched along. 'The young bear.'

'The young bear will be a great warlord and leader in his time,' said Blodwedd. 'And he will never be forgotten.' She frowned. 'I see images of him in far-flung times. They confuse me. They are flat and yet they have life – like patterns drawn upon silk, but bathed in light, moving, alive, huge in the sky. Most strange, it is. Most uncanny.'

'So, Nixie was speaking again of the boy you told me lived in the south-east – in the kingdom of Wessex. The other champion?'

'Yes. He is the young bear. If you survive the coming ordeal, you will meet him, I think. Yes, you will be of service to him, unless you are already dead – and then it must be another.'

'I will not be dead!' Branwen growled, tightening her arm about Blodwedd's shoulders. 'Have no fear on that score. I will endure, whatever Ironfist can throw at me – and we shall travel together to the distant land of Wessex, and we shall see what we shall see.'

'Perhaps we shall,' whispered Blodwedd. 'If hope outstares fate!'

CHAPTER ELEVEN

The morning mists had faded away by the time Prince Llew and his entourage arrived at the gates of Pengwern. The sun burned pale behind thin cloud and the air was so crystalline and clear that an eagle perched on the roof of the Hall of Arlwy could have seen a hare running on the high mountains to the west, or looking eastwards, might even have spied the glinting spearhead of a Saxon sentry walking the walls of Chester.

At least, that was what Blodwedd had told Branwen's band shortly before they had left her in the sick-hut to gather on the ramparts above the inner gate. They stood together, blowing white breath and pulling their cloaks about them against the cold north wind. All Branwen knew now was that she was chilled to the heart, and uncertain of how to greet a man whom she despised beyond words.

Both sets of gates were flung wide for the prince, and

an escort of mounted warriors lined his route as he rode imperiously over the earthen bridge and came to where King Cynon awaited him in the bailey.

Cynon was on a white stallion, his shoulders covered by a great fur cloak that hung about him in swathes, pinned at the neck by brooches of solid gold, encrusted with yellow garnets. The golden circlet of the kings of Powys was about his brow, and a sword in a golden, finely engraved scabbard was at his waist.

At his side sat the representatives of the other three kingdoms, and at his back were gathered his counsellors and captains. And his son was there now, also. Prince Drustan, tall and erect in the saddle, his black hair swept back over his shoulders, his face as strong and proud as his father's, but smooth and youthful, and untouched by the burdens of kingship. Branwen guessed that Drustan must have returned overnight from his mission in the south. She wondered whether Meredith had seen him yet, and if so, what she made of him.

Horns rang out as Llew rode in through the gates and brought his horse up sharp in front of the king. More warriors gathered at the prince's back, reining in their horses. Hooves stamped, cold breath blew. Manes shook. The warriors were silent in the saddle. None moved. There was tension in the air, sharp as tempered iron.

Branwen's hand slid instinctively to her sword hilt.

Unspeaking, Prince Llew slipped down from the saddle and strode the last few steps to the king's horse. Branwen watched with narrowed, suspicious eyes as the prince knelt, reaching up to touch the hem of the king's cloak.

'My undying fealty, my lord king,' called the prince in a loud voice that he clearly intended everyone to hear. 'The saints be praised for the coming of this day when all misunderstandings and all grievances shall be at last expunged from the hallowed land of Powys.'

'Thrice welcome you are, Prince of Bras Mynydd,' replied the king, also speaking so that all the people gathered in the bailey and on the palisade and ramparts could clearly hear his voice. 'What animus or friction stood between our royal heart and the love of our most noble lord is all swept away by the unbreakable bonds of a newer and deeper alliance between our two families.' He gestured towards Drustan. 'My son will wed with the Princess Meredith, and thus shall the kingdom of Powys endure for a thousand years!'

There was a lot of cheering and the beating of swords on shields at this, but Branwen still wasn't convinced. Even when the king dismounted and the two men embraced like long-lost brothers, she still mistrusted Llew ap Gelert.

She was even less happy when she saw Captain Angor

step forward and kneel in front of the prince of Doeth Palas. There was a pretty pair of vipers to hold to the king's bosom! There was foul treachery fermenting in the egg!

Now Drustan dismounted and was enfolded in Llew's embrace, while the rest of the prince's soldiery and wagons came feeding in behind to fill the bailey.

'Close fast the gates!' cried the king. 'Let's to the Hall of Arlwy, where food and fires and friendship await our honoured guests.'

'I've had enough of this,' muttered Branwen. 'I'll not be able to keep down my breakfast if I have to endure any more.' She turned away and pushed through the crowds to the inner slope of the ramparts. The others followed her, and she could tell by their pensive faces and their silence that they were no more convinced by Llew's acts of public contrition and reconciliation than she was.

'But even if Llew's true face is hidden behind a humble mask of devotion, what can he do?' asked Banon as the small band made their way to Linette's hut. 'The king is surrounded by warriors that love him – and there's not one of us who would hesitate to plunge a knife into Llew's dark heart if he proved false.'

'All the same,' muttered Dera. 'I'd sooner he had been dragged here defeated and bloodied than ride in with such pomp and ceremony. How that must swell his treacherous heart.'

'I don't believe Llew will act against the king,' said Iwan. 'Not here – not overmatched by five to one. It would be madness to do that.' He shook his head. 'And yet . . .'

'And yet we do not trust him.' Branwen finished his thought. 'And so we must be vigilant and see what comes.' She held the wicker door of Linette's hut open for the others. 'And in the meantime, let's show smiling faces and merry hearts to our ailing sister.'

'Rhodri, ho!' called Iwan. 'How fares our comely comrade?'

Following the others, Branwen stooped to come in under the low thatch. She heard gasps and exclamations of delight from Aberfa and Dera and Banon and Iwan, who had gone in ahead of her. A moment later she saw the cause of their joy. Linette was propped on furs, a food bowl in her hands – and her eyes were open at last.

Praise be to the Shining Ones, thought Branwen, running forward. *They have brought you back to us, just as I knew they would!*

Linette was weak and ashen, but she was able to speak a little and take some nourishment. Blodwedd sat at her side, lifting every now and then a spoonful of broth to her lips. Branwen saw that she had difficulty swallowing, and behind her eyes was a lot of pain.

The rest of the Gwyn Braw sat around her, all gloom lifted as they told her of the things that had happened while she had slept, and chided her for her lethargy and sloth.

'To fake an injury just to avoid the ride home!' said Aberfa, patting Linette's knee under the fur coverings.

'And are Meredith and Drustan married yet?' Linette asked, her voice so soft that they had to strain to hear her.

'No, you've not been slumbering that long,' said Iwan. 'My guess is that Llew and the king will be doing a lot more talking before any marriage vows are spoken. Llew will want it in writing that his daughter's children will sit upon the throne of Powys. And you can bet he'll demand an amnesty for all his rebellious people and some kind of reward for himself for laying down his arms. I'd not expect to hear the wedding horns ringing out for some days yet.'

'Does the king have more work for us to do?' asked Linette.

'Nothing so far,' said Dera. She stood up, hands on hips. 'I wish he would give us some task,' she said. 'I do not like this inaction. I'd rather be away in the wilderness and carving Saxon flesh than wasting my time hanging around here making small-talk with the king's lackeys.'

And you'd rather be far from the disapproval of your father, thought Branwen. *How cruel that you've lost the affection you crave more than anything else.*

'As soon as Linette is well enough, I will go to the king and seek some assignment in the east,' Branwen said, smiling at the sick girl. 'But for the moment, you must do as Rhodri tells you and be a good and humble patient.'

'A little rest and quiet will help her best,' Rhodri said. 'Go now. All of you.' With a few final words for Linette, they allowed themselves to be shooed like a gaggle of geese to the door of the hut.

'Who's for some training?' asked Aberfa. 'A few passes with sword and spear to drive the cold away.'

As they were about to head for their long house, Rhodri appeared at the doorway. 'Branwen,' he called, beckoning.

She walked back to him. 'What is it?'

He kept his voice low, leaning in so only she could hear. 'Don't let Linette's wakefulness fool you,' he murmured. 'She is still very sick. The hardness in her stomach has not gone away and there are other signs in her body that I do not like.'

Branwen frowned at him. 'But she is better than she was, yes?'

Rhodri looked solemnly at her. 'Yes, perhaps,' he said.

'But she's on a long path, Branwen, and even with all of Pendefig's charms, I don't know how it will end.'

'You worry too much,' Branwen said, resting her hand on his shoulder. 'And I love you for it!' She glanced over his shoulder into the glowing hut, where the owl-girl was making Linette comfortable under her furs. 'I spoke to Blodwedd about her dream. She saw some demon that she feared would destroy me. I'm warned now and all will be well.' She tugged the hem of her cloak close as a gust came searching out of the cold north. 'I think I'll walk the walls a little to clear my mind. I still have a bad taste in my mouth from witnessing the arrival of the prince.' She narrowed her eyes. 'I wish this winter was at an end – I've had my fill of snow!'

'A horseman approaches!'

Branwen had grown weary of staring out over the bleak snowscape of the north and was about to head back to the long house to be with her companions, when the voice from the gate tower stopped her in her tracks.

She ran back up the log steps to the palisade, making her way as quickly as she could along the narrow walkway.

'Where away?' called a voice from the bailey.

'From the south,' cried the first voice, and Branwen saw an arm pointing from the top of the tower.

'Friend or foe?'

'I cannot say.'

Branwen leaned over the parapet of the high wall, twisting herself to try and see the coming rider.

There! A solitary horseman, helmeted and cloaked, carrying something that she took to be a spear. But it was still a few moments before she saw the black beard and knew for sure that the man must be Saxon.

Now more sentries leaned over the walls. Arrows were put to bows as vigilant eyes watched the horse and rider come cantering across the bridge towards the gates.

'Halt and declare yourself!' a warrior shouted from the wall. 'Die, else!'

The rider brought his horse up and untied some strings that bound something to the top of his spear shaft. He shook it out and a red banner fluttered, emblazoned with a white dragon.

'My name is Eanfrid Hunwald,' called the man. 'I have no weapon upon me. I come as emissary from General Horsa Herewulf Ironfist, Lord of Winwaed, commander of King Oswald's armies in Mercia.'

'You come with messages from Ironfist?' Branwen called down. 'Is he to surrender, then?'

'My message is for the ears of King Cynon,' called the man. 'Will you allow me entry?'

There were a few muttered exchanges between the warriors on the wall. Branwen cut through the debate. 'I will come down,' she called to the Saxon horseman. 'You will be given leave to enter.'

She ran quickly down into the bailey, shouting orders to the guards to throw back the bar and open the gates. Although she had no real authority among the men of Pengwern, they were sufficiently awed by her to do as she asked – the great heavy gates were opened within moments.

Branwen strode out to meet the Saxon, her shield on her arm, her hand on her sword hilt. Eanfrid Hunwald swung down from the saddle, and Branwen saw that he wore no armour or mail and had no sword and no visible seax in his belt. But she knew of old that the loose Saxon garments could easily hide a dagger. She was not going to be taken unawares by this unexpected visitor.

He looked at her with this head tilted a little, like a man may look at a young doe he has a mind to bring down. 'Who are you, child?' he asked.

She returned his steady gaze. 'Do you not know me?' she asked. 'Has Ironfist not told you of me?'

His eyes widened and he seemed about to take a step back before he halted himself. 'You are Branwen ap Griffith,' he said. 'The accursed and vile waelisc shaman girl!'

'That is me,' said Branwen.

CHAPTER TWELVE

'You speak our language very well, Master Hunwald, with hardly a trace of a foreign accent,' said Branwen. 'Why are you here?'

'To speak with King Cynon.'

'So you said. But how am I to judge your honesty?'

Hunwald opened his cloak. 'Test my honour for yourself.'

Warily, Branwen moved in closer and patted his clothing for weapons hidden under the folds. There was nothing. 'Follow me,' she told him. 'Bring your horse. He will be fed and watered while you wait upon the king's pleasure.'

She was aware of many eyes watching her as she led the Saxon emissary in through the gates of Pengwern.

Branwen found the king in the Hall of Araith. She waited at the doors while a guard took her message

135

down to where Cynon sat on his throne under the awnings and flags of Powys. Eanfrid Hunwald stood behind her, the spears of two door wardens pointed at his heart.

The hall was a hundred paces long, but even at that distance, Branwen could see quite clearly what was going on at the far end of the high, columned chamber.

Meredith and Drustan sat on low stools in front of the throne, some five paces separated, but facing one another. Behind Meredith stood Prince Llew and Romney, along with Angor and some other of Llew's warriors. At Drustan's back were his mother and a small group of councillors. Representatives of the other three kingdoms were gathered behind the throne, looking on.

Clearly, bride and groom were meeting formally for the first time. But Branwen's mind was entirely overtaken by conjecture concerning what message the Saxon emissary might have brought from Ironfist.

The guard spoke briefly to one of the king's men, and the message was then relayed to Cynon himself. Every head turned to the doors. Branwen stepped into the open and bowed.

'Bring him to me,' Cynon called. Then he spoke some quiet words to the people assembled around him. The peaceful tableau broke up, the women departing to some side-chamber, and the men lining up beside the throne, grim-faced as Branwen led Eanfrid Hunwald forward.

The king sat back in his throne, leaning on one arm and regarding the Saxon messenger with a cool detachment.

Eanfrid Hunwald dropped to his knees in front of the throne. 'Great King of Powys, I bring greetings from my lord Horsa Herewulf,' he said, his voice showing no trace of fear, although Branwen guessed he must be feeling uneasy among so many armed enemies.

'Indeed?' said the king, his voice low and laconic, his eyes hooded as though to conceal any hint of his true thoughts about this unexpected visitation. 'And what words does the warlord of the east have for we whose blood he has so infamously shed?'

Branwen stood close behind the Saxon, her hand on her sword hilt, her nerves tingling and her whole body alert for any treacherous move. One step wrong on his part and her sword would be in his back up to the hilt.

Eanfrid Hunwald raised his head and spoke in a loud, clear voice.

'My lord Horsa Herewulf bids me speak these words to you.' His voice boomed to the rafters. 'Great King of Powys, you have fought with honour these past months, and you should have no shame that you have not done your duty to your realm. But ranged against you are forces so mighty that you cannot ever hope for a victory.

All the lands to the east and to the north and to the south, is my lord Horsa Herewulf emptying, and into his great encampment at Chester are these men pouring in their multitudes. Surrender now to the mercy of King Oswald's great general, and many lives will be spared. Continue in your obstinate refusal to acknowledge the overlordship of King Oswald, and General Herewulf will unleash his armies to flow as an unstoppable tide over your lands. If General Herewulf is forced to come across the borders in arms, be most certain, not a man will be left alive to tell the tale, not a woman will escape servitude, not a child shall live to see freedom again.'

Branwen's eyes flickered across the gathered faces that surrounded the throne. There was anger and outrage in most faces, but trepidation in none. If Ironfist's words were intended to intimidate, then they had failed. Apart from a hard gleam in the king's eyes, Branwen could see no reaction from him.

'Here's our answer!' shouted Angor, drawing his sword and taking a step forward. 'To send you on your way without a head to your shoulders for your impudence!'

The king lifted a hand and Angor halted, his arm shaking with fury.

'We are not barbarians, Captain,' said Cynon. 'We do not kill messengers because we like not the message they have been sent to deliver.' He looked long and thoughtfully at the Saxon. 'These are hard words,' he said at last. 'And we need time to consider them.' He rose from the throne. 'Take this man to where he can find food and drink. Keep close guard on him. He shall be called when our deliberations are done.'

Branwen turned, meaning to leave with the Saxon.

'Branwen, stay awhile,' said the king. 'We desire your counsel. You alone have met General Ironfist face to face.'

Is that so? Then do you forget, my king, that Captain Angor has knelt at his foot and done his bidding in the past?

But Branwen was wise enough to hold back her thoughts – opening old wounds would do no good, and might do harm while the treaty between Llew and the king was so young and tender.

Dark looks followed Ironfist's messenger as he was led at spear-point from the Hall.

'Well now,' said the king. 'What are we to make of this?'

'Nothing, my lord father, by your leave,' said Drustan. 'Only the bully seeks to cow an opponent with haughty words.'

'It's not the words themselves we should sift,' said Llew, 'but the thought behind them.'

'We and the Saxons have beaten our heads together like stags these six months gone,' said one of the king's men. 'Why does Ironfist choose this moment to threaten us so?'

'Indeed,' said the king. 'That is my question also. Branwen? Have you any insights into Ironfist's thinking?'

'None beyond this,' said Branwen, remembering what Iwan had said to her some days previously. 'Ironfist was content to let us fight brother against brother while he stood by and watched. But if word of the marriage treaty has reached him, he may realize his time of standing aside is all but done.'

'So he seeks to frighten us with fell words before setting his dogs loose on us?' said Angor, and Branwen was quick to notice a hint of respect for her in his voice. 'Goes this with the turn of his mind, girl?'

'I think so,' said Branwen.

'Belike he has other motives for such threats,' added Dagonet. 'If all we have been told of the forces mustered outside Chester are true, then he must have an army of four or five thousand in camp. Men in such numbers need much feeding and watering, and many will have horses, too, that will need fodder. How will the town of Chester cope with such numbers? Ironfist's army must be bleeding the town white, and this winter is a friend to us in so far as it has blocked the trade routes from the east and made the bringing of supplies from afar almost impossible.'

'That is a good thought,' said Llew. 'And if true, it means that he must either seek provisions by dint of conquest, or see his army starve.'

'Will he let loose war in such weather as this?' asked another counsellor. 'Surely not?'

'If need drives him, he may have no other choice,' said the king. 'A hard reply from us may force his hand.' He looked around at the other men. 'Are we prepared for the hordes of the east to come at us?'

'We must try to hold him back for a little,' said one of the men from Gwynedd. 'For the passage of a moon, at least, to allow us time to return to our king and have him send the levies across the mountains. Two thousand men can we provide for the succour of Powys, but they cannot be gathered all in a moment.'

'I would say the same,' added Hywel al Murig, among the men of Gwent. 'Can we send some serpentine response that will set him on his heels for a while? King Tewdrig will send warriors now that the conflict in Powys is ended, have no fear, but it is many leagues to the southern kingdom, and many leagues back.'

'A cunning reply, my lord, will maybe forestall an attack,' said Angor.

'But what words of ours might make him think we wish to negotiate a peaceful settlement?' asked Drustan.

'Why do we not suggest an old course of action?' said

Prince Llew. 'In times past, the mayhem of warfare was often averted by the surrender of tracts of land to a strong enemy. Perhaps we could let him believe we will offer to hand over some of our eastern cantrefs to him, if he calls his army off.'

'Land for peace,' said Dagonet. 'That may work, at least to give him pause.'

'He may feel the need to send word to King Oswald before he makes such a bargain,' said Drustan. 'And we can reinforce the eastern citadels while he waits on a reply.'

'Good, good,' said the king, his eyes glinting. 'Gull the mighty general with false promises, then.'

'To lie would make us no better than a Saxon,' blurted Branwen. 'We cannot win the day with falsehoods, my lord. And he will surely not believe we would truly give up our lands to him uncontended?'

'In his arrogance, he may,' said Dagonet.

'But my own home of Cyffin Tir lies on the eastern borders!' cried Branwen. 'He cannot think I would surrender my homeland to him!'

'That need not be a problem,' said Llew. 'We shall tell him that Branwen ap Griffith is dead or fled . . . or devoured by the demons she worships.'

'Or imprisoned by the king for her dark sorceries and insolent ways,' added Angor with a cold smile. 'That would not be hard for Ironfist to believe.'

Indeed, not! As it's something you already wish were true!

'My lord king,' said Branwen, looking into Cynon's unreadable face. 'Ironfist is a liar and an oath-breaker – but must *we* walk that same path?'

'For the charging bull, an arrow to the heart will suffice,' replied the king, eyeing Branwen sharply. 'But for the venomous serpent, slithering through the long grass, stealth and subtlety are the tools best suited to the task.' He raised a hand. 'We will slow the great general of Mercia down with talk of treaties, and of land to be given over to King Oswald. We will send word that we wish for a meeting between our most wise counsellors – his and ours – in some place where the safety of all is guaranteed. Some neutral ground where none should fear ambush.'

'And while we negotiate the terms of this meeting, so we shall send to Gwent and to Gwynedd and to Dyfed for reinforcements,' said Llew. 'I like this council, my lord. And by the time Ironfist realizes he has been fooled, we'll have gathered an army to hold him back!'

The king rose and reached out his hand to the prince. 'And you, my noble lord of Bras Mynydd, shall be our General-in-Chief, to lead our armies to victory.'

Branwen stared at the king in alarm and dismay. This was getting worse by the moment! Cynon was handing over the army to Prince Llew? To the man who had till a few weeks past been seeking his death on the battlefield? It was madness.

'My lord, may I speak with you alone?' she asked the king. She had to make him realize Llew could not be trusted. If Cynon gave the prince of Bras Mynydd command of the army, he might as well hand over his crown at the same time.

'Thank you for your counsel, Branwen of the Gwyn Braw,' said the king. 'Go you now and fetch the Saxon messenger while we debate the exact nature of the words we would send back to General Ironfist.'

'But, my lord—'

'Do as the king commands,' said Angor, glaring at her. 'Or do you think the demons you worship allow you to question the king's wishes?'

'No, Captain, I do not,' Branwen replied, holding back her anger. 'But I know twisted counsel when I hear it, and I would rather face Ironfist in open battle than defeat him by stealth and falsehoods.'

Bowing to the king, she turned and strode quickly from the hall, well aware that malevolent eyes followed her.

'It is called *diplomacy*,' Iwan said earnestly. 'Branwen, we have spoken of these things before. More wars are won by lies and deceits than by swords and axes.'

'I know!' Branwen replied sullenly. 'But I hate it all the same.'

'You are too honourable,' said Banon.

'Maybe I am,' sighed Branwen. 'But this kind of trickery sickens me.' She jumped up. 'Banon! Come, spar with me! I need to clear my head!'

It was the afternoon of the same day. The Saxon messenger had been sent back with the king's reply and as he had departed snow had begun to fall. Although Branwen had brought Eanfrid Hunwald to the Hall of Araith, she had been sent away without hearing exactly what was said to him. Not that she wanted to listen to such shameful, dissembling words.

Now she was with her followers in the long house, joining in with their arduous training regime, trying to block out her apprehension with hard physical effort.

She worked every muscle as she fought sword against sword with Banon. The gangly warrior girl was a wily, lithe opponent who seemed never to be quite where Branwen expected, and who moved around the field of contest like a hare made mad in the spring. Banon was not the strongest of her followers, but all the same, Branwen found it hard to get the better of someone who in two long-legged springs could be behind her and swinging her sword at the back of her neck almost before she could turn round.

They fought till Branwen found an opening in her opponent's guard. Sweeping Banon's sword arm aside, she brought her blade to a stop a hair's-breadth from piercing the lanky girl's exposed stomach. They stood panting, looking at one another with shining eyes.

'One day I shall get the better of you, Branwen,' said Banon.

Branwen gave a crooked smile. 'But not today.' She turned. 'Aberfa? A little exercise?'

'Indeed,' said Aberfa, getting to her feet and hefting her spear.

Branwen spread her feet, raising her shield to her eyes, gripping her sword tightly, preparing herself for battle. Aberfa stood gazing at her. Smiling, she raised a hand and beckoned. Narrowing her eyes, Branwen moved in.

Aberfa was powerful and deadly – it was like attacking a tree, but a tree that could swing around with startling speed and give Branwen a buffet on the side of her head. Two or three times in their contest, Branwen fell back, her head ringing and eyes full of stars.

'Well hit!' Iwan roared as Branwen retreated again from Aberfa's attack, feeling as if wasps swarmed in her burning ears. 'Are you half asleep, barbarian princess?'

'If she was, that blow will have woken her!' declared Dera, watching the contest with excited eyes.

Branwen narrowed her eyes, pushing back the annoyance she felt at having been bettered like that. Had Aberfa's spear shaft been a Saxon axe, her skull would have been cloven in two!

Pay attention! Forget everything but the foe in front of you! Focus your mind!

But that was easier said than done when images of Prince Llew kept drifting into her head, breaking her concentration and making her vulnerable.

Aberfa came at her like a raging bear. Instinct took over from thought in Branwen's mind. She dived forward, curling up, her shoulder striking the ground first as she rolled at the advancing girl's feet.

Aberfa stumbled, taken off balance as Branwen's shoulder and back took her feet out from under her. The ground shook as Aberfa came down in a sprawling heap. Branwen bounded to her feet again, pivoting, her sword held high above her shield, the point angling down.

She came down heavily astride Aberfa's back, the sword point at her neck.

Dera and Iwan and Banon applauded. Aberfa spluttered and shook herself.

'Are we done?' Branwen asked her gasping opponent.

'We are!' puffed Aberfa. 'Put up your sword, before you snick my head from my shoulders in your zeal!'

'Ha!' Branwen sheathed her sword. A moment later,

Aberfa rose up under her like a mountain. Branwen was thrown on to her back as Aberfa's spear point pressed against her throat.

Branwen stared at her in surprise. Aberfa's face was grim, her cheeks flushed red. 'Do you see the lesson I am teaching you, Branwen?' she said, withdrawing the cold iron from Branwen's flesh. 'It is as Iwan has told you – deception is a sure road to victory, when all else fails.'

Branwen sat up.

'And if even Aberfa knows this, imagine how it thrives in the minds of men like Ironfist,' added Iwan.

'What do you mean – "*even* Aberfa"?' asked the huge warrior girl.

Branwen sat looking up at Aberfa, her elbows on her knees, her breathing still rapid from her exertions. 'I was brought up always to speak the truth and to treat even the vilest enemy with honour,' she said. 'Was I taught wrong?'

'I'd not say *wrong*,' replied Dera. 'But to the Saxons, truth is foolishness – honour, a sign of weakness.'

Iwan reached down and Branwen grasped his hand, allowing him to haul her to her feet. She looked from one to the other of her companions. 'If Saxons are deceitful and treacherous,' she said slowly and heavily, 'then all the more reason for us to be honest and truthful!'

'Ahh, Branwen,' sighed Iwan. 'What manner of barbarian are you?'

'An enlightened one, I hope,' said Branwen. 'And one with a throbbing head, thanks to Aberfa!'

'Dera ap Dagonet.' It was a man's voice, sounding out unexpectedly from the door to their private house. They all turned. Branwen recognized the man as one of Dera's father's warriors, who had come with him from Gwylan Canu.

'What is it?' asked Dera, stepping forward.

'Your father summons you,' said the man.

There was a moment of silence. Dagonet ap Wadu wished to speak with his daughter? That was something that had not happened since they had come to Pengwern. Perhaps Branwen's words to the grim warrior in the Hall of Arlwy had touched him after all?

Dera seemed stunned at first, then she quickly stepped forward, her face filled with hope and barely suppressed excitement. 'Then take me to him,' she said.

She left the house without even a backward glance at her companions.

'Well!' said Iwan, blowing out his cheeks. 'And what are we to make of that?'

'Father and daughter reconciled?' puzzled Banon. 'After all these months?'

'Let us hope so,' said Branwen. 'The estrangement from her father eats at Dera's heart like a canker.'

Iwan gazed thoughtfully out through the doorway.

'We shall learn more of it when she returns, I do not doubt,' he said. He turned, whipping his sword from its sheath. 'So now? Who dares stand against the finest swordsman in Powys?' he called, making a few rapid passes.

'Only Powys now, is it?' laughed Banon. 'I thought it was all of Brython!'

'Modesty forbids!' said Iwan with a grin as Banon drew her own sword and lifted her shield to her eyes in preparation for battle. 'With me, modesty always forbids!'

As he advanced on Banon, he winked at Branwen and smiled, and not for the first time, Branwen was puzzled that something so ordinary should set her heart racing.

CHAPTER THIRTEEN

That evening, Branwen and her friends sat in their long house to eat a meagre meal of watery cheese and hard bread and the last of the small, wrinkled apples from the storehouses. All washed down with snow-melt water and thin goat's milk.

Dera had not yet returned, although Fain was making his presence known, having been out hunting somewhere in the wilds and returning with a woodpigeon in his claws. He took his prize up to the rafters. Feathers occasionally drifted down, sometimes with blood on them.

After the meal, Branwen stood at the door, staring out into the ghostly-white night, missing her other companions and wishing Linette would heal quickly so that the Gwyn Braw might be sent off on some urgent mission.

Despite the danger, she would even have been glad to

be ordered east across the river − anything would be better than this endless watching and waiting while Llew and Angor hatched dark schemes for the downfall of King Cynon . . . and probably for her own death as well.

She could feel the heat of the fire on her back, and hear the voices of her companions as they chatted of the things they had seen and done over the long winter months.

Guards moved like wraiths of silk on the ramparts of the citadel, and still the snow fell.

Iwan came and stood at her side, leaning against the doorframe, balancing his knife on his palm, dropping it, catching it deftly, throwing it up to cartwheel before catching it again.

She saw in the corner of her eye the dull gleam of the blade as he tossed and snatched at it, and all the while as he played with the knife, he hummed softly to himself under his breath. It was as though he was idly waiting for her to say or do something.

Branwen reached out and caught the knife by the handle as it was about to drop into Iwan's palm for the twentieth time.

'Do I disturb you, Branwen?' he asked mildly as she handed the knife back to him, hilt first.

'Deeply and often,' she said without looking at him.

'Good. I'm glad,' he replied. 'Then we are even.' There

was a pause. 'You worry me, barbarian princess,' he continued. 'A surfeit of honour in such times as these may catch in the throat and choke a person to death. And I wouldn't have you fall, Branwen – not for the world.'

'I shan't fall,' she said, still staring out into the never-ending snowfall.

'I'd say that was pride running wild if anyone but you said it,' Iwan replied. 'But even you are not indestructible, Branwen. And you're not indispensable. If you die, the Shining Ones will find another . . .'

She turned her head to look at him now, and there was genuine concern in his face.

'It might be as easy as picking up windfall apples in the autumn for the Shining Ones to replace you, Branwen,' he said. 'But there are those among us who will find it much harder.' He rolled the knife over his open palms. 'I'm only saying be careful. You're not as unbreakable as you think.' He shrugged. 'It's a shame, but it's true.'

Branwen frowned. 'Why do you always do that?' she asked.

'What?'

'Turn everything into a joke.'

'Is that what I'm doing?' he said, looking into her eyes. 'Then perhaps it's because I'm waiting for some sign from you.'

She let out a breath, white as steam into the night air. 'We're all waiting on a sign,' she said, her eyes turning broodingly to the west again. 'I'd hoped the Shining Ones would show their goodwill towards us by making Linette better – but she still lingers in the sickbed, and from the looks of Rhodri and Blodwedd, you'd think she might die.' She checked herself. 'She won't, of course – but a quick healing would be some proof that Rhiannon and Govannon are with me still.'

'I see you don't mention the others. Are Merion and Caradoc not your friends, then?'

'Blodwedd believes they may be angry with me – she thinks I made a mistake in coming here against their wishes.'

'Let's hope she's mistaken,' said Iwan. 'Although this endless winter might suggest that Caradoc has little love for you.'

'Blodwedd says the snow is not a punishment,' said Branwen, gesturing to the sky full of snow. 'She thinks Caradoc is at play, full of his own self-importance and willing to do anything to amuse himself.' She gave Iwan a sidelong glance, her lip curled in a smile. 'A little like you.'

Iwan pursed his lips, tapping the flat of his knife against his palm. 'If I had the power of the winds,' he said, 'I wouldn't torment you with blizzards. I'd bring you warm southern breezes and clear blue skies.' He looked into her eyes, no hint of mockery in his gaze. 'And if I had Govannon's power over living things, I'd have the birds sing you to sweet sleep every day's eve.'

Branwen's heart galloped as she held his gaze. His hand moved to push a lock of hair off her face. She lifted her own hand and thrilled at the touch of his skin. Her mouth was dry, her throat tight, and for a few moments it felt as though her legs might fail under her.

'You are a marvel to me, Branwen ap Griffith,' he murmured, his fingers still warm against her cheek. 'This is no time for troth-plighting, not when our lives hang by a thread, but when peace comes at last, if we two are still alive, then we shall speak again . . .' His eyes pierced her to the soul. 'If you wish it.'

'I do wish it,' she whispered. *With all my heart I wish it!*

He smiled, withdrawing his hand. 'There,' he said. 'And all said without a taunt or a tease.' He frowned into the snowy night. 'Let's close the door, barbarian princess – and banish the cold as much as we can.'

And so they drew the wicker door close and pulled the woollen curtain across to keep out the cold. And together, with hands almost touching, they walked to sit with their companions by the cheering firelight.

Branwen was awoken in the middle of the night by a

stealthy step close by the end of her bed. She was alert in an instant, one hand reaching for her sword.

A shadow slid across the ruddy firelight. A familiar shape.

She let go of her sword hilt and got quickly to her feet, wrapping herself in the fur bed covering.

Dera was sitting on a hearthstone, her shoulders hunched, her eyes hidden as she stared into the flickering flames. Branwen knelt at her side, looking searchingly into her face.

'Is all well?' Branwen whispered.

'All is well,' Dera replied softly.

'You were gone a long time,' said Branwen. 'Did you and your father speak much together?'

'We did,' Dera replied. 'Mostly we ate and watched the entertainments in the Hall of Arlwy, but we spoke as well.'

'That's good, isn't it?' urged Branwen, wanting to know more and growing impatient with her taciturn friend. 'Are you reconciled?'

Dera turned her head away. 'I'm tired,' she said. 'Can we speak of this another time?'

Branwen rested her hand on Dera's knee. 'Did he ask you to choose between his love and mine?'

'It is not so simple as you may . . .' Dera's voice faded away with the rest of her words going unspoken.

'I'm tired,' she said again, getting up this time. 'I want to sleep.'

For a few minutes, Branwen knelt alone by the fire.

What had passed between father and daughter?

Denounce the shaman girl and return to the bosom of your family!

No! Never!

Or . . .

Yes! I cannot bear it! I will do as you ask, Father. I will renounce the Gwyn Braw.

Branwen shook her head to rid herself of these pointless thoughts. Dera would not turn from them – the sky would fall first!

Dera was no more forthcoming the next morning when the rest of the Gwyn Braw awoke. All they could learn from her was that she and her father had spoken, and that Dagonet had made no demands on her to shift her loyalties. Beyond that, she remained tight-lipped, although it was clear to Branwen that she was leaving something unsaid.

The morning was spent sparring in the long house and checking that their horses were comfortable and as well fed as possible in the circumstances. In ones and twos they made trips to visit Linette. Branwen noticed she was quieter than the previous day, as though the effort of showing them a brave face had drained her. The ailing warrior girl lay either gazing into the fire or with her eyelids closed, but not asleep.

Some time in the latter part of the afternoon a commotion at the gate alerted Branwen that Eanfrid Hunwald had returned. He must have had quite the gallop to get to and from Chester so rapidly.

Branwen strode impatiently up and down the long house, waiting for a summons from the king, so that she could learn what word had been brought from Ironfist.

She saw the Saxon general's scarred one-eyed face in her mind. He was laughing at her. Mocking her. She snarled and ground her heels into the earthen floor, every sinew tense in her body, every muscle aching to strike out at the jeering vision that filled her head.

In the end she lost patience and stormed across the compound to the Hall of Araith. The doors were closed and guards stood sentry with spears in their hands.

'Let me pass,' she said.

'The king says none may enter,' replied the guard, and she saw his knuckles tighten on the spear shaft.

'Is the Saxon within?' asked Branwen.

'He is.'

'And I am not to know what is being said?'

The guards did not reply.

She considered trying to force them aside – but to

what purpose? If Cynon did not want her in there, then breaking in would do her no good.

This is Llew's doing, she thought bitterly as she turned away. *He murmurs his lies in the king's ears and stops me from speaking to him. Well! If that is the way the wind blows, perhaps my duty here is at an end. Perhaps it's time to take my people out of Pengwern and return to the path the Shining Ones would have me follow.*

The unbidden idea appealed to her; beaming out in her mind like a shaft of sunlight through heavy storm clouds. To be away from the machinations and deceits of the court would be a fine thing indeed. And what further use was she here? She was unloved and feared by almost everyone in the king's service. Who would mourn if the Gwyn Braw rode out through the gates of Pengwern never to return?

And as the idea grew in her mind, so she found herself longing for the freedom of the wild hills and eager to see once again the beautiful face of Rhiannon, the Woman in White upon her milk-white steed, and to look again into the glorious, sad eyes of Govannon of the Wood, lord of the forests.

Yes! I will do it! I will be rid of the fetid stink of this place. I'll no longer be Branwen the witch girl, the tamed and shackled monster of King Cynon's court. I'll be the Emerald Flame! The Bright Blade! The

The urge to escape blossomed in her until she almost felt like running to saddle up Terrwyn at that very moment, to ride out into the dying day. Anything to be out of here as quickly as possible.

But she stifled her growing desire to be gone. Even if she were to take such an extreme step, and even if all her followers chose to depart with her, she would not think of quitting the king's citadel without Linette.

Her enthusiasm waned as reality flooded her mind.

I cannot leave Linette, not even if Llew chose to send an army of assassins to cut me down where I sleep. No, patience will be my guide till Linette is healed.

But then . . .

When the time came, the king would not even know they were gone until they were three leagues from this place, galloping full-tilt westwards to the mountains.

'Rhodri, Blodwedd, go! Stretch your legs – walk on the walls perhaps – or go and sit with the others for a while. You haven't been out of this hut in days!'

Branwen had entered Linette's hut to find Blodwedd sitting huddled with her arms wrapped around her shins and her chin on her knees, watching while Rhodri sorted herbs from a wicker pannier. Linette lay sleeping by the fire, loaded up with woollen cloaks and furs. The hut smelled of the crushed and pounded herbs, not an unpleasant mix of odours, but very strong and pungent and heavy, especially when Branwen first stepped inside from the clear chill air.

Rhodri looked uncertainly at her. 'I'll keep watch,' Branwen assured him. 'If she so much as flutters an eyelash, I'll fetch you.'

Rhodri got slowly to his feet. 'My aching back,' he groaned. 'A walk would do me good, I think.' He gazed down at Blodwedd. 'Will you come with me?'

'I will.' Blodwedd rose to her feet. She padded to their bed and picked up their two ermine cloaks.

Swaddled in furs to ward off the worst of the late-afternoon chill, the two stepped out, Rhodri's arm about the owl-girl's shoulders. Branwen watched them with fond eyes as they went crunching side by side through the mash of grey snow.

The snow had stopped falling and there were tears and rips and holes in the cloud-wrack, through which the sky showed, pale blue and distant, like the promise of a spring that might never come.

Branwen tiptoed to Linette's side and stooped to lift an edge of a fur covering up higher over her shoulder. Linette's eyes fluttered open.

Branwen smiled, although the pain in Linette's eyes clawed at her stomach.

'Well met,' she murmured softly. 'Did I wake you?'

'I heard voices,' whispered Linette. Her breath was unpleasant in Branwen's face – sour, sickly and unwholesome.

'I sent Rhodri and Blodwedd away for a while,' said Branwen, determined that Linette would not see her distaste. 'Rhodri says you are improving mightily with each passing day,' she lied. 'You'll soon be up and about again. By the saints, but you must be sick of this place.'

A weak smile twitched at the corner of Linette's mouth. 'You could do one thing for me,' she whispered. 'Prop me up a little, so I can see out through the doorway. I'd like to see the mountains, if that's possible.'

'Of course.' Branwen carefully lifted Linette with an arm around her thin shoulders, while she tucked furs under her back and head. She tried not to show how troubled she was by the wasted look in Linette's face, nor by her rank breath nor the soft groans that escaped her friend's lips as she was moved.

She went again to the entrance, pinning back the woollen curtain and opening the wicker door.

The distant mountains had torn the clouds open and the snowy peaks were bright as burnished brass where the sun struck them, dark as lead in the deep shadows of the coming evening. Even the looming clouds were tinted pink and orange so that as Branwen gazed out at them, they hardly seemed real.

'The world is putting on its best finery for you, Linette,' said Branwen, deeply moved by the stark beauty of the scene before her. 'It must have known you wished for something glorious to send you sweet dreams.' She turned and looked at Linette. The pale girl was gazing way beyond her, a bright light glowing in her eyes.

Branwen smiled and turned again to the mountains, leaning in the doorframe, her arms folded against the chill air. 'I'd say the Shining Ones sent this twilight to us,' she said with a sigh in her voice. 'They are still watching over us, I know it in my heart.' She paused. 'I have been thinking that it is time we quit the king's employ. What do you say, Linette? Once you are well, shall we be gone from here? Back to the mountains and the forests. I have done my duty, haven't I? My duty to the king, I mean, and my duty to Gavan ap Huw, of course, rest his soul.'

She looked again at Linette. The pale girl's eyes still gazed into the west, but she did not respond to Branwen's words.

'I am worried for the king,' Branwen continued, looking out towards the mountains again. 'He's taking a dangerous course in trusting Prince Llew. Should I stay and protect him against treachery, do you think? I don't know. Is it even safe for me to stay here with Llew in the ascendancy? Might he convince the king to be rid of me once and for all? I wouldn't put it past him . . .' She narrowed her eyes. 'I shall ask Rhodri, he always gives good counsel.' She smiled to herself. 'I already know what Blodwedd's advice would be.' She deepened her voice in affectionate imitation of the owl-girl. '"This small king of men is no more to you than a pebble on a beach, Branwen – yours is a higher calling!"' She laughed softly at the thought. 'That is what Blodwedd would tell me, for sure. And she may be right. All these months with the king may have been time wasted.' Her thoughts shifted. 'Or maybe Iwan will give me wise advice.' Her voice lowered, almost as if she had forgotten that Linette was within earshot. 'I know I could trust him with my life . . .' She let out a sigh, wondering whether to pursue this line of thought. Linette might have some advice for her, or maybe just the act of voicing her confusion aloud might give her some clarity.

'Linette? What does it feel like to be in love? Do you know? My mother and father loved one another very deeply, and it was a calm love – easy, respectful. Is that what love is like always? Because if it is, then I don't know *what* I am feeling for Iwan. Sometimes he drives me to a frenzy with his glib tongue . . . and at other times he is so gentle and kind that . . .' The words stalled in her throat, too big and heavy to be brought up into her mouth. She stood listening to her heart beating. A tingling heat burned under her ribs. She could as easily have wept as burst out laughing.

After a while, she carried on speaking, in a voice little above a whisper. 'Sometimes when he smiles at me, I feel . . . oh, I don't know how to describe how I feel . . . powerful . . . vulnerable . . . strong and weak all at once.' She turned to look once more at her friend. 'Love is such . . . a . . .'

The words died in her throat. She took a faltering step towards her still and silent friend.

'. . . Linette . . . ?'

CHAPTER FOURTEEN

I *must find Rhodri. He will know what to do. He will make her better.*

Branwen ran like a mad thing through the wet snow, her feet slithering under her, the air like arrows cutting into her lungs. A wild panic had hold of her. Something had happened that was not possible. She must have misunderstood. She was no healer. She knew nothing of such things.

She must fetch Rhodri!

Branwen broke in through the closed doorway to their long house, panting, her heart hammering, her head swimming.

Rhodri and Blodwedd were there with the others, sitting around the fire-pit, talking and laughing a little. Not knowing. Not even imagining the horror.

Branwen stumbled to a halt, swaying, dizzy, unable to speak.

'What is it?' asked Iwan, jumping up before any of the others had moved. 'What's happened?'

Branwen tried to gather the wounded remnants of herself. 'Linette,' she gasped, gesturing back the way she had come.

Rhodri was on his feet in an instant and out through the doorway in a breath, Blodwedd bounding along behind him, her hair flying.

The others rushed past Branwen, fear and anguish in their faces. Only Iwan stayed with her, his hands on her arms, his face agonized as he looked into her eyes.

'Is she dead?' he asked, his voice cracking.

'No, she cannot be . . .' She struggled weakly to get away from him, refusing to look at him. 'She cannot be!'

His hands gripped her upper arms. 'Branwen? Be still, now. Is she dead?'

Branwen hung between his hands, all strength, all faith, all hope gone from her.

'Yes,' she choked. 'The Shining Ones let her die!'

The small hut was a place of horror and grief and despair. Rhodri was crumpled at Linette's side, weeping as he desperately spoke his healing rhymes over her in a broken whisper, his two hands holding hers, pressing her flesh and kneading it as though to force life back into her unmoving body.

Blodwedd stood behind him, silent as a stone, staring into Linette's white face with wide, uncomprehending eyes.

Aberfa knelt at the dead girl's head, stroking her hair, her face constricted with grief, her lips a tight, thin line.

Dera and Banon stared on in devastated silence, tears spilling over their cheeks.

Branwen stood in the doorway, stupefied with disbelief, hardly able to draw breath, while white flames danced around the rim of sight. Iwan was silent at her side, one arm circling her shoulders, taking her weight as she leaned against him, the world pitching and spinning around her.

The grievous scene floated like a nightmare in front of Branwen's eyes. Her friends had turned to stone before her, their tears condensed on their cheeks into hard, sharp diamonds. She felt as though she was falling. Falling and falling and falling. Mouths opened and closed all around her – black mouths opening into nothing. Into Annwn. The faces of her companions melted into hideous shapes. Sickness heaved through her. Her bones were water, her blood was ice.

Rhodri looked up, his face contorted with remorse and wretchedness. 'She's gone,' he said. 'I can do nothing.'

Banon let out a choking cry. Aberfa's tears dripped into Linette's hair.

'But she is so small,' Aberfa groaned, staring up at Branwen as though expecting her to be able to do something to change the harshness of the world. 'So delicate. Look – look. See how fine her skin is.' She traced fingertips over Linette's temples. 'How can she be dead?'

Dera turned towards Branwen, her face stiff with anger and pain. 'We are alone,' she said. 'This is proof. The Shining Ones have deserted us.'

'No!' Blodwedd's voice was strangely shrill. 'They would never do that.'

Branwen stared at her, shaking uncontrollably, trying not to hate this messenger of the Old Gods – the Old Gods who had turned their backs on her and let Linette die. 'They have . . . abandoned me . . .' she croaked. 'They have . . . failed . . . me . . .'

'No!' shouted Blodwedd. 'It is *you* who failed *them*. You brought us here – you turned away from the true path—'

'Blodwedd! Enough!' cried Rhodri.

Branwen stared again into Linette's poor dead face. An unquenchable anger boiled up in her. Flames roared behind her eyes. Black clouds filled her brain.

She turned, wrenching herself out of Iwan's grip and running from the hut.

She knew whose fault this was! She knew who to blame.

She began to run pell-mell through Pengwern, racing up the gentle incline towards the two Great Halls, drawing her sword as she ran, red rage clouding her vision.

A guard stepped across the closed doors of the Hall of Araith, his spear raised in warning.

'None may pass!' he said.

But he was not prepared for the fury that struck him. Branwen brought the hilt of her sword up in a hard blow at the side of his head, grabbing his tunic and dragging him aside even as he fell. She pulled the doors open, snatching a torch from its sconce in the wall.

A moment later and she was in the long, narrow chamber, only vaguely aware of the cries of the guard at her back. 'Alarm! Madness has taken the witch girl! The king is in danger! Alarm!'

Branwen saw a servant sleeping under a blanket on the floor. She caught the startled woman by the arm and dragged her to her feet. 'Which is the princesses' room?' she spat into the terrified woman's face. 'Where do they sleep?'

The woman pointed a shaking arm at a door in the side wall of the chamber. Branwen released her and she fell to the ground with a cry.

Bearing the sputtering torch high in her fist, Branwen kicked the door open.

It was a small room, no larger than allowed space for two mattresses and a chest.

'Romney!' Branwen shouted, standing quivering at the foot of the two low beds. 'Romney! Wake up!'

The two curled forms stirred under the covers. Meredith lifted herself up, staring at Branwen with sleepy, frightened eyes.

'Oh, saints preserve us, what has happened?' she gasped.

'Linette ap Cledwyn is dead!' Branwen raged, stooping and using the point of her sword to rip the covers from the other bed. Romney huddled up in her linen shift, torn out of her sleep and utterly bewildered.

'Do you care?' shouted Branwen, stooping over the girl, holding the torch close to light up the drowsy, terrified face. 'Do you care at all that someone died because they were good and noble enough to wish to save your miserable life?'

'Merrie! Help me!' wailed the small girl, kicking with her feet as she tried vainly to get away from Branwen's wrath.

'Branwen, don't hurt her,' pleaded Meredith, clambering across to Romney's bed and gathering her sister up in her arms.

'Branwen, by the saints, *stop*!' called a voice at her back. Iwan's voice. His hand caught her sword arm by the wrist, dragging it down. 'What are you doing here, Branwen? What madness is this?'

'Linette died because of her!' Branwen spat. 'She died to save a selfish, spiteful, mean-spirited child! I want Romney to know what that means! I want her to feel the pain of it!'

'On the point of a sword?' cried Iwan, still trying to pull Branwen back.

Branwen twisted to stare at him. Then she gazed down at the blade as it gleamed in the torchlight. The sight of it suddenly horrified and sickened her. Had she been so consumed and blinded with anger that she could have used the sword on a defenceless child?

'No!' she gasped, half speaking to Iwan, half to herself. 'Of course not!'

'What is this turmoil?' It was one of the king's warriors, newly arisen from bed, it seemed, a cloak thrown over his shoulders, a sword bare in his fist.

'It is nothing!' said Iwan, wresting the sword from Branwen's fingers and slipping it into his belt. 'It is over. Let us pass.'

'By the saints, I'll not!' roared the warrior. 'Not till I know more of this treachery!'

'It is no treachery, my lord,' called Dera from beyond the doorway. 'Grief had got the better of our leader, and she acted without thought. One of our number has died this eve. Let us look to Branwen ap Griffith. We will take her from here and keep her safe till the fury of her grief is past.'

More warriors had gathered now, staring in at Branwen, their eyes and weapons glittering.

Voices murmured.

'The shaman girl has been taken by madness!'

'This was long in the coming – did I not say so?'

'More deadly than the Saxons, she has always been!'

'Take her! We'll see justice done on her at last!'

'Upon my father's honour, put up your swords, my lords!' Dera shouted. 'Do not stop us from leaving, or blood will be spilled to no purpose! Iwan, come! Branwen, let's away from here before every warrior in Pengwern falls upon us!'

Shivering and broken, Branwen allowed herself to be led by Iwan out of the princesses' bedchamber and away through the gathered warriors. She felt their hatred beating on her as she passed among them in the protective circle of Iwan's arm.

'Take me to my death,' she mumbled in Iwan's ear as she stumbled along beside him. 'I cannot bear this! For pity's sake, let it be done.'

'Eat something, Branwen. You must eat.'

Branwen looked up with hollow, aching eyes to where

Banon stood over her.

She had no true idea of how long she had been sitting at Linette's side, but she was aware that a faint light was growing beyond the door. Dawn already?

This was not the first time Branwen had sat benumbed at the side of the dead body of someone she loved. She'd had good practice at this over the past year!

Who had been the first? Geraint, her brother, of course. Slain by a Saxon rider at Bevan's farm while she stood trembling at the forest's eaves and did nothing to help him. And her dear father, cut down from his horse at the gates of Garth Milain and hurt to the death because she had chosen to go to the aid of her mother. And she could never forget Gavan ap Huw, staunch warrior of the old wars, defender of kings, Cadwallon's standard-bearer, brought to his death by a foolish girl's pride, fallen in a woodland ambush that could have been so easily avoided.

Yes, the tally of good people at whose side she had mourned grew long – too long by far. And how soon before it would be her body that was laid out cold and lifeless on the ground and some other soul torn asunder by her death? Rhodri, perhaps. He would grieve, yes he would, faithful and loving friend! Or Iwan. What had he said, just a brief time past? *You are a marvel to me, Branwen.* A marvel still, with the worms gorging on her flesh? A marvel, with the ravens pecking at her eyes? A marvel, with so many deaths on her lifeless, skeletal hands?

'We must give thought to her funeral,' said Iwan, speaking for the first time since they had returned to the hut.

'We shall build her a pyre fifteen ells high,' said Branwen, not looking at him. 'She shall depart this world among leaping flames.'

'I don't think that will be possible,' said Banon. 'All cut wood is needed for winter fuel, and fresh-hewn timber will be wet and hard to stack and to burn.'

Branwen sighed. 'No pyre, then? Does it matter? Shall we toss her from the walls and let the animals of the wild have their fill of her. Would that be honour enough?'

'There are stones enough in Pengwern to build a cairn,' said Aberfa. 'The ground will be hard, but we will be able to dig her a grave. And then over her head we will pile stones to keep her safe from harm.'

Rhodri began to whisper a snatch of an old song.

Dig her grave both wide and deep,
That she shall be disturbed not in her sleep,
And on her breast plant a weeping willow tree,
To show she died for love of thee and of me . . .

'Say rather she died to save a stupid child,'

muttered Branwen darkly.

'Romney is not to blame,' Iwan said. 'She ran the wrong way, that is all. Blind fate did the rest. Blame fate and this cruel winter.'

'And who brought the cruel winter down on us?' asked Aberfa.

Branwen glared at her. 'Caradoc of the North Wind,' she said, giving voice to the thoughts flooding her mind. 'One of the Old Gods, whom I so arrogantly defied. If it be his wrath, or his sport, then . . . the blame rests with me.'

'I did not mean that,' Aberfa muttered.

'You are too quick to apportion blame!' said Blodwedd, sitting apart from the others by the doorway, staring out into the growing daylight. 'Is every death then the result of ill judgement or malice? If Branwen ap Griffith chooses unwisely, is the death of every bird that falls from the sky to be laid at her foot? And when man makes war upon man, is Branwen ap Griffith there as each man gasps out his final breath?' The owl-girl stared at Branwen, her eyes burning golden. 'Death is not in your hands, Branwen,' she said solemnly. 'No more than is life. There are births. There are deaths. The world teems. The world rejoices. The world mourns. It's none of your doing!'

'And what of the Shining Ones?' asked Banon.

'Did they promise that no harm would ever come to you and yours?' Blodwedd asked Branwen. 'Did they ever say to you "follow our lead, and all will be well"?' She frowned. 'You do not know of the mercy and love that the Shining Ones bestow on this world!'

'"Mercy and love"?' said Iwan grimly. 'I see precious little of that coming out of the west. If you have such faith in the benevolence of the Old Gods, go and find them, Blodwedd – ask them to bring the torment of this winter to an end, ask them to breathe life back into Linette's body. Ask them to show us the true meaning of devotion.' His voice trembled with anger. 'Ask them what measure of blood spilled will be sufficient to please them. Ask them how much blood it will take to set Branwen free!' He drew his knife and held it to his upturned wrist. "I'll give freely enough, if one body will suffice.'

'Stop it, Iwan!' Branwen said, pulling the knife away from his wrist. 'They need no blood sacrifices.' She forced down her grief and looked keenly at Blodwedd. 'I do not know what to do,' she said. 'When Linette was well enough to travel, I had intended to take you all out of Pengwern and to go back to the mountains to seek a new path. But what purpose would that serve, if the Shining Ones deny me? What end would we come to but an ignoble one in the deep snows, our bones gnawed by the wild wolves, our souls mourned by none?'

'I'll not travel west to do service to the Old Gods,' growled Aberfa. 'I'd rather ride full-tilt into the east and die in battle with the Saxons.'

'That would be a futile gesture,' said Rhodri, sitting red-eyed among the scattered remnants of his ineffective herbs and potions.

'Indeed, it would,' said Blodwedd, rising to her feet and staring fiercely at Branwen. 'I will do as Iwan suggests,' she said defiantly. 'I will go alone into the western forests. I will seek my lord Govannon. I will hear his words and I will return. Do not throw your life away in the east, Branwen. Not till you have heard what word I bring from the Shining Ones.'

Branwen looked at her, too tired to argue. She nodded wearily.

'Dawn is come,' said Banon. 'We should give thought to the departed.'

Most eyes turned to Branwen, but she looked away, losing herself for a moment in the glow of the fire-pit.

'We shall pass through the gates when morning has come,' said Aberfa. 'We shall bury our dear friend in some fitting place where she can see the mountains of her home.'

'Yes,' agreed Iwan. 'We'll find some sheltered spot upon the ridge to lay her to rest. And then Blodwedd shall travel westwards and we shall return here to be the king's eyes and ears for a while longer.' He frowned. 'Dera has been gone a long time. Need we go and find her?'

Dera had not returned to the hut following Branwen's manic incursion into the king's Great Hall. She had stayed behind to try and pacify the ants'-nest that Branwen had stirred up, to explain her leader's wild behaviour and to seek forgiveness and compassion for them in their grief and loss.

But that had been the whole night ago. And yet there was still no sign of the daughter of Dagonet ap Wadu. She had not sat vigil over their lost comrade with the others of the Gwyn Braw. She had not been there to share their grief.

Branwen wondered again whether Dera's loyalties had been stretched to the breaking point. Was she still one of them – or had her father's love sent her down a different course?

CHAPTER FIFTEEN

The sky was cloudless, a bright, burning sapphire blue and so huge that Branwen felt herself to be little more than an insect crawling on the rind of the world as she and the Gwyn Braw rode out towards the long hill that lay to the west of the king's citadel.

As the sun had risen that morning, so the snow clouds had slipped away, sliding slowly into the north on a curiously balmy southern wind. Everyone in Pengwern felt the change in the weather. People emerged with puzzled, delighted eyes to see such a sky and to feel such a wind on their faces. The geese cackled and the goats bleated and the few remaining cattle lowed and snorted in their pens.

It was almost as though spring had come all in a single morning.

Branwen was riding on Terrwyn at the head of her solemn, melancholy band. A stretcher was tied to

Aberfa's horse. Linette lay upon it under a white shroud. None but the Gwyn Braw had passed through the high gates of Pengwern. No one else cared that Linette ap Cledwyn was dead. A few soldiers watched them without interest from the walls. The gates had been drawn closed at their backs.

But not all of the Gwyn Braw were in the mournful cavalcade. Dera had not retuned to be with them, and no one had gone to seek her out. She knew what must happen that day – let her come and find them if she was still one of them. If not – then so be it.

The snow was crisp and fragile under their horses' hooves, crackling and crumbling, the thin crust hollowed out by the warmth of the sun. They wound slowly up the hillside towards the leaning huddles of bare trees.

Snow fell from the branches as they passed. The tree bark glistened wetly.

Branwen found an open place between two clumps of trees. She halted, her eyes narrowed against the sunlit white snow, her head throbbing from all the raw light that poured into her skull.

They all dismounted. They had brought tools with them. Picks and spades to hack at the iron-hard earth. They also carried stones in leather bags – as many as each horse could carry. Stones enough to cover Linette's grave and hold her in the earth.

They took it in turns to dig – all except Aberfa, who wielded an iron pick and who would not pause or rest. Gradually, the hard ground relented and a mound of dark soil grew in the snow as the grave deepened.

The sun climbed to the crest of the sky as they worked, and they sweated under their winter cloaks until they had to shed them for relief.

It was a little past noon when the steady thud and thunk of pick and spade was broken into by the sound of hooves on the hillside.

Dera rode up silently to the graveside. She dismounted, her face closed and grief-stricken. Without speaking, she held out her hand for Banon's pick. Without speaking, Banon gave it to her. Still without speaking, Dera jumped down into the grave and began to dig as though her life depended on it.

At last the awful work was done. Aberfa and Dera were hauled up out of the pit, their reddened faces running with sweat. Iwan and Rhodri lowered Linette into her grave and all stood around the dark slot, hands clasped, heads bowed, tears running.

The long, mournful silence was broken by a soft chant, as Rhodri began to speak a song Branwen had never heard before.

She rides now as the sun sets upon her

Taken from us, glad and true and full of hope
Far, far into the deeps, on the winding path to Annwn
She rides to the court of Arawn, the great huntsman

Branwen lifted her eyes and gazed into the west.

The snow was a formless dazzle under the flood of sunlight. But was there something out there between the long hill and the mountains? A shape? Man-like, yet not quite a man. She screwed her eyes against the glare. Did she see antlers rising from a high forehead? Did she see from afar a faint glint of green, like emerald eyes shedding emerald tears?

Did she?

Gatherer of souls, eternal chieftain
She will feast now with the departed,
Feasting and fighting and rejoicing for all time
In the great halls of the merry unliving

And was there a gentle, shimmering movement out in the fathomless snow? A lady in white riding upon a white horse? And did the horse turn away and did the lady beckon?

Branwen felt that her heart was stilled in her chest. A small figure followed the lady in white as she rode away through the snow. A slender shape, walking lightly on lithe legs. And the head turned, and the hair was a tumble of curls the colour of new-ripened corn, and the eyes shone and the lips smiled.

> *She rides now as the great doors close behind her*
> *We shall see her nevermore*
> *Glad and true and full of hope*
> *Taken from us, we who loved her so deeply*
> *steeped in the pain that she has left behind*
> *We who mourn.*

As the song ended, so Branwen felt a profound silence come down over the world. The air was still. The sun halted in the sky. Not a twig stirred. Not a breath was taken.

The sound of a horse approaching from behind broke the spell and the pulse of the world seemed to miss a beat and when Branwen looked again to the place where she thought she had seen Linette and Rhiannon, there was nothing but smooth, endless snow.

'Are we come too late?' asked a familiar voice. Branwen turned from the grave. Drustan had brought his horse to a halt on the hilltop, a few paces away from them. Seated before him in the saddle was Romney, swathed to the nose in a thick winter cloak. Behind him, also swaddled deep against the cold, sat Meredith.

'Too late for what, my lord?' asked Dera.

'To show respect,' replied Prince Drustan. 'Will one of you help Princess Romney down? She is not used to riding and she is afraid that she will fall.'

For a moment no one moved, as though none felt inclined towards helping the child whose actions had caused Linette's death. But then Branwen looked into the small, round, petulant face and saw under the selfishness and the pride, a genuine spark of sorrow. She came up to the horse and lifted her arms. Romney reached down and with Drustan's help, the little girl was set safe on the ground.

The prince and Meredith also dismounted, and Branwen noticed how they held hands as they moved to the graveside.

So, a love-match after all. How fate can smile when it chooses to.

The others parted to allow them to come to the brink of the dark hole. Romney followed, pressing herself in between them, taking a grip on Meredith's hand, staring down at Linette's body under its white shroud.

'How did you get leave to come here?' Dera murmured.

'I am the king's son,' Drustan replied. 'I need no permission.'

'Does their father know of it?' asked Iwan.

Drustan lifted his head and looked into Iwan's face.

'I did not think to ask,' he said. 'Meredith and Romney sent word that they wished to speak with me. I came to them and they told me that they wanted to pay their respects at the graveside of your fallen comrade. And so we are come.'

'I hope we do not intrude on your grief,' said Meredith. 'The wish to do this came from Romney.'

Branwen looked at the little girl in surprise. She had assumed Romney had been forced to come against her will.

'I wanted to give her something,' Romney piped, her voice thin and strained. 'She was nice to me and I was not nice to her and I'm sorry she's dead and I wish she was still alive.' And so saying, she took something from within the folds of her cloak and dropped it down into the grave. It shone on the white cloth. A golden brooch. 'There,' she said. 'I'm sorry. I want to go back now.'

'Well, there was a marvel of sorts, to be sure,' breathed Iwan as they watched Drustan and the two princesses riding back to Pengwern. 'I would not have thought the little brat had such a heart in her. Do you think she did it of her own will, or was there coercion?'

'I think it was as Drustan said,' replied Branwen. 'I think she was genuinely saddened by Linette's death.'

Aberfa picked up a spade and thrust it into the mound

of fresh earth. She took the heaped spade to the graveside. 'Farewell, sweet sister,' she said. 'We'll meet again, anon.'

'But not too quickly, I hope,' murmured Iwan, taking another spade and joining Aberfa in heaving earth into the grave.

The white shroud gradually vanished under the brown earth. For a while, they heaped the earth over Linette, working in diligent silence while the day wore on. At last, they beat down the filled grave with the flat of the spades and then fetched the grey stones. Branwen watched, standing slightly apart from the others, while Banon and Rhodri and Blodwedd ferried the stones from the saddlebags and Iwan and Aberfa positioned them over the grave.

Dera came and stood silent at her side.

'You were gone a long time,' Branwen said. 'I thought perhaps you had made a final choice.'

'I made that choice last summer,' said Dera. 'I have not changed my mind since then. I am yours, Branwen, for all that is worth.' A miserable edge came into her voice. 'But it is hard beyond endurance to feel the displeasure of my father.'

'And so you are torn,' said Branwen. 'I understand.'

Dera looked sideways at her. 'There is more to it than that,' she said. 'My father's blessing would mean a great deal to me, it's true, and I linger at his side to show him that I remain his loving daughter.' She frowned. 'But there is something else. He is uneasy . . . he will tell me nothing in plain words – but I believe that this truce between the king and Prince Llew worries him.'

Dera now had Branwen's full attention. 'He fears treachery?'

'If he was sure that Llew ap Gelert was false, he would speak out,' said Dera. 'But I see him watching the prince and Captain Angor at times, and he has a troubled brow, as though he senses something bad is brewing – like a faint rank smell on the air.'

'And has he spoken to you of what word the Saxon messenger brought from Ironfist?' asked Branwen. 'Was he there when Ironfist's message was delivered?'

'He was not. The king and Prince Llew spoke to Hunwald alone in an antechamber, but the word is that some trysting place has been agreed – neutral ground where all may feel safe – and that emissaries of King Cynon and General Ironfist will meet there soon to talk terms. Apart from that, I know nothing else.'

Branwen looked into Dera's eyes. 'If you learn more, will you tell me of it?'

'On my honour, I will,' said Dera.

'And meanwhile we must kick our heels and bury our dead and hope for better weather . . .'

Dera gazed up into the clear blue sky. 'Is this bright

day not enough, Branwen?'

'I was thinking of the bitter winds and stormy clouds that gather in Pengwern,' said Branwen, also looking up into the crystalline sky. 'Of this . . . I do not know.'

Blodwedd looked at them, as though she had somehow guessed what had just been said. She walked forward, her arms outstretched. 'It is the Lord Caradoc who has given us this day,' she said. 'Do you think it happenstance that the wind blows from the south on this day of all days?'

'A curious compassion, it is,' growled Aberfa, standing up from having placed the final stone at Linette's head. 'To strike Linette down with an avalanche, and then to have the sun shine down upon her burial. Too much and too little, I'd call that.'

'You do not understand the workings of the Shining Ones,' said Blodwedd.

'Then enlighten us, Blodwedd,' said Iwan, leaning on his spade. '*Make* us understand.'

Blodwedd frowned, as though thinking. 'There is a story from long, long ago,' she began as the others gathered around her. 'A Druid priest and his wife came to do homage to Lord Govannon once on a time. They rode through the forest on a great white stallion that was their pride and joy. They came to ask the Lord Govannon to bless them with a child, for they had been childless in ten years of marriage.'

'And did Govannon help them?' asked Banon.

'Lord Govannon killed their horse and told them they would never have children,' Blodwedd said dispassionately. 'Then he sent them from him.'

Iwan blinked at her. 'And this is a story to show us how the Shining Ones love us?' he asked in amazement.

'Hush,' said Branwen. 'There is more.'

Blodwedd continued: "What Lord Govannon knew but the man and his wife did not, was that the woman was ill to the death. She would have died within the week had Govannon not blessed her with life. But a life had to be forfeit for the woman to remain in the world, and so Lord Govannon took their horse in her place.'

'A strange tale,' breathed Dera. 'But why were they left childless?'

'Because it was foretold that their firstborn would grow evil and madness, and that upon his twentieth birthday, he would slaughter his parents in their sleep.' Blodwedd looked around at the puzzled faces that surrounded her.

'And how does this twisted tale relate to us?' asked Iwan.

'Because we cannot know what purposes drive the actions of the Shining Ones,' Blodwedd responded solemnly. 'Only a fool judges the depth of a lake from the shine upon its surface!' She turned to Branwen. 'Now, with your leave, I will ride west as I promised.'

'Go,' said Branwen, moving forwards and putting her arms around Blodwedd's narrow shoulders, stooping a little to hold her close. 'Be swift as you can, and bring back good word from the Shining Ones. We will wait.' She released Blodwedd from her embrace. 'Rhodri? You may go with her if you wish,' she said.

'No,' Blodwedd said quickly. 'I must travel alone.' She walked over to where Rhodri was standing and took him by both hands. 'I will return to you, my friend,' she said, her voice low and full of emotion as she looked up into his eyes. 'Look to the west and think of me when you may.'

'I will,' said Rhodri. 'Be safe for my sake.'

Blodwedd smiled and moved away. All eyes followed her as she walked among the horses, but Branwen could not begin to imagine what thoughts were in those looks. The wish, perhaps, that they still had the love and protection of the Shining Ones, despite what had happened? Or the hope that they would be rid of the Old Powers and free to live and love and fight and maybe die among their own kind?

Just as Blodwedd was about to mount the horse that had carried her and Rhodri to the hilltop, Rhodri broke into a run, pounding through the snow towards her, his face twisted with love and concern. She turned, hearing him coming, and she held out her arms to him.

They clung to one another as though their hearts would break at the parting, and Branwen saw the owl-girl's face tilt up to Rhodri's, and his head come down so that they kissed – and that was something Branwen had never seen happen between them before.

And as they kissed, the world turned and the sun beat down and the wind blew soft from the south.

CHAPTER SIXTEEN

Branwen spent the latter part of the day alone in the small hut where Linette had died. Occasionally, footsteps crunched through the snow close by, but no one came in; at times she heard voices, but no one called out to her. She was, as she had wished, utterly alone. She wallowed in her solitude, needing it and hating it at the same time.

Mostly, she sat gazing into the fire. She had hoped for some kind of enlightenment to come to her – some understanding, some explanation of why her comrade had died – but her mind was heavy and blank and the time passed in miserable monotony. Not even the spirit of Linette ap Cledwyn lingered with her in that dreadful place.

As the day faded, Branwen threw herself down by the fire and floated on sleep's troubled surface, often awake, sometimes asleep but dreaming she was awake, her eyes always full of the brawling of the red flames, whether they were closed or open.

A hand on her shoulder brought her out of her stupor.

She gazed up at the figure crouched by her side, the face bathed in ruddy light. It was Dera.

'I have grim news,' said the young warrior girl. 'We must act, Branwen – or the king will be betrayed.'

Branwen sat up, shaking her head loose of dreams. 'What has happened?'

'My father asked that I sleep in his chamber in the Hall of Araith,' Dera began urgently. 'I obeyed, wanting to do all I could to please him. And so we doused the candles and prepared for slumber. But I could not sleep and I felt the need to be with my comrades in the long house. Once I was sure my father was asleep, I crept from his chamber, meaning to quit the hall. But as I was about to depart, I heard men speaking privately just outside the doors.' Her eyes burned. 'One was Angor, and the other was Prince Llew. They were discussing the meeting that is to take place with the Saxons.'

'The meeting where land will be offered as tribute to hold Ironfist's army back?' Branwen's mind was sharp as flint now. 'What of it? What did you hear?'

'The arrangements have been made,' Dera said urgently. 'The message that Hunwald brought from the Saxon general was that Ironfist would only agree to discuss a treaty on the condition that the king and Prince Llew meet him face to face.'

'That would be madness,' gasped Branwen. 'Ironfist will betray them to their deaths!'

'It is not Ironfist's treachery we need fear,' Dera said grimly. 'Listen to me close, Branwen. The meeting is to take place on the mound of Bwlch Crug-Glas in the east.' Branwen knew of the place – a bare and solitary tumulus crowned by an ancient ring of standing stones. It was no more than half a morning's ride from Pengwern. 'The king and Prince Llew are to ride out at dawn this very morn, with a troop of twenty-five armed warriors,' Dera continued, speaking rapidly now. 'The warriors are to be left at the foot of the mound, and Llew and the king are to ride to the crest alone and without weapons. There they will meet with Ironfist and one of his captains – also unarmed.'

'Ride into ambush?' interrupted Branwen.

'Worse than ambush!' growled Dera. 'I heard Llew command Angor to pick twenty-five warriors of Doeth Palas as the escort – twenty-five men who are loyal to the prince. And when Llew rides at the king's side to the top of Bwlch Crug-Glas, it will be to betray the king and to hand him over to Ironfist!'

'No!'

'By my soul, yes!' hissed Dera. 'Once the king is in

Ironfist's hands, Llew ap Gelert will be crowned the puppet king of Powys, and will allow the Saxon armies to enter Brython – and our beloved land will be in Saxon thrall for a thousand years!'

Branwen jumped up, burning with hatred and anger for the faithless prince of Bras Mynydd. 'So, it is as I thought,' she cried. 'This treaty between him and the king is all sham and pretence!' She swept up her shield and drew her sword. 'Let's to his chamber and take the head from his neck while the opportunity is there!'

'No!' Dera's voice was sharp. 'He is surrounded by warriors. We would be cut down before we came close, no matter how fiercely we fought.'

'Then we go to the king!'

'Our word against Prince Llew's?' said Dera. 'Cynon would not believe us.'

'He will, by the Old Gods!' growled Branwen. 'I'll see to that!'

'I think not,' insisted Dera. 'Remember, he trusts Prince Llew – even to the point of making him overlord of all the armies of Powys.' She rested her hands on Branwen's shoulders. 'Besides, he knows we hate the prince – he will think that we purpose the prince's downfall for our own reasons.' Branwen looked into Dera's eyes, knowing she was speaking the truth. 'I have a better plan, Branwen. A surer plan that will reveal Llew ap Gelert's treachery in a way that cannot be refuted!'

'Tell me.'

'We two should depart Pengwern upon this moment,' explained Dera. 'We should go to Bwlch Crug-Glas and hide ourselves among the standing stones and await the coming of the king and Llew and Ironfist. They will be unarmed, as was agreed – but we shall keep our swords at the ready! And the moment that Prince Llew seeks to betray the king, we will rise and strike!'

'By the Old Gods, I like that plan!' said Branwen. 'Three birds killed with but one stone! The king rescued, Llew ap Gelert exposed and, with luck, Ironfist run through with cold iron! But we should not go alone, Dera – we should take the others of the Gwyn Braw with us!'

'I think not,' Dera said again. 'Two may hide among the stones and hope not to be seen, but our chances of being revealed too soon would increase with a greater number. And besides, we two may quit Pengwern unremarked, but if all the Gwyn Braw leave, word will get back to Prince Llew, and his suspicions be roused.'

Branwen frowned. 'There's sense in that,' she admitted. 'But what of the twenty-five that will follow? How shall we keep them at bay?'

'If Llew is dead, I believe they will kneel to the king,' said Dera.

Branwen smiled grimly. 'Then Llew shall die,' she

said. 'At my hand shall the treacherous prince meet his end – and if fate allows, my second blow will be to the heart of General Ironfist!'

Leaving Pengwern at dead of night was accomplished without too much difficulty, despite the guards on the gates. For Branwen the hardest part was creeping past the long house of the Gwyn Braw to secure their horses, without rousing her comrades for the adventure that was to come. But Dera was probably right – six riding out together would cause too much of a stir. And there was another, perhaps stronger reason why Branwen was prepared to leave her followers slumbering while she and Dera departed.

She feared that more of her comrades might die. If the Shining Ones had chosen not to protect Linette, why should Branwen assume any others of the Gwyn Braw were safe now? Better to ride into danger with Dera alone, than to drag her friends to potential destruction.

'Who seeks to pass?' demanded the gate guard, standing besides a blazing iron brazier and wrapped head to foot in a cloak of thick furs. His eyes narrowed as he saw who it was that had led their horses to the outer bailey. 'What is your business outside in the deeps of the night?'

'I have heard word,' Branwen said, reciting the

explanation that she and Dera had practised. 'The Shining Ones wish to speak with me.' She regarded the guard captain with a cold eye. 'The Old Powers will not be denied, master gate warden,' she said in a low voice. 'Either you let us out to speak with them, or they will come here. The choice is yours.'

The man's eyes widened in panic and a few moments later one of the gates was opened a fraction to allow Branwen and Dera to lead their two horses out into the night. As they mounted up and rode along the causeway, they heard the timber bars being thrown into place. None in Pengwern wanted to have dealings with the Shining Ones. Let the shaman girl go and meet with the old demons, if she was moonstruck enough to wish it!

The wind had shifted in the evening so that now it flowed down like an icy river from the north, bringing thick snow clouds along with it, although for the moment no fresh snow was falling. If Caradoc had sent the blessing of that warm, bright day to them so that they might bury Linette in peace, then his benison had ended with the sunset, and the weather had turned foul again.

So, under a deep and starless night sky, Branwen and Dera turned their horses to the north and rode at the canter around the high walls of Pengwern, taking then an eastward path towards the banks of the frozen River Hefren.

They arrived at the isolated mound of Bwlch Crug-Glas a little before dawn. It rose before them, a smooth flat-topped hillock, its crest lifting some five fathoms above the snow-clad fields and forests that surrounded it. It stood there, brooding under the heavy sky, bare and white and eerie in the strange winter's night. It was crowned by a ring of age-old standing stones, erected there in the far-flung mythic times ere even the Romans came to conquer and to settle.

Legends swarmed about the place, legends of ancient rites and festivals, legends of the Druid priests of old, wielding their magic sickles, brewing their spells with the aid of mistletoe and myrtle. Calling on the stars for power, gathering at the four quarters of the year to speak the lost words and to perform the forgotten rituals at sunrise and sunset. Branwen had heard these forbidden tales from her brother, whispered in the dark night when all others slept. She had never forgotten them – she had never forgotten the images that capered in her mind when she thought of them.

Of course, in these days of the Three Saints, when men denied and feared the Old Ones in equal measure, the hoary old hill had lost much of its magic. It lay abandoned and unheeded in disputed lands where the borders waxed and waned between Powys and Mercia.

The old stones, leaning now at odd angles against the horizon, were no more than curiosities. But as Branwen tethered Terrwyn in a hidden forest glade and climbed with Dera at her side up the soft, swelling slope to the top of the hill, she was sure that she could feel a subdued power still, the slow heartbeat of the hill, throbbing under her feet as she trudged through the snow.

Dera carried a bunch of twigs with her, using their whipping ends to sweep the snow level behind them so that their tracks would not be seen.

They came to the crown of the hill just as the first gleam of sunlight glowed in the far east.

'Shall we hide together or apart?' asked Dera in a rush of white breath.

'Apart would be better,' said Branwen. She pointed northwards. 'Go find a stone where you can see but not be seen,' she said. She turned towards the opposite side of the ring. 'I'll do the same. When they arrive, do nothing till you hear me cry out – then move swift and sure and have your sword ready.' She looked into her comrade's face. 'If I fall, you must kill Llew ap Gelert.'

Dera nodded. 'I shall.' She handed Branwen half of the twig bundle.

'So. We hide and we wait,' said Branwen. She almost added *may the Shining Ones look over you!* but left the words unsaid.

Cold! So cold! Cold to the very marrow of her bones. Branwen huddled in the lee of one of the standing stones of Bwlch Crug-Glas as the sun slowly crawled up over the clouded horizon and a pale, colourless light began to creep across the land.

She tucked her hands into her armpits to try and keep some shred of heat in her fingers. There would be little point in leaping out to reveal Llew's treachery if her hands were too numb to grip a sword.

She wished Iwan and Aberfa and the others were hidden nearby. Had she been wrong to agree to Dera's plan? Was it a bad idea that the two of them were here alone?

She lifted her head so that her eyes peered over a nick in the stone. How long before something would happen? How long before Llew ap Gelert's blood would stain the snow?

Branwen heard the faint thud of hooves in the snow. The creak of leather. The dull rattle of metal. Cautiously, hardly daring to breathe, she lifted her eyes over the stone.

Two horsemen were approaching from the east.

One of them was a bearded Saxon man she had never seen before, bearing in his hand a Saxon pennant: a rearing white dragon on a field of blood red.

The other was General Ironfist. He was riding a tall black stallion, his red cloak spread out over the horse's rump. There was gold at his neck and wrists, and upon his head was a round helmet chased with filigree patterns of gold and silver. But it was his face that held Branwen's attention. A face she knew too well – a black bearded face scarred from hairline to jaw on the right side, a brutal face with a reddish blemish where once a cruel blue eye had stared. A ruined face clawed to the bone by Fain the falcon.

Branwen sought for some sign of weapons on the Saxon general, but no sword hung from his belt and she saw no axe or spear or seax knife. Not that he wasn't capable of hiding a dagger in his clothes!

The two riders brought their horses slowly to the very centre of the ring of stones, and there they halted, the horses snorting clouds, the men breathing white mist. Neither spoke. Against the formless grey of the clouds, they sat there in silence, staring into the west.

Time passed.

The standard-bearer spoke and Ironfist replied tersely. Branwen had no idea what had passed between them. Maybe the other had asked *will they come?* and Ironfist had replied *yes, be patient!* Or might it have been: *my dagger is to hand*, with the response *good! Strike swift and hard!*

The steady, snow-muffled beat of hooves came out of the west. Branwen turned her head and saw two riders slowly lifting above the curve of the hill. Her breath hissed and her right hand slipped to grasp her sword hilt, her left tightening on her shield.

Riding side by side, Prince Llew and King Cynon made their way through the stones and out on to the flat hilltop. Both were dressed in fine cloaks and clothes, and the king had the crown of Powys on his head.

Ironfist sat up erect in the saddle, watching with a glittering eye as the king and the prince approached.

Ironfist was the first to speak. *'Nytan laedenspraec, cyning?'* he called.

Cynan brought his horse to a halt some three paces from the two Saxons.

'General Herewulf,' he said. 'Forgive me. I do not understand you.'

Ironfist grinned like cold iron. 'I asked whether you speak my language, King of Powys,' he said in his heavy accent, a hint of mockery in his voice. 'The question is answered.' He looked at Prince Llew. 'It is good to meet at last, my lord prince,' he said. 'Let us hope this meeting will bring us all that we would wish.'

'I believe it will, my lord general,' replied Llew. Did Branwen detect a hint of deference in the prince's voice? Like a man speaking to his overlord rather

204

than to his sworn enemy?

'So is the tribute to hand, King of Powys?' asked Ironfist. 'Have you come here with the thing I requested of you?'

'I do think it is so,' said Cynon. 'My scouts tell me it is close by.'

Branwen frowned. That was strange. Surely this was a meeting to discuss what lands might be handed to the Saxons to prevent their invasion? So, what 'thing' was it that they were talking about?

'And when the tribute is in your possession, General Herewulf, shall we have peace?' asked the king.

'Say rather that we shall be upon the road to peace,' Ironfist replied. 'I shall hold back my armies for now, and our counsellors and wise men shall debate the question of the disputed borders between Mercia and Powys.' Ironfist lifted his chin, his single eye flashing. 'While the talks last, I shall not strike, you have my word.'

'Agreed, my lord general,' said King Cynon.

Ironfist leaned forward in the saddle now, and there was a wild and hungry look on his face, like a wolf that has scented prey. 'Give her to me, King of Powys! I would have her now!'

Her? Branwen's mind spun. The tribute that the king was to hand over to Ironfist was a *woman*?

A moment later, Branwen heard a stifled cry from the

far side of the circle of stones. There was a flurry of movement. Dera plunged into view, running hard, her face livid with dread and anguish.

'Branwen, we have been tricked!' she screamed. 'Fly! It is a trap!'

A large dark shape loomed up from behind the same stone. It ran forward, snatching at Dera, grasping her around the waist, the other hand coming up over her mouth.

Dagonet ap Wadu!

Dera's father lifted her off her feet, stifling her cries with one hand while she struggled and kicked in his grip.

Branwen rose to her feet, drawing her sword with a single hissing motion. But she had not taken a single step before she heard a rushing sound at her back. She turned to see a dozen armed men pounding up towards her. Not Saxon men – but warriors of Powys.

And at the same instant, more soldiers rose from behind the stones – Saxon archers, each with an arrow on the string.

Each aiming their arrows at Branwen.

She spun this way and that, her mind reeling as she tried to take in what was happening. The archers must have slipped up here as the sun rose, stealthy as spiders, lurking in silence to spring the trap on her.

'Take her alive!' roared Ironfist. 'The man who kills

her forfeits his own life!' Then he shouted again in his own language – as though giving the same command to the Saxon bowmen.

Branwen put her back to the standing stone, lifting her shield to her eyes, hefting her sword in her fist – standing ready as the swordsmen approached her up the hill.

'Branwen ap Griffith,' shouted Llew. 'If you fight you will die, that is most certain – but you will not die alone! Listen to me, witch girl! Throw down your sword, or when I return to Pengwern I will have all of the Gwyn Braw slaughtered. Do not doubt me!'

Branwen hesitated, her heart flooded with anger and despair. How had she misjudged the situation so catastrophically? How had it never occurred to her that this might happen?

The men were close to her now, moving more slowly, their eyes uneasy as they came forward. They knew too well her prowess in battle. None wished to be the first to feel her sword.

'I have archers with me who can shoot a cherry from the branch at fifty paces, shaman girl of the waelisc!' called Ironfist. 'If you do not drop your sword, I will order them to fire at your hands. Consider how well you will fight with nothing but the stubs of fingers!'

She lunged forward, shouting, sweeping the air with her sword. The soldiers drew back, fear in their faces. She turned and scrambled up on to the head of the tall stone, planting her feet firmly, turning to face the four horsemen.

'Am I to be sacrificed?' she called out to them, her eyes on the king. 'Am I the price of peace, my lord?'

King Cynon looked at her, his face calm and emotionless. 'You are,' he said.

'I will not surrender!' Branwen cried. 'I'll die before I am handed over to the Saxons!'

'So be it,' called Llew. 'Then we shall ride back to Pengwern over your dead body and cut the throats of all who followed you.' His voice was raven-harsh in her ears. 'And then we shall ride north to Garth Milain and we shall cut out your mother's heart for having cursed this land with such a fiend as you!'

Branwen gaped at him. Not for a heartbeat did she doubt his word. He would do these things. He would murder Iwan and Aberfa and Banon and Rhodri – and then he would go to her homeland and kill her mother.

He would! She knew it as certainly as if she could already see their bleeding corpses in front of her shrinking eyes.

She looked down to where Dagonet still held the squirming and kicking Dera.

So it's all done, is it? At least I die knowing that Dera did not betray me. She was as fooled as was I, that much is plain.

The conversation between Llew and Angor must have been staged for her ears. They knew she would come to me, and they knew I would act as I did. And so I walked open-eyed into the trap they prepared for me. Branwen the honourable fool. And what of my ancient guardians now? Where are they when the Emerald Flame is about to be snuffed out, when the Bright Blade is to be broken? Maybe this is how the Shining Ones punish those who turn away from them.

Or perhaps this was always the end of destiny's path for me.

Her heart breaking, she threw down her sword and let her shield drop from her grip.

Ironfist smiled. Saxon swordsmen surrounded the stone upon which she was standing.

Dera finally wrenched herself free of her father's hands. She dropped to her knees. 'Branwen! I'm sorry! I did not know!'

'But your father knew *you* well enough, Dera ap Dagonet, the saints help you to come to your true senses!' said the king. 'He said you would act as you did – and he was right.' He smiled a cold smile. 'Happy is the father who knows his child so well.'

'No!' screamed Dera. '*No!*'

Dagonet hauled his daughter to her feet, ripping her sword from her belt.

'Silence, child!' he growled. 'It's done!' He gestured

to a couple of warriors, who came forward and dragged the weeping Dera away between them.

'We return to Pengwern,' said the king. 'Farewell, General Herewulf. I shall send ambassadors to Chester in due time to debate the terms of a full and final peace between us.'

'And I shall welcome them, King of Powys,' Ironfist replied.

The king and Prince Llew turned their horses and rode away down the snowy hillside, the warriors of Powys following after them without a backward glance.

Branwen was alone, desolate and unarmed among her enemies.

Ironfist rode up to the stone where Branwen was standing.

'Well now,' he said. 'I have got what I came for.' The chilling smile widened across his ravaged face. 'Will you return with me to my camp willingly or bound to a horse's tail? Either way, I will not be denied the joy of your company.' His voice hardened. 'We have much to discuss – we must speak of how you murdered and mutilated my only son. We have that and many another deeds of yours to debate.' His pale-blue eye flashed with an evil that made Branwen's heart falter in her chest. 'I have a welcome prepared for you in Chester,' he continued with horrible relish. 'A welcome the like of which you cannot even begin to imagine!'

CHAPTER SEVENTEEN

Branwen huddled under scabby furs, her head tucked into her shoulders, her knees clamped to her chest, her arms wrapped around her empty belly. She stared up at a single narrow slot high in the stone wall, a thin, raw gap just under the ceiling through which the meagre, watery daylight oozed. It was the only glimpse she had of the world outside her cell.

That lean sliver of light was a blessing and a curse. Through it she could see a fraction of the sky. On good days when the clouds were being herded along under the whip of the wind, she would sit staring up for hours at the constantly changing shapes that coiled and rolled across her field of vision. On bad days, it was blank white or grey or yellowish and had no life to it at all. Early on in her imprisonment, snow had fallen frequently, sometimes so thickly that it almost blocked her view. But more recently there had been no snow. She guessed that in the world outside her prison, the long hard winter was finally coming to an end.

Sometimes the cold air would trickle down the wall from the raw slot and come creeping across the floor like icy water. Sometimes the gap allowed a vicious wind to gust into the cell and bite at her with its frozen teeth.

Voices and other sounds of everyday life in Chester bled down to her in her chilly cell. The shouting and calling of Saxon men and women – sometimes the laughter of a child. The pattering of feet. The creak of wheels. The clop of horses or the muddled percussion of hooves and the plaintive bleating of animals being driven to market. On days when the bustle of the busy townsfolk was especially loud, she longed for the absolute silence of the black night. To know that people were living free lives just beyond her reach was a torment that she found hard to bear. And yet, in the throbbing dark, she yearned for some sound to prove she was not dead and in her grave. By day and by night the torture in her mind never ceased.

'Rhiannon!' she cried in her despair. 'Govannon of the Wood! Come to me! Help me!'

But the Old Gods did not come.

I am no longer of use to them – no longer under their protection, no longer destiny's chosen child.

She had lost count of the days she had been here in

this sunken box of cold, sweating, lichen-stained stone. Once a day the heavy wooden door opened a fraction and a hand would throw in some scraps of food and a wooden bowl of water. Sometimes the bowl tipped over on the uneven floor and the water was spilled. Then she had to soothe her parched lips with muddy rainwater dripping from the gash in the stones. When it did not rain, she went thirsty.

Branwen had given up shouting and beating on the door – it gained her nothing but a ragged throat and bruised hands. No one ever came in response to her howls, no one cared when she threw herself with all her strength at the solid oak of her prison door. She was like a caged animal, kept barely alive and in torment for the amusement of unseen eyes.

All her possessions had been taken from her – sword, shield, her leather hunting clothes, the golden comb that her mother had gifted her and which she had carried with her always. Her slingshot and the leather bag of stones, her tinder and flint. Everything. She had been thrown in here wearing nothing but a brown linen shift and with nothing but a pair of mangy hides to keep out the cold.

They didn't. She was cold all the time. So cold that sleep seemed impossible – and yet she did sleep, fretfully, shallowly, waking often from hideous nightmares to a nightmare that was even worse, and from which there was no way of waking.

She had not seen Ironfist since she had been thrown sprawling in here and the door had slammed behind her with the crack of hard timbers and the clang of iron.

At first she had dreaded the moment when the cell door would be flung wide and soldiers would rush in to drag her to her death. As days followed days and nothing happened, dread turned to anger, and anger to bewilderment, and bewilderment to dull apathy. She dreaded now that the soldiers might *never* come – that she would be left here frozen and hungry for the rest of her life. Sometimes in the deep dark silence of the night, she wished she had something sharp that she could draw across her wrists to put an end to her dreary, aching, wretched existence.

Sometimes her own thoughts terrified her more than anything that happened outside her head.

Sometimes she thought of Iwan and Rhodri and Blodwedd and Dera and the others, but as the hellish days bled one into the other, she found she could no longer see them in her mind – no longer hear their voices.

It was as if the hunger and the cold and the misery and the loneliness were hollowing her out from the very roots of her soul and leaving her as nothing but wasted skin over a frame of brittle bones.

Branwen gnawed at the chicken carcass, holding it to her mouth with both hands, pulling the bones apart, tearing at the scraps of meat with her teeth. A whole carcass was a rare delicacy and despite the fact that most of the meat had already been cut off, there was still plenty to eat for someone famished enough to grind the gristle and sinew and cartilage between her teeth.

She was barely aware of the guttural, animal noises she was making as she ate; of how she squatted in the corner of her cell, her knees up to her chest, her feet splayed filthy on the straw-matted stones, the fur hides draped over her shoulders, her hair matted and tangled, her hands black with grime.

She lifted the bowl to her lips and swigged the icy water. It went down like knives into her stomach. She made a grunting noise and attacked the chicken bones again, her eyes darting this way and that as she ate.

It occurred to her that she was losing her mind. But what did that matter? Who would ever know or care?

Her head snapped round at a sharp noise from the door. Her mad eyes narrowed. What was this? She had been fed. Why was the door opening? What was happening now?

Two Saxon soldiers armed with spears entered, one of them carrying a thick round chunk of log. They saw

Branwen squatting in the corner and they turned their spears to point at her, their eyes wary, as though they feared she might fly at them with nails and teeth. The log was placed in the middle of the floor.

A third man swept into the cell. Branwen bared her teeth at the sight of him.

Ironfist!

The general was wearing his great red cloak, and there was a sword at his hip, but he wore no armour and seemed to be at his ease. He said something to the two guards and they left, slamming the prison door behind them.

He looked around the cell and sniffed, pursing his lips at the stink that Branwen no longer even noticed. Then he sat astride the log, as a man might sit on a stool, his elbows on his wide knees, his back bent and his chin in his hands as he looked at Branwen with his one good eye.

His one *bad* eye, rather – blue as ice and filled with wickedness. The eye of a snake staring out from a mind that seethed like the blood of wolves.

For a long time the two of them stared at one another without speaking. Until a growing pain in her chest made her suck in air, Branwen had not even been aware that she was not breathing. She had not used her voice for so long that talking seemed odd.

'How long have I been here?' she croaked.

'Thirty-five days,' Ironfist replied blandly.

'So,' she said, 'are you here to gloat over me or to kill me at last?'

'Neither, Branwen,' Ironfist replied, his voice strangely soft and mild. He straightened his back and let his two hands dangle between his knees. 'I've come to see if we can come to some understanding.'

She glared at him, waiting for treachery and malice.

'We have quite the history, don't we, Branwen?' he said after a few moments of heavy silence. 'It was on my orders that your brother and your father were killed and your home burned – and it was on your orders that my son Redwuld was murdered in the forest and his head impaled on a spike.'

Branwen lowered the gnawed carcass to the ground. 'What of it?'

Ironfist sighed. 'Do you know what they call you in Pengwern?' he asked, his voice strangely casual, as though they were passing the time of day in some ordinary market square. 'They call you the thorn that has no rose,' he said. 'And sometimes they call you the flea that worries the hound. And when they are feeling especially vindictive they call you the . . .' He paused, shaking his head. 'No. I'll not repeat it – I'm sure your dealings with the Old Powers are not so base as that.'

'What do you want?' Branwen murmured.

Ironfist rubbed his two hands together. 'What do I want?' he echoed. His pale eye glittered. 'I want you to understand that we need not be enemies.'

Branwen gave a hard croak of laughter.

'You disagree?' he asked with a trace of disappointment in his voice. 'Listen, Branwen, and tell me the truth – were you loved by the people of Powys? Were you cherished by them?'

Branwen rose slowly to her feet, drawing the hides around her. She didn't answer him. But she was very aware how he kept using her name. *Branwen*. Over and over. As though they were old friends. A new trick to addle her mind?

'You need not answer,' Ironfist said with a wave of his hand. 'I know the truth of it. They hate you. They loathe and fear and despise you, those people to whom you have given every last breath of your life.' He shook his head. 'Did you see how readily Llew ap Gelert and the moist-handed king gave you up to me? Do you know how long it took them to agree to hand you over into my custody in the hope of saving their own skins?' He snapped his fingers, a sharp sound that startled Branwen. 'That is how long! They were glad to be rid of you, Branwen. Trust me on this; they were pleased that the thorn without a rose was taken from their sides.'

Branwen wiped the back of her hand across her mouth,

suddenly aware of the chicken grease and scraps that clung about her lips, suddenly embarrassed by her appearance. 'I never asked for their love,' she said. 'I did what I had to do to save my homeland from you and your savage hordes. I'd have done the same had every last man and woman and child in Powys spoken out against me.'

'Well answered,' said Ironfist. 'You'd follow your destiny wherever it led you, is that so?'

'I would!' Branwen said, a rekindled defiance and pride glowing in her heart.

'And your destiny has led you *here*,' said Ironfist. 'And where are your guardians now, Branwen? Where are your Old Gods?'

Branwen's eyes glittered. 'Do not dare to ridicule them, Saxon,' she warned. 'You've seen what they can do – you were there at Gwylan Canu when Govannon unleashed the wind that sank your ships and set loose the forest creatures that devoured your men. Don't laugh at them, for they have long ears and long arms and they will not be mocked.'

'I do not mock them,' said Ironfist. 'I respect them. I bow down in awe to the power of the Old Ones.' He stood up now, and she found herself backing away although he had made no move to approach her. 'Listen to me, Branwen,' he said. 'We are not so very different, you and I. We hold to the old ways – we revere the ancient powers and we follow the paths set out for us by them.' He sighed and a curiously sad look passed over his face. 'Do you know where I would be, Branwen, if fate allowed? I would be on my estates in Winwaed in the north, riding to hunt through the long days of summer, feasting and merrymaking and listening at the winter fireside to the old sagas.' A wistful tone came into his voice, and Branwen got the impression he was seeing faraway things. 'Winwaed once belonged to the kingdom of Elmet – before you were born, Branwen. It was a broad and prosperous land, bordered by rivers to the east and west, with the kingdom of Deira to the north and the vast expanse of Mercia to the south. It was a fine place, my homeland, swallowed up long ago by King Oswald of Northumbria.'

The kingdom of Deira? Where had Branwen heard that name before? Yes! She remembered. Rhodri had been born in Deira – it was the homeland of the half-Saxon boy's mother.

'But destiny had other plans for me, Branwen,' Ironfist continued. 'Destiny decreed that I become a warrior, a *general* – a man of violence and conflict.' He looked at her, tilting his head slightly, angling it as though to focus better on her face with his one eye. 'Is my destiny so very different from yours?' he asked.

'Yes, it is,' she replied grimly. 'Because you want to conquer and to kill, and I want only to protect what is mine.'

'Is that so?' said Ironfist. 'To protect what is *yours*, is it? Do you think your family ruled in Cyffin Tir since the world was formed, Branwen? No, they did not. Before your father's family came, your homeland was governed by the Romans. And before the Romans came, there were other peoples. And before them, yet other folk, who had in their turn conquered and killed those that came before them, and so on and so on through to the dawn of time when the first man set foot upon the soil that is now called the kingdom of Powys and claimed it for his own.'

Branwen stared at him.

'The tides of man are a constant swirl,' said Ironfist. 'Powers come and powers go as fortunes and destinies ebb and flow.' He rested his hand on his chest. 'At this time, in this season of man, it is we Saxons who are in the ascendancy, Branwen. It is the natural order of things.' His eye glowed with fervour. 'And as the Saxon armies move, so their gods move with them. And thus are the destinies of the gods themselves in constant flux. Our gods grow more powerful, and the gods of Brython diminish. The great Lord Ragnar is a mighty and a benevolent god, Branwen. He will love you if you put your faith in him. He will show you a better destiny – a truer destiny.' He spread his arms wide, his head tilting upwards. 'And you will be loved, Branwen. I promise you this – in my world, the followers of the Old Powers are loved and revered and honoured. If you choose, you will be a priestess of the Old Ways, and your life will be filled with purpose and meaning and a greater destiny than the Shining Ones of Brython could ever imagine.'

She stared at him in shock. Now she understood the point of his soft and persuasive words. He wanted her to turn her back on the Shining Ones and offer herself to Ragnar, hellion of the Saxons, blood-letter and reaver.

'You'd have me put my trust in Ragnar?' she asked incredulously. 'A petty god I saw fly beaten and wailing from Merion of the Stones and Caradoc of the North Wind? I should betray all that I hold dear to sit at the feet of one such as he, feeble and weak as he is?'

There was no trace of anger or impatience in Ironfist as he responded. 'Ragnar is neither weak nor feeble, Branwen,' he said. 'His power is waxing as the powers of the Shining Ones diminish. Come, join with me – with us – use your strength and your wits to a better purpose. What would you rather have, Branwen? Your old life among people who detest and dread you, or a new life of joy and fulfilment with people who will honour and adore you?'

He smiled encouragingly. 'I don't expect you to change allegiances all in a moment. I will leave you now. Think over what I have said.' He looked around the filthy cell. 'This is no place for one such as you, Branwen. This terrible hole! Had I known you were being kept in such circumstances, I would have done something about it. Forgive me, other duties have detained me. But later is better than never. Give me but a few moments and I shall send servants to you, so that you be washed and fed and found finer accommodation.' He turned and thumped on the door with his fist. 'Be the shaman girl of the waelisc no more, Branwen – be all that you can be! Be a priestess of Ragnar!'

'The gown suits you, my lady. You have a fine strong shape, and the material hangs very well upon you, do you not think?'

Branwen stared emptily at the elderly servant woman, unable to come up with a response. She was some distance away from being able to think clearly about anything at all, never mind how clothes looked on her.

Enough time passed after her outlandish encounter with Ironfist for her to feel certain that the whole thing had been set up to confound her and to amuse him. But then her prison door had opened and servants had bustled in and she had been led out and taken to a room above ground. There she had been bathed and fed and had the tangles combed out of her hair and the grime pared from beneath her fingernails. Sweet-smelling oils were rubbed on her body and fine garments laid out for her to put on.

She allowed herself to be dressed in a kind of daze, as a puzzled child might. The gown was of a fine, slinky material she had never encountered before, the flowing skirts coloured brown while the close-fitting bodice was covered in silvery embroidery, trimmed with gold thread. The gown was gathered at the waist by a belt of supple leather, etched with intertwining Saxon designs and held at the front with a golden clasp of intricate workmanship.

And as if to make her confusion complete, attached to the belt was her golden comb, and her pouch of flint and tinder – and even her slingshot with its accompanying leather poke filled with small rounded stones.

'General Herewulf has told us that you do not like to have your hair braided or styled,' said another of the servant women, standing in front of Branwen and using her fingers to arrange Branwen's long dark hair over her shoulders. 'Is that so, my lady?'

Branwen gazed absently at her and nodded.

'Then you are quite ready!' said the first woman.

Branwen blinked at her. 'Ready for what?'

'Why, for the feast, of course, my lady. For the great feast in your honour!'

Branwen had been in the Great Hall of General Ironfist once before – but in very different circumstances. That time she had crept along the high walls, cloaked in the invisibility of Merion's magical stones, seeking Gavan's daughter as the revelries of her enemies went on around her.

Now she found herself seated at a long table at Ironfist's side, surrounded by cheering and howling Saxon warriors and with a dish piled high with food in front of her and an overflowing wine cup in her fist.

It was as if the world had turned upside down between sunrise and evening. She could not have been more stupefied by events if she had walked from her prison cell to find the sky turned green and the long winter changed to burning midsummer!

As she gazed amazed around the high, crowded chamber with its long tables filled with Saxons and its walls hung with enemy flags and banners, she was aware of a chant rising around her. She frowned, not understanding at first what was being said. Then her own name leaped out at her.

'*Branwen aefter Ragnar! Branwen aefter Ragnar! Branwen aefter Ragnar!*'

The chant grew louder and louder, the warriors now beating on the hollow tables with knives and fists and cups and even with their wooden platters.

'*Branwen aefter Ragnar!*'

The repeated words echoed to the rafters, ringing in Branwen's ears.

She turned to Ironfist, and saw that he too was pounding his fist on the table and calling out along with all the others.

'What does it mean?' she shouted over the noise. 'What are you saying?'

Ironfist grinned at her, his face glowing from drink, but his eye still sharp and cunning. 'They are calling out a hope for the future,' he said, leaning close so she could hear him over the racket.

'What hope?' demanded Branwen.

'The hope that you will become a priestess of Ragnar,' Ironfist declared. He made a sweeping gesture of his arm around the room. 'See, Branwen? See what can be yours if you turn away from those that hate you and join with us at Ragnar's table? See what delights will be yours for the taking? What honour? What glory?' He leaned closer to speak into her ear. 'Let me tell you of the future that is coming, Branwen. The snows are all but gone, and all talking is done. Within a few days I shall lead my army into the west. We are a mighty force. We will take Pengwern, and King Cynon will be slain. Then Prince Llew of Doeth Palas will kneel to me and all of Powys will be mine. And with Powys in my grasp, it will only be a matter of time before I hold all the Four Kingdoms in the palm of my hand. You can be part of that, Branwen. Say but the word, and all past enmities between us will be forgotten and forgiven and you will ride at my side as my most trusted captain.'

She stared at him, nonplussed, bereft of hope, feeling herself standing at the brink of some dreadful precipice. 'What word would you have me say?'

He smiled. 'It is as they say – *Branwen aefter Ragnar* – Branwen for Ragnar.'

'And what of my friends? What of my mother?'

'You have my word that you will be reunited with the Gwyn Braw, and that they shall not be harmed.' He nodded enthusiastically, as if all the wine he had quaffed was getting the better of him. 'Indeed, if they agree to remain under your command, they shall keep their weapons and ride with us to victory. And your mother shall be allowed to dwell in rebuilt Garth Milain in honour and peace.' He thumped his chest, spilling wine. 'My oath upon it!'

'And all this shall come to pass if I turn from the

Shining Ones and pledge myself to Ragnar?' Branwen asked. 'I'll be revenged on those who hate me, and I will be revered among the Saxons?'

'Oh, but you will, Branwen,' said Ironfist.

She looked closely at him. 'And I have your *oath* on this?'

'You do!' She saw his eye shining now, as though he knew his triumph was close.

'And if I refuse?' she asked.

He frowned. 'Do not refuse,' he said. 'Be true to yourself, Branwen – do not turn from this new life I am offering you.'

She leaned back in the chair, her forehead creasing, her eyes roving over the revelling Saxons that hemmed her in on all sides. She had a very clear vision of the options that lay in front of her. To do as Ironfist asked and to live, or to deny him and probably die.

And who in Powys would care if she died? Not the king, for sure – and certainly not Prince Llew. Not Dagonet ap Wadu, nor any other of the soldiers of Powys. They would be glad to be rid of her. The Gwyn Braw would mourn of course, and Dera would never forgive herself for having led Branwen to this end. But what would it matter? Ironfist's army would still sweep over Powys – the Gwyn Braw would most likely die in the defence of Pengwern. Garth Milain would fall and her mother's grief would be brought to a swift and sharp end.

And if she agreed to become a priestess of Ragnar? What then?

The Shining Ones did not deserve her loyalty – they had shown precious little of that to her in her time of great need. They had discarded her, after all the things she had done for them. They had left her to rot in a Saxon prison.

She saw Blodwedd's face in her mind – rounded, huge-eyed, framed by the feathery fall of tawny hair. The amber eyes pierced her and she heard the owl-girl's voice quite clearly in her head over the cacophony of the Saxon feasters.

'*Do not do this thing, Branwen. Remain true to your homeland. Remain true to your heart.*'

Yes, that was the one thing she could cling to in all her misery and despair and loss. The true voice of her own heart.

The heart of a warrior maiden. The heart of a child of Powys. The heart of the proud daughter of Griffith ap Rhys and Alis ap Owain.

Branwen turned her head to look at Ironfist. There was greed in his face, and a hint of the victory that he seemed certain would be his.

'Do I have your oath on all that you have told me?' she asked. 'Your deathless oath, General Ironfist?'

'You do!'

She laughed then, throwing her head back. 'Then I understand fully the value of all these things you offer, Saxon!' she shouted, her eyes flashing hatred at him. 'They are as worthless as your word, faithless and vile lord of a brutal and merciless people!' She sprang up, seething with anger. 'Do as you will, you filth! I'll never turn away from the land of my birth! I'll never worship Ragnar!'

Ironfist surged up out of his chair, his face contorted by frustrated anger, his hand rising, a metal goblet in his fist.

She laughed in his fuming face. 'So now your true aspect is revealed once more, Saxon cur!' she shouted. 'That is good – your pretences of civility sickened me to my stomach!' She spat at him. 'Know this – I would gladly die a thousand deaths before I betrayed Brython.'

'Then die you shall, shaman of the waelisc!' Ironfist bawled. 'Die and be damned!'

He brought the heavy cup down with vicious strength against her skull. White agony exploded in her head and Branwen fell forward into oblivion.

CHAPTER EIGHTEEN

To awake at all was something of a surprise to Branwen. She had expected to die, her head hammered to a pulp by Ironfist in his thwarted rage – her life snuffed out in a few frenzied moments. But she was alive – the agony that pulsed in her head was proof enough of that, not to mention the cold stone floor under her and the hideously familiar stench in her nostrils.

She lay still for a few moments, gathering herself. Then she sat up and saw that she was back in her cell and that her grand clothes had been torn off her and the filthy, ragged shift thrown over her body once more.

She shivered, pulling her furs around herself as she sat there in the dim light. It was day. The day following the feast, she assumed.

Despite her wretchedness, a steady, clear flame burned deep within her. Not hope – nothing *like* hope – but resolve and determination. She had thrown Ironfist's temptations back in his face. No matter what was to come, she had bested him, and that small victory tasted sweet in all the sour debris of her life

But now what?

Was Ironfist dreaming up some appropriate way to punish her for her impudence? Would she starve to death in here now? Or would she be dragged out for some more public penance and execution?

'*Caw!*'

She turned at the sharp croak. A bird stood watching her from the far side of the cell. She puckered her eyes, trying to make sense of the large black shape.

How had it got in here? It was too large by far to have flown in through the stone slit. And yet, here it was.

The bird stepped towards her, its heavy body swaying, its eyes so bright and fierce a red that it was as though its head were filled with fire.

She knew the malevolent stare of those red eyes. She had encountered this evil creature before.

'Mumir . . .' she murmured.

It was the raven that Ragnar had gifted to the great warrior Skur – a terrible creature with a dark heart and a beak sharp enough to peck out the very soul.

'No, child,' came a sinister, rasping voice from the raven's mouth. 'Not Mumir . . . although I have taken his form so that we may speak awhile together.' The eyes flared. 'I'd have you know your doom, child of the Dying Gods.'

'. . . *Ragnar* . . .' Branwen mouthed the cursed name, her heart freezing in her chest. But she would not give the terrible Saxon god the satisfaction of knowing how she dreaded him. 'I do not fear you,' she said defiantly. 'I saw you bested in the mountains. I saw you flee from the Shining Ones.'

The monstrous bird moved towards her, and as it came closer so Branwen saw that its body seemed to boil and billow, to swell and heave as though some inner force were trying to break free – as though the dark spirit of Ragnar could hardly be contained within the feathered form. Where it stepped, the ground burned black.

'Upon the morrow, will you be utterly destroyed,' the bird croaked. 'My faithful servant Herewulf has invented a new manner of execution especially for you. Your body will be mutilated and ruined while the crowds cheer and mock.' The sinister eyes shone like furnace fires as the black bird rose on ponderous wings, forcing Branwen's eyes to follow as it drifted across the cell and came to rest on the lintel above the door.

'But *you* shall not die, Branwen of the Weak Gods . . . I will keep you alive, even though your body be ripped into bloody-boned pieces. I shall have them cut off your head, my child, and impale it upon a spike.' Branwen stared up at the evil raven, sick with horror. 'Even then you shall not die,' continued the hideous voice as the raven took to the air again, swooping low so that Branwen was forced to flinch as its wings brushed past her. 'I will have them slice off your eyelids and bear your living head before them as they ride into the west to the conquest of Brython,' intoned the creature as Branwen turned again, unable to tear her eyes away from the deadly apparition. 'And thus shall you see all! And even then, when all of Brython squeals and writhes under the heel of my faithful servants, and when the Shining Ones are thrown down into the deepest pits of *Hel*, never more to rise, even then I will not let you die, child. A temple will be set up in my honour – a temple upon the hill that is called Garth Milain. And that temple will be named *Neahdun Cirice Ragnar* – the Hill of Ragnar's Temple. And your head will be placed in that temple, child – alive yet not alive, trapped for ever in the limbo between life and death.' The voice rose to a dreadful, harsh crescendo as the monstrous bird loomed above her, fouling the air with the slow flap of its wings. 'And there you will dwell, child!' it screamed. 'For all time!'

As the ghastly scream echoed in Branwen's skull, so the bird's body finally split apart from the inner pressure and Ragnar's boiling darkness gushed through the tiny cell, as heavy and dense as floodwater, driving Branwen to the floor and holding her there as she gasped for breath.

Two great burning red eyes glared down on her as the darkness penetrated her body and writhed in her mind, blotting out all memory of sun and warmth and life and love.

Ragnar was the only thing that existed in the world.

Ragnar was everything Branwen had ever known.

Ragnar was all.

'So, Branwen, how have you been?'

The well-loved, impossible voice woke Branwen from a sleep as heavy and suffocating as deep water.

She sat up. 'Geraint?'

'Who else?'

The world about her was still pitch black, but her dead brother stood in the utter darkness, as bright as a candle flame.

She scrambled to her feet. '*Geraint!*'

She ran forward, then paused, puzzled. She took another step towards him. Without having moved, he was still the same distance away from her. She reached out but could not touch him.

'Are you a ghost?' she breathed.

Geraint grinned and rubbed his nose. 'I have no idea,' he said cheerfully. He shook his head and rested his two fists on his hips. 'What kind of a mess have you got yourself into, little sister?' he asked. 'Can I not leave you alone for half a day?'

'Half a *day*?' gasped Branwen. 'You have been dead for half a year or more, Geraint!' Anger rose in her throat. 'How could you?' she demanded. 'How could you have been so stupid as to attack those Saxons at Bevan's farm? Did you think you'd be a hero? You weren't, Geraint. You were just another dead boy covered in blood.' Tears pricked behind her eyes. 'And I had to sit with you, and guard your body. How could you leave me like that?'

Geraint sighed and shrugged. 'These things happen in war, Branwen,' he said. 'I was doing well. Two arrows loosed and two targets hit. That's not bad, is it? Admit it – that was pretty good shooting on the run.'

'But they killed you!' wailed Branwen. 'And I was all alone!'

'You still had mother and father,' Geraint replied, an achingly familiar tone coming into his voice. Peevish and stubborn – just as she remembered him. Eight months in Annwn had not changed him, it seemed. 'I'd taught you all that I knew. It was time for you to strike off on your own.'

'Was it?' she cried. 'Do you see where I am? Do you see what I've made of my life?'

Geraint wrinkled his nose. 'You have made some curious choices, I'll admit,' he said. 'Those Old Gods,

236

now. Who would have thought they'd come awake all at once like that and join in the fight against the Saxons? I wish I'd survived to meet them. What was it like, Branwen – coming face to face with the Shining Ones?'

'Don't burden her with such questions,' came her father's voice, and Branwen saw that he was standing at her brother's side, although she could not have said when he had appeared. 'Can't you see she has enough to think about?'

'Papa?' Branwen gasped. 'I'm sorry. I'm so sorry.' Perhaps she could have saved him in the battle under the walls of Garth Milain – but she had chosen to go to her mother's aid, and so he had died.

'I know, child,' he said gently. 'You did the right thing. How could I have lived on if your mother had fallen? It would have been worse than death.' He smiled. 'And things are not so very bad in this place. We feast and we hunt and we tell old tales here.'

'As you shall soon discover for yourself,' added a third voice. Gavan ap Huw stood now with her brother and father, the old warrior of the old wars, come to visit her from beyond death in the nothingness of her prison cell.

Branwen stumbled forward, desperate for absolution. The three forms floated away without movement in the black void. 'You were right!' she cried, weeping now as she looked into Gavan's weathered, scarred old face. 'We should never have gone into the woods. I should have listened to you. You died because of it. My fault!'

'Hush now, child,' said Gavan. 'My death is not on your hands. With eyes wide open I chose to go into the woods. I was the author of my own fate. As are we all. As are you.'

She trembled. 'Will I die tomorrow?' she asked in desperation. 'Or did Ragnor speak the truth? Will I *never* be allowed to die?'

'Ravens aren't the only birds,' said Gavan.

'What do you mean?'

'Saxons aren't the only horsemen,' added her father.

'Ragnar isn't the only god,' said Geraint with a smile. 'Remember what I told you, little sister. Be calm, be silent, be swift, be still.'

The three men began to fade from sight.

'And remember what the goraig told you!' called Geraint, almost as an afterthought, his voice echoing from a vast distance. 'Beware the eyes like two black moons!'

'*Caw!*'

The harsh sound brought Branwen to her senses. The darkness in her cell was not so impenetrable as in her dream . . . or her vision . . . or whatever it had been when the three dead men from her past had spoken with her. A sliver of grey striped the dark above her head and a faint light filtered in.

'Leave me be!' Branwen shouted. 'Are you so petty a god that you must taunt me even on the day of my doom?'

'*Caw! Caw!*'

But it was not the deep, guttural cry of the raven – it was a lighter, more carping, more insistent voice. She frowned, rubbing the sleep out of her eyes with her hand.

'Fain?'

A grey sickle shape flew down from the slot of dawning light. Instinctively, Branwen raised her arm and the falcon came to rest on her wrist, his claws digging into her flesh.

'*Caw! Caw! Caw!*'

Shaking with the thrill of absolute astonishment, Branwen raised her other hand and gently stroked the falcon's chest feathers with the back of her fingers. 'Are you real?' she murmured.

Fain pecked at her hand.

'Ow!' The pain was sharp and immediate, and there was a spot of blood on the side of her thumb where his beak had struck.

The falcon let out more cries, his eyes bead-bright and knowing.

'I don't understand you, my friend,' she crooned, delighting in the exquisite pain in her hand, her spirits lifted by the arrival of the bird. 'Would that Blodwedd were here to translate. But you have found me at last, and that is a fine thing.'

'*Caw! Caw!*'

But does Fain bring me good news, or is he here to say farewell? she wondered, as the reality of her situation drowned her hopes. *I am in the middle of an army of thousands, and I fear that I shall die today.* Her forehead contracted as she remembered the words of the Saxon god. *Or worse than die. Far, far worse.*

Fain stared at her, treading with his claws, his eyes diamond-hard on her.

There were so many questions she would have asked if she could. *What became of my Gwyn Braw when Llew and the king returned from betraying me?* She knew she would die without ever learning the answer. *Were they allowed to live? Were they killed for fear that they would avenge me? And Dera, poor Dera. I wish I could speak with her. One word. One word of forgiveness, so that she might know I do not blame her for what happene*d. She drew the falcon to her face and pressed her cheek to its warm chest feathers. Fain endured this familiarity without resistance, as though he knew how it comforted her.

Did Blodwedd return from the west? Does she know why the Shining Ones turned from me?

Branwen spoke aloud at last, her voice choking hopelessly in her throat. 'Fain, Fain! Will Powys endure?

Or will Ironfist destroy my homeland as he has threatened?' Her whole body shook. 'Please, do not let Ragnar take me. Please!' She did not know whom she was pleading with – the Shining Ones, or some other, greater power? The 'She creator' that Merion had spoken of long ago in her mountain cave?

Was there any power in the world that could save her now?

Clank!

Branwen twisted her head at the sudden noise.

It was the sound of the door being unlocked.

Fain flew from her wrist. In a flurry of grey wings, he headed for the rectangle of light and was gone from the cell before Branwen had time to draw breath.

She stood, turning to face the opening door.

Three Saxon guards stood there, two armed with spears, the third with a sword. Their faces were forbidding and pitiless.

'Will you give me a weapon?' she asked, her voice firm and steady although her heart was faltering in her chest. 'So that I may die like a warrior.'

A fourth and fifth man appeared through the doorway, one with an axe, the other with a net in his hands.

Her muscles bunched under the ragged shift. She rose on to the balls of her feet. She would not be taken like this! She would not be led meekly to her death!

With a scream of rage, she flung herself headlong at her enemies.

She would die on her own terms.

CHAPTER NINETEEN

It had been a futile effort – Branwen's attempt to force the Saxon guards to kill her in her cell. They knew too well the price they would pay if they failed to deliver her alive and in one piece to the marketplace in the town of Chester on that bright and cloudless morning.

As she rushed at them, so they beat her to the ground, kicking her and stamping on her arms and legs to subdue her, then hauling her upright again, so she hung breathless between them, gasping and spitting blood.

But she refused to be dragged along by them. At the very least she would go to her death on her own two feet. Surrounded by the guards, she climbed an uneven stone stair and came into daylight. She blinked in the unfamiliar sunshine as they passed through a high arched doorway of cut and shaped stone and stepped into a wide, open area where an expectant crowd was gathered. Most were on foot, but behind the throng she could see warriors on horseback, chatting among themselves or straining forward to get a better view.

She knew where she was. She had seen this open space before in daylight, when she and Blodwedd had infiltrated the Saxon town of Chester in search of the casket-prison of Caradoc of the North Wind.

The cell in which Ironfist had incarcerated her for the last month was in the bowels of a huge old Roman structure, long ruinous and decayed.

A susurrus murmur rose from the gathered townsfolk and soldiery as Branwen appeared in front of them. She stumbled but balanced herself quickly, refusing to show weakness. Above her, the cracked shell of the Roman building lifted to the clear sky, its impossibly tall walls rounded, and circled with broken stone pillars as thick as forest oaks.

General Ironfist was there, decked out in his finest clothes, his cloak as red as fresh blood, spilling down off his broad shoulders and foaming at his feet. A golden helmet was on his head, etched with coiling serpent shapes, their scales of inlaid silver, their eyes green jewels that flashed and sparkled as he moved under the burning morning sun.

'Welcome, Branwen of the Petty Gods,' he called, spreading his arms to her as she walked forward in the ring of armed men. 'The sun shines down upon us on this most blessed of days.'

'I see I've drawn quite a crowd,' Branwen called to him, staring unafraid at the multitudes with their eager faces, greedy for bloodshed. Women were there as well as men, their expressions choked with blood lust even as they gathered their children close to watch the evil shaman girl meet her doom. Further off, the helmets and spear tips and chain-mail of the mounted warriors flashed in the sunlight.

Branwen eyed them all with a stony face, determined to show Ironfist and the gawping Saxons no hint of the fear that clenched so hard and fierce in her stomach.

'Indeed you have,' said Ironfist. He turned to the gathered people and shouted something in his own language. The congregation let out cheers and catcalls and jeers of laughter.

Ironfist turned back to her. 'I would not have you die alone and friendless, Branwen,' he told her, his single blue eye glinting in his ugly face. 'Call upon your gods, shaman girl. Beg the Shining Ones to save you.'

Branwen lifted her chin and stared challengingly at him, saying nothing.

She knew better than to cry out for help from Rhiannon or Govannon or Merion or Caradoc. They would not come, and her pleas would only serve to amuse the Saxon spectators. She would not perform for them like that! She would show them what fortitude a child of Powys could present as death took her.

'No?' Ironfist said, thrusting out his lower lip in pretence of disappointment. 'Well, if you will not, you will not.' He walked over to her. The guards stepped aside to let him through. He put his hand on Branwen's shoulder and turned her, pointing upwards with his other hand.

She followed the line of his finger. Upon the head of one of the stone pillars perched a large raven, watching her with baleful eyes that flickered with an unhallowed red fire.

'To tell you the truth,' Ironfist murmured in her ear, as though passing on some amusing secret, 'had they come, they would have been unable to do anything but watch you suffer. In this place, Branwen, in *this* land, Ragnar reigns supreme.'

Such a horror came into Branwen's heart as she looked up at the hideous raven that she didn't dare to speak in case her voice broke and let her down.

Ironfist stepped back and said something to her guards in his own language.

Branwen was held by the arms as four horses were led forward. Branwen watched them with growing apprehension. Was she to be trampled to death? It would be a horrible way to die, but it was hardly the dreadful new manner of death that Ragnor had threatened her with.

Four Saxon guards began unravelling coiled ropes. They brought them to Branwen and each tied a rope around her elbows and knees, knotting them excruciatingly tightly.

Biting her lip to prevent herself from crying out with the pain, Branwen saw the four ropes being fed out to where the horses stood, stamping their hooves and tossing their heads.

Four ropes and four horses.

Branwen shuddered as an inkling of what Ironfist had planned for her came into her mind.

The other ends of the ropes were knotted to the horses' saddles. Ironfist shouted instructions and the four horses were led away from one another, two to points at Branwen's left, two to her right.

More soldiers moved through the crowds, parting them so that four wide aisles were formed. Nausea filled Branwen's throat. Her legs weakened under her and had she not been held to the pillar, she might have fallen to her knees.

The long ropes hung slack between her limbs and the four horses. The animals now faced outwards to where the four passages had been cleared in the crowd.

Blood pounded in Branwen's head, louder even than

the growing noise of the excited Saxon audience. A chant grew among them, swelling and swelling till it sounded like thunder.

'*Waelisc abreatan! Waelisc abreatan! Waelisc abreatan!*'

Ironfist swung round to face her again, his face exultant. 'They call for you to be destroyed, shaman girl,' he shouted over the howling of the crowds. 'Would you beg for clemency, Branwen? Even now, if you give yourself to Ragnar, you will be spared.'

Branwen swallowed hard. 'Let it be over!' she shouted, her voice sounding frail and weak against the tumult of the crowd and the beating of blood in her temples. 'I die for Powys! I die defiant! Brython will never be yours, Ironfist! Never!'

'So be it!' howled Ironfist, lifting his arm. Four men stood holding the bridles of the horses. Four others stood at their rumps, armed with thick wooden staves, holding them ready to be brought down hard on the animal's backsides to spur them forwards.

On Ironfist's command, the struck horses would gallop away from Branwen. The ropes would tighten, thrumming as they became taut. There would be a torment of utter agony as Branwen's limbs were jerked from her body.

She would be torn apart.

'*Caw!*' She stared up in pure terror. Ragnar was glaring

down at her, and in the raven's fiery eyes she saw her fate revealed.

Not to die. To be ripped to pieces, but to survive.

To be a trophy of the Saxon armies.

To live for ever in agony and despair.

To see Brython overrun.

To witness everything she had ever loved be destroyed.

To never know peace.

Ironfist's voice rang out. '*Nu oa!*'

Now!

The four rods came down hard on the horses' rumps. The four animals sprang forwards, kicking up dust. The ropes hissed as they straightened out.

Branwen closed her eyes and filled her mind with the image of her dear mother. A final shred of comfort as she prepared to meet her doom.

CHAPTER TWENTY

A sharp sound made her force her eyes open again in wide surprise. *Thwick!* It was a familiar sound. The sound of a speeding arrow. She felt a pulling and then a release of tension in her right arm.

And at exactly the same moment she heard a murmur of consternation rise in the crowd, while above her head she became aware of yet another noise – a humming, buzzing turbulence coming down to her from high in the air.

She saw a second arrow come whizzing over the heads of the crowd. Aimed sure and true, it cut the rope that led from her right leg. And even as the rope fell slack, she saw cloaked figures dart from the crowd, arms raised, shouting, standing in the way of the two horses that were still drawing out the ropes from her left side.

The horses came to a startled halt, one of them rearing so sharply that it lost balance and fell back on to its rump. It writhed on the ground, trying to find its feet. But before it was able to get up again, the cloaked and cowled figure leaped forward and slashed at the rope.

Meanwhile, the other figure had hold of the last horse's bridle and was holding it steady while its sword stroke severed the final rope.

Branwen stood dumbfounded in her bonds.

Not ripped apart!

Not destroyed yet!

A raucous darkness swept down over her. She looked upwards. She was under a shadow cast by a great flock of owls. The birds came flooding in their hundreds over the top of the stone building, gathered together as dark and thick and threatening as thunderclouds scudding across the sun.

The raven demon gave a cry of fury and anger, taking to the air as the owls swarmed, but their great downy bodies surrounded and engulfed it.

A bellow of rage took her attention away from the upper airs. Ironfist had his sword in his hand. He was howling orders to his discomforted men. But a moment later a third arrow flew, striking Ironfist in the chest, glancing off his chain-mail, but sending him staggering backward with its force. He stumbled and fell, his golden helmet rolling in the dirt.

Scores and scores of owls descended upon the crowds,

screaming now, reaching out with their huge claws, raking the air so that the terrified people cowered and fell, or fled in panic, trampling one another in their desperation.

But in all the chaos, Branwen saw two horses riding towards her, ignored by the owls, buffeting their way through the milling throng.

One of the horses bore two cloaked and cowled riders, the other, slightly in the lead, carried just the one figure, his cowl stripped back, a bow across his shoulders and a bright sword flashing in his hand.

'*Iwan!*' Branwen's voice escaped involuntarily from her throat.

It was Iwan, beyond all hope, beyond all delusion, beyond all reason – it was *Iwan*! Iwan ap Madoc come to save her!

One or two soldiers, rallying themselves in all the mayhem, blocked Iwan's path. He cut them down like dry grass as he urged his horse out through the mêlée and galloped towards her, his bloodied sword spinning in his fist.

'Gwyn Braw!' he shouted. 'Gwyn Braw to Branwen!'

Gasping in wonder and disbelief, Branwen now saw who rode the other horse. It was Banon, with Blodwedd clinging on behind. And the two figures that had stalled the wild gallop of the roped horses were Dera and Aberfa.

The Gwyn Braw had come to her rescue!

Sweet gods of water, wood and stone! Am I to be saved?

Bringing his horse up short, Iwan leaped down from the saddle. His sword flashed in front of Branwen's eyes – once, twice, three times. The ropes fell away from her and she lurched forward into his arms.

'Do exactly as I say,' he panted, pulling her after him as he ran to one side. 'Say nothing. Trust me.'

He drew her into the space between two of the stone pillars, pressing himself up against the ancient stone wall, holding her tight against him in both arms. She was shaking so much that she could hardly stand. She felt him press something small and hard and cold to the side of her neck.

'Be silent!' he hissed.

Too shocked and stunned to disobey, she leaned against him, breathing hard, her face up close to his, her eyes staring into his eyes. He grinned a fierce grin and winked, lifting his mouth to kiss her forehead, then bringing his lips close to her ears.

'I have two of Merion's crystals,' he whispered. 'Blodwedd brought them to us. If we keep still and make no sound, we may go unseen in all this uproar. Do not fear – we have a plan.'

Merion's crystals. Six small white stones that the Mountain Crone had imbued with a part of her powers, so that anyone wearing one of the stones against their flesh would be able to move unnoticed among their enemies. Not invisible as such – but unobserved so long as the eye of a foe was not drawn to them by a sudden word or action.

Branwen huddled against Iwan, feeling the heat of his body seeping into her through the thin rag that covered her, feeling his breath warm and sweet on her cheek, feeling his arms enclosing her.

'Give me your sword,' she hissed. 'I must fight!'

'No!' he insisted, his arms tightening around her. 'Let others do it – they are better equipped to escape alive! Be calm and still, for pity's sake, Branwen! I know what I'm doing.'

A terrible conflict was taking place in the airs above Branwen's head. She could hear screaming and hooting and croaking from the mass of owls that had mobbed the raven. But Ragnar was no easy prey. Every few moments, the body of an owl would come tumbling down from the affray, bloodied and torn and bereft of life, to thud pitifully on to the ground. A few of the injured creatures tried to move, but most lay stiff and still, their feathers clogged with gore.

But the remainder of the great flock was still causing disorder and pandemonium among the Saxons, tearing flesh, pecking eyes, beating at faces and limbs with their wide, sturdy wings. The occasional soldier stood his ground, swinging blindly with a sword, or thrusting into the air with a spear, his other arm flung up to protect his face. But most had scattered or lay writhing under the ferocious weight of the attacking birds.

The passage of events was too swift for Branwen to take in. It seemed to her that only a few beats of her heart ago she had been on the brink of a horrible fate – but now, in the blink of an eye almost, it seemed – the turn of a head, the time it might take to draw in a breath – the world had come alive again around her and she was filled with new hope and new anxiety and new life.

She watched in a daze as the owls rose and gathered, leaving blood and dread and disorder in their wake. She saw them flocking above Blodwedd and the others of the Gwyn Brawn. She saw that Dera and Aberfa were horsed now. She saw Banon turn her steed away and go riding hard and fast towards the gate of the city, Aberfa and Dera close behind.

Ironfist staggered to his feet, roaring orders to the remnants of his soldiery, running after the fleeing horses. And through the power of the white crystals, Branwen could now understand his words, even though he was speaking his own tongue.

'Stop them!' he howled. 'To horse! They must not get away! They have the shaman girl with them! A bag of gold to the man who brings down the waelisc witch!'

Iwan whispered in Branwen's ear again. 'See now what we had planned? Dera will lead the others to the bridge and over the River Dee while you and I slip quietly away in the opposite direction.'

'They will be run down and killed!'

'With good fortune, they will not. The owls will do all they can to cover their escape! They are loyal birds and brave fighters, and they will do Blodwedd's bidding, even to the death. While the owls keep Ironfist's men busy on the bridge, Dera will lead the others north and around in a wide circle. If they outrun the Saxons we will meet with them in a place we have already chosen. The two of us shall approach it from the south, and there will be no Saxons on our trail.'

'And if they do not outrun the Saxons?'

'Then you at least shall be saved,' Iwan replied. 'The Chosen One of the Old Gods will not be lost, and neither shall the great destiny that she is meant to fulfil.'

Branwen stared into Iwan's dancing eyes. 'How did you know where to find me?'

'That's a tale for a less precarious time and place,' said Iwan. 'Are you able to walk?' His eyes were anxious. 'You are grown so thin,' he said under his breath, a catch coming into his voice. 'I've fretted for this day for a month and more!' He touched his forehead against hers. 'I feared you were dead, Branwen. Truly, I did!'

She lifted her hand to touch his lips. 'Hush, now!' she said. 'I'm alive, Iwan. And I can walk, barefoot though I am and half naked in such cruel weather!'

'In that at least, I can help you.' Iwan undid the clasp that held his cloak and threw it around her shoulders, pulling it tight around her and clipping it at her throat. He looked into her face again, and for a moment the longing in his eyes took her breath away. But then he lifted the hood to cover her head and leaned forward, peering out over her shoulder.

'The plan goes well,' he said. 'Let's slip away now. Remember – move as quietly as possible and say nothing. We will need to pass close by the army camp, and I'd not count much on our survival if they get wind of us!' She shivered. 'Have you seen their numbers, Branwen? I'd say Ironfist has mustered six or seven thousand.'

'I've seen them,' Branwen replied. 'Come, Iwan. Give me the crystal.'

He opened his palm and she took the small, cold crystal and closed her fist around it. She looked up. The sky was clear now, but she had noticed that there were no black feathers among the tawny bodies of the slaughtered owls. It seemed that the raven had fled. But where might he have gone, that was the question.

Ragnar was not a demon to be defeated by owls, no

matter how thick they flocked around him.

So where was the dark god of the Saxons?

Where was Ragnar?

Branwen and Iwan made their stealthy way to the south gate of the town. On the way, they were often forced to step aside or to dart into cover as warriors came running past them in the opposite direction. From the centre of Chester, battle horns were blowing a strident call as Ironfist gathered his troops to hurl them in pursuit of Dera and the escaping Gwyn Braw.

Branwen watched the passing Saxon soldiery with angry, narrowed eyes, wishing she had a sword to hand so that she could strike them down. She felt again that slightly dream-like state created by Merion's crystals – the eerie sensation of being present but unseen, of being among her enemies, and of hearing their voices speaking a language she hardly knew, and yet at the same time being able to understand their speech.

The Saxons were evidently in some confusion.

'What has happened?'

'Have the waelisc mountain rats attacked?'

'I think not! More likely something has gone amiss at the execution of the witch girl. Did you see the owls? They were not here by chance! Remember how they flocked to save that demon creature last summer? They're bringing some similar mischief now, I'd swear that by Wotan's beard!'

'Cut out your jabbering and run, you fools! The general needs us!'

Keeping tight to the walls, Branwen and Iwan managed to slip away through the open gate. Ironfist's mighty encampment confronted them now. When Branwen had been brought this way the previous night to attend the feast in the Great Hall, she had only been able to guess at the size and scale of the army – but now she saw it under a clear sky, and her heart turned cold.

Stretching away as far as the eye could see was an ocean of tents and huts and paddocks, of smithies, and storehouses and barns. There were horses by the hundred, wagons loaded with weapons, barrels filled with arrows and spearheads. The camp had become a whole city of dwellings and work places to house and support the vast Saxon army.

And despite the scores that had run at the summoning of the horns, thousands upon thousands of warriors still swarmed in the camp.

Iwan tugged gently at her sleeve and Branwen turned away from the awesome and fearsome sight, following him as he slipped alongside the outer southern walls of Chester towards the River Dee.

'We can't risk crossing the river here,' he murmured

close in her ear. 'Someone might notice the disturbance in the river. We'll head south a way and find some secluded spot to swim over.'

She nodded silently, her mind still glutted with the image of Ironfist's gigantic army. She could almost see them in her mind – flooding through Powys like an unstoppable disease.

Even if she survived – even if she returned alive and battle-ready to Powys – how could she ever hope that the warriors of Brython could hold back such a tide of hate and death?

They followed the meandering loops of the river southwards, till Chester and the army camp were lost behind hills and ridges and bare winter woodlands. Then they travelled silently a little further into the wilds, seeking for some place where the river seemed less wide.

They found a likely crossing place at last, where the river narrowed between high, grassy strands, backed by thick woodlands. They slithered down the muddy, pebbled banks and stepped hand in hand into the icy flow.

But the moment that Branwen's foot touched the water, it began to bubble and churn, foaming and spitting and drawing away from her. She gave a cry of surprise as the running water pulled back, revealing a broad arrowhead of muddy, pebble-strewn riverbed.

'What's this now?' hissed Iwan, staring at the boiling and eddying lips of retreating water. 'What new tricks have you learned while you were in prison, Branwen?'

'None, I've learned *none*,' she breathed. 'This is not *my* doing.'

They grasped each other's hands again, fingers twining tightly as they watched the waters curl back into two long, seething bulwarks of frothing and swirling foam. The dank riverbed lay exposed now in a deep water-walled ditch all the way to the far bank.

'Run!' said Iwan. 'Quickly. While we can.'

Branwen went leaping down with him between the rising dykes of ever-moving water. The bubbling crests of the two poised walls rose high above their heads, roaring like cataracts, spitting a fine hail of drops down on to them as they pounded along the slithery and slippery channel.

Branwen glanced anxiously from side to side as they flung themselves towards the western riverbank, their heels kicking up mud and ooze, their lungs gasping for air in the fine haze of water droplets.

The towering, howling, thundering banks of racing water would give way – they *had* to give way! This was beyond all reason! They would be crushed under the weight of falling water.

Yet they were not. There was a final frantic scramble up the far bank, their feet sinking deep in the slime, mud squelching between their fingers. And then, breathlessly, they were up out of the river and on to firm, dry land again.

Branwen hardly had time to turn before there was a crash and a boom and a great spurt and fountain of white spray, as the vertical walls of water fell in on themselves. The water moiled and eddied for a moment, then the foam spread out and vanished and the river was flowing again as it had ever done.

'That was Rhiannon's doing,' Branwen murmured in a daze of astonishment. 'It must have been.' She turned to Iwan. 'She has not forsaken me!'

'So it would seem,' he said with a grin. A moment later he frowned. 'But why has she waited so long to hold out her hand to you? Were you being punished for refusing Merion of the Stones – and is that punishment over?'

'Maybe so,' said Branwen, feeling light-headed. 'Or perhaps the Lady in White was not able to come to me in Saxon land.' She turned to Iwan, the full realization of what had happened dawning on her. 'They have not abandoned me, Iwan!'

'No, they have not!' Iwan took her hand and together they walked up through the black-boned trees that bordered the river. They came to a small clearing, and as though to offer them yet more comfort, the sun burned down hot in that lonely place. They stood facing one another, dry from the miracle of the river crossing, but still cold and exhausted and far from home.

Wherever home might be now!

'Where must we go?' Branwen asked. 'To meet with the others?'

'West, and then north,' said Iwan. 'We need first to find some high ground so I can judge where we are. A shame we have no horses – I think we have a long slog ahead of us, Branwen.'

She gave him a glad smile. 'I am alive and whole,' she said. 'That is enough for now. Wishing for horses might be—' She stopped, hearing sounds through the trees.

Iwan drew his sword and stepped in front of her. His bow was still across his back, but Branwen saw that there were no arrows.

'Saxons?' she whispered, stooping and feeling through the leaf-mulch for any handy missiles.

'Perhaps.'

She stood up again, a decent-sized rock in either fist. The first soldier to come at her would get a well-aimed stone in his face before he laid a hand on her, she was determined of that.

'Horses,' Iwan whispered. 'Two or three, I think.'

'Yes! I see them.' Dark shapes moving through the trees. One horse for sure, maybe more. Branwen judged the weight of the stones in her hands, ready to hurl them as soon as she saw a target.

They stood poised as the horses came closer.

Thub-thub-thub-thub through the trees. The faint snort of horse breath in the stillness of the woods.

Iwan wiped a lock of hair off his face, licking his lips as he shifted his balance from foot to foot.

The dark forms drew closer. Branwen's blood pounded in her head. Two horses. But with no riders!

Iwan straightened up, his sword arm drooping as he stared at the two horses that came clopping into the clearing. They were saddled and bridled, and on the saddles of both were strapped bulging leather panniers. Upon the saddle of the leading horse hung a shield and a sword.

'What's this new wonder?' Iwan asked in astonishment as he stared at the two familiar horses. Branwen recognized them as well, a dun mare with a cream-coloured coat and a black mane and tail, accompanied by a tall bay destrier with a fiery eye. 'These are our own horses, or my eyes are playing me false!' he gasped. 'Gwennol Dhu and Terrwyn in the very flesh! But how?'

'I do not know,' said Branwen with a thrilled smile. 'But see their eyes! They are a gift!'

She had noticed the green light in the eyes of the two horses from the moment they had emerged from the shadows. She had seen that same flickering emerald light before – in the eyes of animals under the enchantments of Govannon of the Wood.

'The Shining Ones again!' Iwan breathed, sheathing his blade and stepping forward quickly to grasp the hanging reins of Gwennol Dhu. He stared at Branwen in amazement. 'Their favours come thick one upon the other, Branwen. This is welcome relief, indeed.'

'Yes, it is,' said Branwen, her throat thickening, tears of joy pricking behind her eyes. She threw her arms about Terrwyn's broad, muscular neck, breathing in his scent for a moment. 'I never thought to see you again, my lad!' she murmured. 'This meeting is a great joy.' Terrwyn nodded his great head and snorted.

Branwen moved to the saddle and opened the pannier. She found warm clothing and a cloak within, as well as cheese and bread and a stoppered bottle of water. She would have wished for her mystical white shield to have been returned, but any weapons were welcome in the wilderness.

'But why now, when the Old Gods could have come to our rescue a thousand times in the past?' asked Iwan.

'I don't know,' Branwen gasped, hardly able to speak for the solace and bliss that filled her. 'Blodwedd always said we could not fathom the ways of the Shining Ones.' She looked at Iwan. 'But we are saved! We have food and clothes and beloved horses to bear us!'

He smiled a true, merry smile for the first time. 'We are saved,' he agreed. 'I will ask no more questions. Come, give me back my cloak and put on the clothes Govannon has sent you. Bear the shield on your arm and strap the sword about your waist, they are surely meant for you. We can eat on the way! And it would not surprise me to find that these steeds have a clearer idea of our destination than we have!' He laughed aloud as he looked at her. 'Branwen of the Shining Ones! Branwen the shaman girl! You are a marvel to me, by all the saints, you are!'

CHAPTER TWENTY-ONE

Iwan had been absolutely correct – the two horses had known where to take them. No sooner had they climbed into the saddles, than the beasts had turned and set off at a lively canter through the trees, down the long hillside and northward through the heather and spinneys and wild grasslands of eastern Powys. The speed of their travelling made conversation virtually impossible, and so Branwen had to wait a while longer for answers from her rescuer.

As dusk descended they were riding at a tireless trot through a long, narrow valley, and as the moon came up full in the starry sky, they found themselves under a high cliff of pale, bare rock. Without warning, the two horses stopped.

Branwen peered around. 'And is this the place where we were to meet the others?' she asked.

Iwan shook his head. 'I don't know where we are.'

'Our steeds do, it seems,' said Branwen. 'What should we do, do you think? Dismount and make camp for the night?'

'It's a bleak place to seek for shelter,' said Iwan.

'All the same.' Branwen was certain that they had been brought here for a reason. She swung down from the saddle; but as her feet hit the ground, she felt the world tremble under her.

With a deep creaking, growling groan, the face of the grey cliff yawned open in front of them like a sideways mouth. The horses stood calm and unperturbed, their heads down to tear at the long grass, seemingly indifferent to the uncanny gaping of the raw stone wall. Iwan jumped down to be at Branwen's side, his eyes wide and thrilled.

The fissure in the cliff face became still and the ground was quiet again under Branwen's feet. A broad, low-roofed cave was revealed, and in the middle of the even, earthen floor, under the sheltering arch of solid rock, a fire of hewn wood was burning brightly.

Branwen moved forward and rested her hands on the cold cliff face. 'Thank you,' she called. 'Merion of the Stones – thank you!'

They unsaddled the horses, tethered them where there was good grass to eat, and carried the panniers inside.

They ate and drank, seated close to the jumping flames, and for the first time in an age of torment,

Branwen felt genuine warmth and comfort seeping into her body so that her cheeks glowed and her fingers and toes tingled with new life.

'Now will you tell me how you came to save me at the very last moment?' Branwen asked Iwan, basking in the heat of the fire and watching his face through the licking flames.

'It's a long story, if you want to know it all,' he replied.

'I do. Leave nothing out.'

And so he told her the tale of how the king and Prince Llew and twenty-five warriors on horseback set off for their tryst with Ironfist, and how the Gwyn Braw stood on the walls of Pengwern, staring into the west, waiting for Branwen and Dera to return. And it was not only the two warrior girls who had vanished – Fain was gone, too. Rhodri guessed the faithful bird had departed with Branwen, but no one knew for certain.

Neither Fain nor the two maidens returned that day, but the king and the prince did, in the early evening, full of good news from the east. The talks had gone well and Ironfist had been bought off with vague promises and the offer of further negotiations, they were told. What the Gwyn Braw did not notice was the swathed and gagged figure who was bundled into the citadel and locked away in a chamber of the Hall of Araith. Thus they had no inkling then that Dera had been brought back as a captive.

Days passed and still Branwen and Dera did not return from the west. Rumours circulated that the two girls were dead, or that they had fled the king's citadel in fear of Saxon attack. Others said they had indeed met with the Shining Ones and that the Old Gods had devoured them.

'We did not believe this last tale,' Iwan told her, grimacing at evil memories. 'At least, the others did not. I was not so resolute at first, and the thought that I had lost you for ever seared me through and through . . .' He paused. 'It was Rhodri who convinced me to have faith. He never doubted the Shining Ones for a moment. He was certain that you and Dera would return, and the rest of us fed off his belief.'

Branwen smiled tenderly at him; dismayed to think that he had known such grief, but glad that Rhodri's stout heart had brought them all through.

Then, Iwan told her how the passage of a whole moon went by with no word from Branwen or Dera. At the same time, scribes and wise men were sent to speak with Ironfist's representatives in the east, while reinforcements began to arrive from Dyfed and Gwynedd and Gwent, swelling the numbers in Pengwern and preparing for war.

'And then, when some were beginning to lose all hope, Blodwedd came back to us,' Iwan carried on. 'I don't know how she got into the citadel – certainly not through the gates – but she woke us at dead of night as we slept in the long house.' He stopped, snapping his head around to face the cave mouth. 'Someone is out there!' he hissed, standing up and drawing his sword.

A small figure stepped into the firelight. A slender shape with a tumble of tawny hair and with great, reflective golden eyes in her round face.

'Well met,' said Blodwedd. 'I came first to be sure you were not enemies, although I guessed what I would find!'

Branwen leaped up, running headlong towards her friend. She grasped Blodwedd in her arms, clinging to her, burying her face in the long hair. Startled as she was by this display of human affection, the owl-girl smiled and patted Branwen's shoulders. 'Well met, I say again, Branwen of the Shining Ones,' she said. 'I bring good news from the west.'

'I know it!' cried Branwen, almost too choked with emotion to speak. And as though seeing Govannon's messenger again after so long were not enough, Branwen saw the others of the Gwyn Braw step forward into the cave mouth. Dera and Banon and Aberfa gathered around her, laughing and weeping and throwing their arms about her. And Rhodri, too – his dear face wreathed in smiles as she turned to embrace him.

'I would have come to your rescue,' he told her,

hugging her tight to him. 'But there were only six stones — so one of us had to stay back. And you know these women!'

As if these blessings weren't enough for Branwen, Fain came flying in under the roof, crying out again and again as he circled the joyous gathering.

'But how did you find us?' Iwan asked as they all gathered around the fire.

'Fain came to me and told me that you were under the protection of the Shining Ones and that you had been brought to this place,' Blodwedd told her.

'The owls held back the Saxon horsemen long enough for us to get far away from them,' said Aberfa. 'And I'll warrant they'll not find us now.'

'Let's hope not,' said Dera, looking at Branwen with a haunted light in her eyes. 'I was such a fool, Branwen — to have led you into treachery.'

'All's done, Dera, my friend,' said Branwen, reaching out to grasp her hand. 'I do not hold you to blame for what happened to me. Others must bear that burden!' She looked around at them. 'But I would know how you came to me at that last moment in Chester.' She turned to Blodwedd. 'Iwan told me you returned to Pengwern at dead of night.'

'Indeed I did,' said the owl-girl. She reached out her long slender fingers to Branwen, the white nails curling.

'See now, Branwen, what I saw. See how you are loved!'

As Blodwedd's fingers touched her forehead, Branwen felt a sudden giddiness. The world spun in an arc of whirling red flame and she felt herself tumbling and tumbling.

It was an uncanny sensation, one that Blodwedd had forced upon Branwen once before. She felt as though she were no more than two watching eyes, bodiless, remote, floating on the air, as events unfolded before her.

She saw Blodwedd climbing into forested hills, deep in snow, and somehow she knew that the owl-girl had been wandering in the cold mountains for many a long and weary day. She saw Blodwedd standing upon a lonely crag, calling out in a loud, urgent voice.

She saw a creature making its way through the dark trees towards her. The shape warped and distorted as it moved, so that sometimes it looked to Branwen like a huge eagle drifting under the branches on wide, still wings, and sometimes like the tall, green-hued and antlered stag-man that she had seen once before. Govannon of the Wood.

'Govannon! Govannon!' cried Blodwedd. 'Have you deserted the Emerald Flame? She is alone and afraid. Will you not come to her?'

A deep voice boomed in reply. 'My part in her journey

is done, Blodwedd of the Far-Seeing Eye. Others must aid her now.'

'But this winter has no end, and one of her followers is dead at Caradoc's hand,' called Blodwedd. 'Can you not make him withdraw his long white claws from the land? Can you not force him to lift his frozen breath from us?'

A second shape emerged from the trees, and Branwen saw Rhiannon, seated upon her white horse as it padded forward through the thick snow in a jingle of silvery bells. 'We cannot tell the wind which way to blow,' she said. 'We are bound to the earth, child – we cannot bring this winter to a halt.'

'Nor would we!' croaked another voice, as dry and cracked as sun-parched rock. The stooped and gnarled figure of Merion of the Stones stepped forward with a rowan staff clutched in her knobbed hand. 'He runs free and wild, does my beautiful brother, and answers to none of us.'

Blodwedd fell to her knees, bowing down low in the face of the three Old Gods of Brython. 'May I take then no word of comfort back to the Warrior Child?' she cried. 'Is she alone and unloved?'

'She is not,' said Rhiannon, her eyes flashing. 'We will speak with our airy brother, we will entreat him to show mercy. But the Bright Blade must know, we do not have the power over life and death – had this been warm and sun-bright summer, still would her companion have died. It was none of our doing – but it was nothing we could have prevented.'

'And take these tokens,' added Merion, reaching out a clawed fist to Blodwedd and dropping six white crystals into her hand. 'You must return to the citadel of that petty king of men. You will find Dera ap Dagonet held captive in the Hall of Araith. Free her with stealth and then tell the followers of destiny's sword these words.' Her voice rumbled like distant thunder in the mountains. 'The Warrior Child is held captive by treachery and malice. You must set her free. Fain will lead the way. Travel with speed or not at all, for if you come too late, she will be lost to you for all eternity.' Merion smote her staff on the ground. 'Tell them that!'

'And if you come in time, and the Warrior Child is saved, say this also,' added Rhiannon. 'Tell her that we three are bound to the land, and that we cannot intervene again to alter the outcome of the great battle that is to come.'

'Go, now!' roared Govannon. 'Run like the wind, Blodwedd of the Far-Seeing Eye – there is not a moment to lose!'

As Branwen watched, Blodwedd turned and scrambled off the rocky peak and wildly down through the trees.

Now Branwen saw a small curved-winged shape come flying from the branches. Fain, cawing loudly as he followed after the racing owl-girl. And even as they plunged together down the mountain, so Rhiannon's voice echoed after them.

'Remember these words!' she called. 'We three are bound to the land and cannot be called upon to hold back the army that is coming! Tell her exactly these words, Messenger of Govannon – and hope that she understands!'

Branwen came to her senses with a gasp, startled by the faces that surrounded her and the fierce firelight that danced in her eyes.

'Yes,' she gulped. 'Yes, I saw all.' She rubbed the heels of her hands into her eyes and took in deep breaths to anchor herself back in the real world.

'As soon as we heard what Blodwedd had to tell us, we crept by dark of night into the Hall of Araith and found Dera bound and gagged in a side-chamber,' said Banon. 'Setting her loose, we armed and saddled our horses to depart. The gate wardens tried to detain us, but we would have none of it.'

'We had to break a few heads to get out of the citadel,' added Aberfa. 'But we cared not, for Dera had told us all that happened at Bwlch Crug-Glas, and we were filled with anger at the king's treachery,'

'Then we rode like the wind,' said Rhodri, 'while Fain guided us. And it did not take long for us to understand where he was taking us.'

'We were upon the hill overlooking the city of Chester ere the sun rose the following morning,' said Dera. 'Only five could go into the Saxon den – a stone was needed for you, Branwen – so you could be taken from there unseen.'

'And the rest you can guess or know already,' finished Iwan. 'Using the power of the crystals, we infiltrated the city.' He grinned. 'And using my uncanny marksmanship, I fired off two arrows to cut two of the ropes that held you, while Aberfa and Dera prevented the other horses from dismembering you.'

'And I called upon the owls,' said Blodwedd. 'Many died, but they did not resent the sacrifice. They knew that they perished to keep the sinister shadow of Ragnar out of their forests.'

'And here we are,' said Rhodri. 'We few, together again – against all hope!' He glanced around at the gathered faces, then his eyes fixed on Branwen. 'But where are we to go?' he asked. 'Not back to Pengwern, surely – for that would be nothing short of walking wide-eyed into a noose. But if not to the king, where does our destiny lead?'

'We are seven against seven thousand,' said Iwan. 'We

cannot fight alone. And we are surely in no doubt that we *are* alone – the words given to Blodwedd by the Shining Ones is proof enough of that.'

Branwen frowned, staring into the fire, hoping to find patterns or logic or hope in among the play of the flames. She saw none, but at the fire's core she did think she discerned a heart of utter blackness.

'What of Ragnar?' she asked, remembering the great black bird. 'What harm can he do us?'

'We are in Brython,' said Rhodri. 'His powers are less fearsome in lands where the Shining Ones hold guardianship – but we should still beware him, whatever we may choose to do.'

Blodwedd closed her eyes, her face tight and pale, her hands trembling.

The flames licked and cracked, and for a moment Branwen imagined she saw a familiar sight in among the burning branches. A lone hill crowned with a palisade of timber. A solitary mound in a wide wilderness.

She lifted her head, and gazed around at her companions. 'I know where we must go!' she said. 'Where dark treachery gathers, we must seek out the one place where love and honour still hold sway. We shall go to my mother – we shall go to Alis ap Owain and to the rebuilt citadel of Garth Milain!'

CHAPTER TWENTY-TWO

Several times in the night, Branwen awoke with a start, her mind choked by dreams that she was back in her prison cell. She would open her eyes, startled to see the firelight and to feel its warmth on her body. Iwan lay close enough for her to touch him, and even in sleep, his hand was on his sword hilt.

Branwen would remain awake for a little, leaning up on one elbow, gazing at Iwan and her other slumbering friends in wonder before lying down again and slipping slowly back into the discomfort of her deceitful nightmares.

They were together again, all save for poor Linette, may her soul rest easy in Annwn. And this time no power in the world would separate them. Not if Branwen of the Old Gods could prevent it.

It was a cloudy morning, and the wind came down chill

from the east as Branwen and the Gwyn Braw rode northwards towards Garth Milain. Fain was often on the wing, flying high, then returning to her shoulder without giving voice. Branwen knew that if he cawed, it would mean he had seen something that he recognized.

There were wide leagues of wilderness between them and the southern marches of Cyffin Tir, but on every high point of their journey, Branwen puckered her eyes into the north and hoped to see some familiar landmark to show they were drawing near to her homeland and her dear mother.

The longing to see Alis ap Owain grew in her with every passing moment. For long months she had refused to let these feelings into her mind, knowing that they would torment her, knowing that it was an impossible wish. But now that fate had led her down this path, and she realized she would soon be in her mother's strong arms, she finally allowed herself to accept the homesickness that she had so long denied.

She hoped that if any of her companions noticed the tears that ran down her cheeks, they would think them drawn out by the chill wind, and not the product of the emotions that churned and swelled in her heart. She was still their leader, and after all that had happened, this was not the time to let them sense weakness in her, not even the weakness of a daughter who longs for the loving embrace of her mother.

The morning was half done and dark clouds were gathering from the east when Rhodri quickened his horse and came riding up alongside Branwen with Blodwedd, as ever, clinging on behind.

They were upon a bare hilltop and Branwen had been deep in daydreams of the coming reunion with her mother. She had been imagining the two of them walking the ramparts of a rebuilt citadel, talking over old times and banishing sadness with hope of better fortunes to come.

She had not seen Garth Milain rebuilt after the fire – but she had heard that Alis ap Owain had seen to it that the fortifications were as formidable as before, and had called on many warriors of the cantref to man the timber palisades. There had not been time to rebuild the Great Hall – that would be a task for a more peaceful time, and Branwen hoped to be there to help her mother, once all her other duties were fulfilled.

Branwen turned to look at Rhodri's worried face. Behind him, Branwen's forehead was creased and her eyes were filled with distress.

'What is it?' Branwen asked sharply.

'A great weight lies on my heart,' said Blodwedd. 'A fear has been growing in me through the morning. This east wind brings more than rain-clouds, I'll warrant.' Her golden eyes burned. 'I feel a darkness brewing.'

'Saxons?' asked Branwen. 'An ambush, perhaps?'

'No. Worse.' Blodwedd winced and flinched, as though some invisible thing had flown into her face. 'Far worse.'

'What is this?' called Dera, riding up to Branwen's side. 'What do you sense, Blodwedd?'

'Ancient evil,' growled the owl-girl. She turned her head to the east, her fingers tightening on Rhodri's shoulders. 'It comes!' she gasped. 'With the speed of the forked lightning, it comes!'

Aberfa stared eastwards. 'I see nothing!' she cried, drawing her sword. 'By the saints, what is it you fear, Blodwedd?'

There was a hiss now as swords were drawn. The horses whickered uneasily. Iwan rode to the eastern rim of the hilltop, staring into the sky. 'I see nothing save the clouds,' he shouted back. 'What should we be looking for?'

Blodwedd threw her hands up over her eyes. 'The roaring darkness!' she cried. 'Save me! It comes!'

'The Three Saints preserve us!' gasped Banon, her horse rearing under her, its eyes rolling. 'What is *that*?'

Branwen saw it now. They all saw it. A fist of absolute darkness high in among the grey swirl of the rolling clouds. A careening heart of pure black, streaking towards them out of the east. The clouds boiled and split open as it came screaming down the skies towards them, limned with lightning, roaring like thunder, black as hatred, swift as malice, red-eyed and dreadful.

'Ragnar!' Branwen howled. 'It is Ragnar!'

The black mass congealed and reshaped itself and was a raven. Fain flew recklessly at it, but the gallant falcon was beaten aside, tumbling to the ground in a flurry of tangled feathers.

Ragnar descended on them, cloaked in midnight, staining the air to ebony as it spread its wings. The horses reared and screamed and kicked at the darkening sky. Banon and Iwan were thrown to the ground, their horses bolting in terror. Aberfa only just managed to keep in the saddle as she flung a spear at the onrushing demon. The beak gaped. The spear was engulfed. With a cry, Aberfa was flung backward from her mount.

Rhodri slashed at the sky with his sword, shouting defiance. Behind him, Blodwedd screamed and clawed the air. Then their horse tumbled sideways and they were thrown to the ground.

Branwen fought to master Terrwyn, pulling hard on his reins, gripping with her knees, uncomfortably aware of the strength she had lost in captivity. She raised her sword arm, the white blade pointing at the raven's blazing eyes.

'Seek to harm me and the wrath of the Shining Ones will smite you, monster of the benighted east!' she howled, hardly knowing where the words were coming from. 'By the power of the forest, I defy you!' Green lightning flowed down her sword and burst out towards the plummeting god. 'By the power of sweet water I defy you!' Silver sparked and flared at the point of her sword, flashing in the demon's fiery eyes. 'By the power of ancient stone I defy you!'

All around Terrwyn's stamping hooves, pebbles and stones were pulled upward out of the very ground. They gathered, swirling around her sword, whirling faster and faster and then flinging themselves upwards into the face of the great raven.

Squawking and screeching, the black bird was thrown back by the force of the green and white shafts of light and the volley of flying stones.

The world convulsed, emerald and diamond-white lightning stabbing through the enveloping blackness, while dreadful, inhuman voices shouted and wailed and screamed in Branwen's ears.

But in all the turmoil and chaos, Branwen stayed in the saddle, keeping her sword raised while the Old Gods warred above her head.

The hill heaved under her. There was a blinding burst of white laced through with hissing green shafts.

A stillness came down over the hilltop. Branwen reeled and gasped, her ears ringing, lights exploding behind her eyes. Her companions were scattered, the hill was burned black and smouldering.

But a slithering darkness was fleeing into the east, skimming the treetops, leaving a wake of black smoke.

Branwen blinked, keeping Terrwyn steady as she struggled to clear her sight. Close by, Dera and Aberfa were clambering to their feet, looking dazed.

'Ragnar is defeated!' Branwen cried. 'See how he runs from us!'

Banon tottered upright. 'Are we all unhurt?' she gasped.

'Only my pride,' gasped Iwan, scrambling up, staggering a little before he caught his balance.

'I am well enough,' said Rhodri, sitting up and rubbing his head. 'Bruised but with no bones broken.' He reached an arm towards Blodwedd, who was sitting on the burned earth with her head hanging between her knees. 'How have you fared, Blodwedd?' he asked. 'Are you all of one piece?'

Blodwedd shivered under the touch of his hand.

Branwen frowned down at her, worried to see her

friend's limbs shaking so badly. 'Blodwedd? Are you hurt?'

A low, guttural laugh came from the owl-girl.

'Oh, no, Warrior Child,' she growled. 'I am not hurt.'

Branwen slipped down out of the saddle and walked forward, puzzled.

She paused, her heart beating loud as Blodwedd's head rose slowly. For a moment, the thick tawny hair veiled her face, then the curls fell back and Branwen's heart stopped in her chest.

Three raw and bleeding cuts etched parallel grooves across Blodwedd's face, ripping her flesh open from the right temple to the left jaw line, masking her lower face in a curtain of red, like some terrible blood-sacrament from before the dawn of time.

'Oh, dear gods, no!' Branwen murmured, feeling her legs almost give way as she stared into Blodwedd's disfigured face and saw two lightless and lifeless eyes staring back at her.

Two great circular staring eyes that had grown as black as the pits of *Hel*.

Eyes like two black moons.

CHAPTER TWENTY-THREE

Rhodri shrank back as Blodwedd rose slowly to her feet, her head tilted down, her deadly eyes fixed on Branwen, a small, sharp smile revealing her pointed teeth.

'Blodwedd, no!' groaned Branwen. 'Please – no!'

'You were warned,' croaked an abominable, discordant double voice, half Blodwedd and half Ragnar. 'Do not say you were not warned! A creature of the Old Powers I have always been, Warrior Child. But see you now that I have slipped the grasp of the lesser gods of Brython and become a new thing, a better thing, a more powerful thing.'

'Blodwedd, for pity's sake, fight it!' cried Rhodri, reaching out to her. She turned like a snake and hissed at him, her fingers curling into claws.

'I am not *Blodwedd*!' she cried. 'I am Ragnarok. I am the end of days. I am the doom of all mankind! I am the Warrior Child's final destiny!'

With a terrible strength, she grasped Rhodri's arm, laughing as she twisted it. He cried out, driven to his knees by the pain.

Dera leaped forward, her sword aimed towards the owl-girl. 'Release him, or I shall smite you!' she cried. 'You've been taken by a Saxon hellion, Blodwedd! Be yourself again!'

Snarling, Blodwedd turned to her, giving Rhodri's arm a final cruel wrench before releasing it. With a speed beyond Branwen's ability to follow, the owl-girl came upon Dera, passing her sword point unhurt, driving her to the ground. Claws gripped the fallen girl's neck as Blodwedd's jaws opened at her throat.

'No!' shouted Aberfa, hurling herself forward, her spear thrusting at Blodwedd's side.

Hissing and spitting, Blodwedd slipped adder-quick out from under the spearhead. It stabbed into the ground and even as Aberfa fought to wrest it free, Blodwedd sprang, wrapping her long, wiry limbs around her, howling as she bore the tall, powerful girl backwards. Struggling to prize the demonic owl-girl free, Aberfa staggered across the hilltop until a snag caught her heel and sent her crashing.

Iwan and Banon were upon them before Blodwedd's teeth could meet in Aberfa's throat. They dragged Blodwedd back, kicking and screaming and clawing.

'Do not hurt her!' cried Branwen, coming out of a kind of stupor of disbelief. 'She's possessed by Ragnar! We must set her free!'

Eyes like two black moons.

The warning had referred to Blodwedd all along. The owl-girl had understood something of it – she had intimated as much when they had been together on the ramparts of Pengwern. What had she said?

When you see the eyes like two black moons, do not hesitate – not for love, nor honour, nor compassion nor friendship.

But how could Branwen not hesitate?

Kill it before it can kill you.

How could she kill someone who had sacrificed so much out of loyalty and devotion? How *could* she? There had to be another way to release Govannon's Messenger from Ragnar's thrall.

Branwen ran forward, but too late. Blodwedd writhed loose, leaping like a feral beast at Banon. Blood spurted and Banon fell back, clutching at her shoulder. Turning, as lithe as a serpent, Blodwedd flung herself headlong at Iwan, knocking his sword out of his grasp, reaching with curved nails for his face.

Even then, Branwen could not bring herself to strike at her friend with cold iron. She lunged forward, snatching a handful of the owl-girl's thick hair, digging her heels in hard as she hauled back, ripping the ravening monster away from Iwan – seeing how the hooked claws had already dug bloody crescents in Iwan's cheekbones.

Using all her strength, Branwen heaved Blodwedd backward, swinging from side to side to prevent the berserk girl from regaining her balance. But she was not prepared for how mercurial and how agile Blodwedd had become. The owl-girl squirmed and thrashed in her grip, spinning to face her, the crooked nails now stretching towards her eyes.

Unprepared for Blodwedd's sudden shift of weight, Branwen fell over backward, striking the ground hard so that the air was beaten from her body and the sword jarred from her hand. Blodwedd came down on her like a thunderbolt, straddling her chest, her long hair hanging, her face frenzied and inhuman, the black eyes like holes in the world.

Blood and spittle showered Branwen's face as the insane owl-girl laughed, her hands gripping either side of Branwen's head, the nails like splinters of flint scoring her flesh.

'Govannon!' Branwen cried in desperation, wrestling to throw the owl-girl off. 'Rhiannon! Save her! Release her!'

'They cannot!' howled Blodwedd. 'I am no longer theirs to command. It is too late.'

Branwen snatched hold of Blodwedd's wrists, trying to prise her hands free. 'Fight the demon,

Blodwedd,' she gasped.

'"Fight the demon"?' snarled Blodwedd, her open mouth curling into a terrible smile. 'I *am* the demon, Warrior Child! I have always been the demon – did you not know that?' Slowly she raised her arms, Branwen's fingers still clinging to her wrists. 'The Emerald Flame, you are called, Branwen of the Petty Gods. But let us see how you follow destiny's path with only the pits of lost eyes to guide you!'

Branwen let out a cry as the curved fingers came raking down towards her face, the nails stretching for her eyes.

'One eye you took from Earl Herewulf's face,' raved the gravelled voice from Blodwedd's mouth. 'One eye from my lord's most trusted servant! As forfeit, you shall pay with both of yours!'

As Branwen looked in horror into the owl-girl's face, she knew the truth: Ragnar had taken her friend body and spirit – there was no more Blodwedd. There was only Ragnar – a savage and murderous *thing* housed in Blodwedd's body, a hellish beast that stared down at her with black, dead, ferocious eyes.

'Blodwedd!' A shape loomed in the corner of Branwen's eye. It was Rhodri, stumbling forward, his arms out towards the demon that had once been his beloved friend. 'For the love I bear you, Blodwedd, stop!'

For a moment, the furious strength of Blodwedd's

arms lessened a fraction. She turned her head, staring at Rhodri, as though some tiny shred of the person she had been had ignited a spark of memory in her mind.

Now Branwen did not hesitate. She released Blodwedd's left wrist and flung her arm out. Her fingers caught the hilt of her sword and closed about it. Screwing her eyes shut to avoid seeing the thing she was about to do, she angled the blade upwards and thrust deep.

Blodwedd let out a wild screech as the sword drove through her body.

'No!' screamed Rhodri. '*No!*'

The owl-girl's dying body convulsed on top of Branwen, the back arching, the neck stretching, the mouth gaping.

Blodwedd fell writhing to one side, ripping the sword from Branwen's hands, clutching at it as though trying to pull it out from between her ribs.

Overwrought with horror, her eyes flooded with tears, Branwen crawled to where Blodwedd lay twitching on the ground. With a final burst of strength, the owl-girl jerked the sword out of her body and flung it to one side, her breath coming rapidly, blood blossoming on her clothes.

Rhodri dropped to his knees at Blodwedd's side, shouting his futile denials as he bent over her, one hand pressing against her bloody wound, the other cradling the side of her face.

Branwen crouched by Blodwedd's head, weeping, distraught, wrung with guilt and grief.

The owl-girl's eyes opened as she turned her head to gaze for a moment into Branwen's face. Branwen bit back a sob when she saw that her friend's eyes were golden once more.

'Do not weep,' Blodwedd whispered, blood tricking down the side of her face and into her hair. 'You had to do this . . . I would have . . . killed you all . . .'

Branwen tried to speak, but her voice would not come.

Blodwedd's eyes began to glaze over. 'I am free now. Soon I shall be at Govannon's side – soaring the great wide sky-fields once more. Blodwedd of the Far-Seeing Eye.' She turned her head one final time to look into Rhodri's face. 'I have . . . a gift . . . for you . . . Rhodri . . .' Now her voice had become very faint and Branwen could hardly hear her words. 'Come . . . closer . . . dearest . . . friend . . .'

Rhodri leaned close over her, his shoulders heaving as he sobbed. She lifted her hands and held his head between them, bringing his face down to hers and softly kissing his eyes. 'Forgive me . . . sweet Rhodri,' she breathed. 'This is . . . not . . . an . . . easy burden . . . to bear . . .'

Her fingers loosened, her arms fell limp.

The light faded from her golden eyes.

Blodwedd the owl-girl lay dead upon the hill.

CHAPTER TWENTY-FOUR

Rhodri let out a scream of utter agony, his body jerking upwards, his hands coming up to his face. Branwen stared up at him in alarm as he knelt there, swaying, shuddering, grinding his hands into his eyes as though fighting intolerable pain.

She ached to comfort him – but how could she do that – killer as she was of her friend's great love? She had to suffer his agonies as well as her own. She deserved no better!

Through her tears, Branwen was aware of figures moving forward across the hill. Iwan was the first to reach Rhodri, stooping, taking the howling boy's broad shoulders between his hands as though to halt the rolling of his agonized body.

Rhodri's screams ended abruptly and he slumped sideways, almost dragging Iwan down with him as he crumpled to the ground.

Strong hands lifted Branwen to her feet. 'Are you hurt?' It was Dera's voice. "Branwen? Are you injured?'

'No.' The word was like a knife in her throat.

'There was nothing else you could have done,' said Banon, holding a bloody rag to her wounded shoulder. 'Ragnar had taken her over – she would have killed us all.'

Kill it before it can kill you.

Blodwedd's own words.

'Why did they not protect her?' shouted Branwen. She turned, facing west, screaming her anger into the grey sky. 'Why did you not protect her? She was your creature! Did her life mean nothing to you? Are you so cruel?'

But the clouded sky gave her no answer.

It was a vision, or a dream, or a . . . *visitation*. Branwen stood on air. She was far above the hill, gazing down. Between her floating feet, she saw *herself*, seated on the blackened ground at Blodwedd's side, her head hanging, her sword flung aside. She saw Rhodri lying close by, a cloak covering him to the chin while Banon and Iwan lifted his head and used a wetted rag to bathe his forehead. But Rhodri's eyes were closed and from such a distance, Branwen could not even be sure that he was breathing. Three horses were tethered on the hill – Aberfa and Dera were busy rounding up the others that had fled when Ragnar had come.

Fain was there also, on the ground, preening his ruffled and disordered feathers, shivering but otherwise unhurt after his encounter with the evil raven. That at least was a blessing.

Branwen looked up, her mind strangely empty, wondering how much time had elapsed since she had slaughtered her friend.

'You had no choice, you know that.'

Branwen turned her head and saw that Linette stood at her side on the empty air. The girl was dressed all in white, and there was a light radiating from her face that made it almost impossible for Branwen to look directly at her. Brighter than the noonday sun, Linette's face had become.

'I'm cursed,' Branwen said. 'All who come near me perish.'

'When war stalks the land, many die, Branwen,' said Linette mildly. 'Yet you are right – you are cursed. You bear the curse of leadership.'

'No. I'll not lead any more. Let them choose another. Let Dera or Iwan guide them now. I'm done with it. I'll not lift a sword in anger again. I shall take the path into the forest and live out my days in solitude. That way no more lives will be lost on my account.'

'You can't do that and you won't,' came Linette's

gentle voice. 'You have a long and weary road ahead of you, Branwen. The only way you could make it worse is if you seek to avoid it. Do you not know that by now?'

'I don't care.'

'I think you do.' Linette sighed. 'Besides, you cannot leave poor Rhodri to his fate.'

Branwen frowned. 'What of Rhodri? What do you mean?'

'Blodwedd has given him a gift that he will find it hard to bear alone.'

'What gift?'

'The gift of the awakening blood. It will rise in him like a fever and when it boils behind his eyes he will not know himself. But he will speak truths to you, and you would be wise to listen. Iwan has long called him Druid, in jest – but it is jest no longer.'

'Must I return then?' Branwen asked. 'Is there to be no respite?'

'You know the answer to that already.'

Branwen gazed down at Blodwedd's sad, slender corpse. 'Why did they not save her?' she asked, her tears falling, glimmering in the sunlight.

'Because they could not,' Linette sighed. 'Do you think they are not bereft, Branwen? Do you think you are the only one that grieves?' Her hand touched Branwen lightly on the shoulder. 'Follow the path, my friend, my leader, my captain. Go south and do great deeds.'

'My path lies northwards,' said Branwen, narrowing her eyes as the light from Linette's face grew brighter and brighter.

'No,' said the echoing voice. 'It does not.'

'And when all my tasks are done, shall I then be given time to grieve over Blodwedd's death?' Branwen called as the light engulfed her. 'Shall I ever know peace, Linette? *Ever?*'

But there came no answer.

Branwen was aware of shapes moving in front of her in the gaping whiteness, and of hollow voices speaking in the void.

'Does she even know we are here?'

'How long must we wait? The day is all but ended, and still she sits like a stone upon the hill and responds to nothing!'

'It's the grief, for pity's sake. Can you not see that?' Iwan's voice, Branwen realized. 'She killed a dear companion; it has broken her spirit.'

'We cannot camp upon this hilltop till doomsday.' That was Aberfa. 'The question is, will she be able to ride, or must we find some other way to bear her? And what of Rhodri? His injuries are slight, but he will not awaken.'

'Bear her where?' Banon, now. 'Do we still go to Garth Milain, as she intended? Who will lead us?'

'I shall, if no other takes the challenge.'

Branwen smiled a little at Dera's voice. Yes, Dera would wear well the mantle of leadership, if it came to it.

'Did you see that? Her lips moved.'

The wasteland of empty white light began to fill with coherent sights and shapes now. Branwen jerked back as Aberfa's face loomed close.

'Are you with us again, Branwen?' asked Iwan, kneeling at her side. 'We feared your mind had gone.'

Branwen bowed her head, trying to make sense of what was happening around her. 'Help me up,' she said, lifting her arms. She swayed and almost fell, but arms supported her. 'How long was I . . .' She faltered, not knowing what words to use.

'You strode about the hill for a while, smiting at the air with your fists and shouting oaths and threats,' said Dera. 'Then you came and sat at Blodwedd's side and became still.'

'You made no move nor spoke any word, nor saw nor heard anything for the whole of the afternoon,' said Banon.

'And Rhodri?' Branwen asked, avoiding looking at the place where Blodwedd lay, a cloak thrown over her face and upper body.

'Out of his senses,' said Iwan. 'Alive, but beyond us to rouse.'

Branwen shook herself free of helping hands and walked unsteadily to where Rhodri lay. She crouched, extending her hand, touching his face with her fingertips. What had Linette told her? Druid in jest no more. But what did that mean?

'Will you awake now?' she asked him in a low voice. 'Even if it is to hatred and despair, I want you to wake up now, Rhodri.'

'By the saints, look!' gasped Banon. Branwen saw it too, a fluttering of the eyelids, a movement of the lips, a turn of the head.

Rhodri's eyes opened and he looked straight into Branwen's face. She gasped, standing up, quivering. His eyes were golden – like discs of amber threaded with sunlight. His eyes were the colour of Blodwedd's eyes!

And then his body heaved and he sucked in air and struggled under the cloak. He sat up, panting, his teeth gritted, his head lowered.

Then his head snapped up and he stared at Branwen – and his eyes were his own again – and there was a look of such pain and anguish and hatred in them that Branwen took a step backward and lifted her hands as though to ward off a blow.

'You killed her!' he cried, scrabbling to his feet, his

fists bunching. 'She did not need to die! I could have saved her.'

He flung himself towards her and it was only the quick actions of Iwan and Dera that prevented him reaching her with his flying fists. He struggled in their grasp, his face enraged, his eyes blazing.

'Blodwedd knew this would happen,' Branwen replied, her voice dull and stoic. 'She told me – she told me that I would have to kill her.' She gave a wracking sigh. 'Do you think I wanted this? Do you think I wanted *any* of this?'

Rhodri pulled himself upright. 'Leave me be!' he said in a suddenly loud and commanding voice. 'None may touch the son of *Y Ladi Wen*!' Startled by the change in his voice, Iwan and Dera stepped back. Rhodri spread his feet apart and raised his arms, his fingers stretched wide, stabbing at the sky. 'I see the high pool of Deheubarth, where my mother held the mirror to the sun and all the world was burned. I see the bright-browed Taliesin, teller of the ancient tales. I see Mabon the son of Modron, bearing the gift of the ocean's child. *Bachen rhyfeddol*, they called me! Child of wonder! But that was many years ago and I am grown mighty in power and lore now. I am the strange marvel of my people.'

And now he seemed to see Branwen, as though for the first time. His eyes widened, his finger pointing. 'When the owls depart, you must ride south,' he roared at her, his face blazing with such majesty that she truly believed he might be some ancient Druid lord brought back into the world. 'Ride to Pengwern and deal with what you will find there! And remember well the words of Rhiannon of the Spring. Remember, and find you wisdom!'

And then the light went out of his eyes and the fervour left his face and he crumpled on to his hands and knees as though felled by an axe.

Rhodri was unconscious again, lying under a cloak, breathing deeply and steadily, but impossible to awaken.

The others were gathered together, sitting in a ring on the hill as the sun dipped low in the west, debating what they should do.

'Ride south when the owls depart?' mused Dera. 'What did he mean by that?'

'Could he have been referring to Blodwedd's death?' asked Banon.

'In which case should we not already have quit this place?' asked Aberfa.

'Are we to do as he says?' wondered Iwan. 'Is it not possible those were the ravings of a man bereft of his wits?'

'Those were not ravings,' said Branwen heavily. 'Something has happened to Rhodri, for good or ill. As she died, Blodwedd passed something to him . . . some spirit or power or . . . I do not know! Something that has come alive within him. Something that has stirred in him the blood of his ancestors.'

'Druid blood?' asked Iwan.

Branwen nodded.

'So shall we go south to Pengwern?' asked Dera, her voice dubious. 'Is that wisdom when the king wants none of us?'

'King Cynon is *not* Powys,' said Branwen. 'It is the land itself that we must serve, not its passing lords.' She frowned. 'But I do not understand about the owls.' She glanced to where Rhodri lay. 'Should we wait for him to awaken?' She stood up and walked restlessly about. 'Instead of hints and riddles, I would like for once to be given some clear sign of what I must do!'

Iwan straightened his back, his head cocked. 'Listen!' he said. 'What is that sound?'

Branwen heard it too. A low thrumming in the air. 'Where is it coming from?' she asked.

'From the west!' cried Dera, springing up and pointing.

A dark shape was moving towards them above the tumble of the wildlands. It looked at first like a low cloud, but it was moving against the wind, and it did not have the form of any cloud that Branwen had ever seen.

'It is birds!' cried Aberfa. 'A whole host of birds!'

'Owls!' gasped Branwen as the flock came closer.

The legion of owls came sweeping up the hillside, flying low so that all but Branwen ducked as they passed over them. Branwen guessed there must be a hundred or more of the great majestic creatures. They wheeled about her, their eyes burning, their wings hardly moving, their voices stilled.

And then, as though acting with some powerful instinct beyond human understanding, the wings cupped, the eyes shifted and the whole congregation of huge birds descended to the ground where Blodwedd lay. The greater part of the hill disappeared under their tawny bodies. Branwen stood her ground, but her companions drew back, silent in awe, their eyes wide.

Then the owls gave voice.

Their melancholy hooting filled the air, a lament at the passing of a beloved kinswoman, a sound to break the heart.

Branwen dropped to her knees, tears flooding her face.

While the hilltop still reverberated to the dirge of sad hooting, the owls took again to the air. They swarmed and wheeled and then flowed away into the west.

And where Blodwedd had lain, there was just a scattering of tawny feathers.

Branwen wiped the tears off her cheeks. She got to her feet, her heart clamouring in her chest, her blood flowing strongly through her veins.

'I asked for a sure sign,' she called to the others, all doubt and confusion gone from her mind. 'We have been given it! Come, gather the horses, we ride into the south! We ride to Pengwern!'

CHAPTER TWENTY-FIVE

They rode until night took the land. Rhodri did not recover, and they had to tie him to his horse, one rope around his waist to hold him in the saddle, and another under the animal's belly, linking his ankles. In that manner, he rode safe enough, slumped low over his horse's neck, while Aberfa took the trailing reins.

Fain had an injured wing – he could fly, but only for short distances, clumsily and with evident discomfort. Branwen rode with him perched upon her shoulder, grieving that she would never again know what his shrill cries meant. She had lost that advantage when she had rammed sharp metal into Blodwedd's body.

No! Don't think of it. It's done. It is past.

Don't think of it?

As though that were an option.

In the dark of night, they made camp in woodland by a thin stream of clear cold water. Banon gathered wood and lit a fire. They lay Rhodri close to the warming flames then clustered around it like tiny insects drawn to a candle. Although the long and bitter winter was relenting at last, the air was still deathly chill, and they sat shrouded in their cloaks, their faces ruddy in the welcome heat.

'I did not think to ask,' said Branwen as they gnawed dried meat and tore stale bread apart for their meagre supper. 'Are Drustan and Meredith wed now?'

'Not when we left Pengwern,' said Aberfa.

'Is it the prince's doing?' asked Branwen.

'Nay, it is the king who forces the delay,' said Iwan. 'He has a serpent's wisdom in this, I think. Once the marriage is sealed, Prince Llew will have all that he wishes. Why then should he obey King Cynon's commands? No, the king desires to keep the prince on a tight leash, so he makes Llew wait for his prize, like a dog kept hungry and keen for the fight while food is dangled out of reach.'

Dera nodded. 'The king's no fool in this,' she agreed. 'Knowing Llew ap Gelert's dark turn of mind, it would not come as a surprise to find Cynon struck down by some unknown ailment on the night following the wedding!'

'You think he'd kill the king?' asked Aberfa.

'If it made his own daughter queen of Powys?' said Dera. 'Why not?'

Branwen winced. 'Is there to be no end to treachery in Powys?' she groaned. 'Sometimes I think the Shining Ones have chosen a poor race of folk to champion.'

Iwan looked at her. 'Do you really think the Shining Ones were given a choice in the matter?' he asked. 'Is that not like questioning the wisdom of a river that runs through a barren valley or a tree that grows on a windswept hill? The Shining Ones are surely part of the land – they cannot pick and choose the realms they protect.'

Branwen gazed at him. 'You have come a long way since we first met, my friend,' she said. 'Can you imagine those words coming from the mouth of Iwan the merry prankster of Doeth Palas?'

He laughed ruefully. 'We have all travelled far,' he said.

'Those of us who survived the journey,' added Dera, glancing at Rhodri as he lay under a cloak close by. 'Survived with our wits intact, I should say.'

'What has happened to Rhodri?' asked Banon, looking at Branwen. 'What spirit possesses him, do you think?'

'A Druid forebear, perhaps,' said Branwen.

'Hush!' said Aberfa, leaning close to Rhodri's head. 'He is saying something. I can't make it out. A word. Repeated over and over.'

Branwen scrambled around the fire and knelt at

Rhodri's side, bringing her ear down close to his moving lips.

'. . . Caliburn . . . Caliburn . . . Caliburn . . .'

'Rhodri? Can you hear me?'

'Call in greatest need . . . and Caliburn shall come to you . . .'

'Rhodri? I don't know what you mean.' She pressed her hand against the side of his face, turning his head towards her. 'Who is Caliburn? What are you saying?'

'. . . remember Rhiannon's words . . . call for Caliburn when all is lost . . .'

'Rhodri! Rhiannon has never spoken of Caliburn.' She patted his cheek, hoping to rouse him. 'You must tell me more.'

But the lips ceased moving and Rhodri said nothing more.

'A troubling oracle, he may turn out to be, if he cannot make his meanings more clear,' said Iwan. '*Ride to Pengwern and deal with what you find there*, he told us. But with no hint of what we might find nor of how to deal with it.' He shook his head. 'This half-Saxon and half-Druid may well be the death of us all!'

They struck camp at dawn, heading south-west, looking to come across the Great South Way as it wound through Powys. The ancient earthen track traversed the length of the entire kingdom, stretching from the northern sea-shore to the deep southern cantrefs, linking hamlet and citadel and farmstead as it made for Pengwern and beyond.

The sun was high in the eastern sky when they rode to a cliff edge and saw at last the long-awaited sight in the valley below. The road lay like a brown ribbon beneath them, cutting through the wild lands, pointing the way to their destination.

Branwen would have had them travel at the gallop if she had been given the option. But they needed to take care of Rhodri, and even at the trot, there was the risk of him falling and being injured.

As they rode, she puzzled over his cryptic words. Banon had been right to ask the question – who or *what* had taken hold of her wise, kind, gentle friend? It had come from Blodwedd, she believed, and so she had trusted it – but what if she was wrong? What if something of Ragnar had been put into Rhodri's mind? What if he was leading them to their doom?

An inner debate occupied her mind as they followed the road.

No. If this was evil, it would make itself clearer, I think. The riddling nature of his words makes it more likely to be something to our benefit – if we have the wit to untangle the message! Oh, why is it always so hard?

Because to strive is part of the purpose.

Perhaps. But to strive and to fail is my fear!

You have not failed so far.

Indeed not? Tell that to the ghosts of Geraint and Griffith ap Rhys and Gavan ap Huw and Linette and Blodwedd . . .

Have you not learned the lesson yet, you fool?

'Smoke rises over Pengwern!' cried Dera. 'I fear we come too late!'

Branwen had been so wrapped up in her thoughts that she had not realized they were approaching the long hill that rose to the west of the king's citadel. Here, little more than a month ago, the Gwyn Braw had ridden hard out of the snowy mountains, bearing Meredith and Romney along with them, pursued by Saxon war bands.

She stared into the eastern sky. Dera was right. A veil of smoke hung in the air beyond the crest of the hill.

Branwen slapped the reins, kicking her heels into Terrwyn's flanks to urge him on. Dera was also riding hard for the hill, Iwan at her side and Banon close behind. Only Aberfa had not joined the wild gallop to the hill – but even she had brought her horse to a brisk trot, riding alongside Rhodri's horse, one strong hand holding him by the collar so he would not fall.

As they rode up the flank of the hill, Branwen began to hear strange and disturbing sounds faintly from beyond the fast-closing horizon. Dark smoke drifted high, staining the pale clouds.

Branwen was the first to come to the crest of the hill. She rode between thickets of woodland, reining Terrwyn up hard, staring down with horrified eyes into the long valley that lay between them and the king's citadel.

A dreadful sight met her eyes.

The valley swarmed with Saxons. As thick as bees in a hive, they gathered below her shrinking gaze and her heart withered in her chest to see their numbers.

Even as she reeled in the saddle, the noise of warfare came bursting in her ears, loud and confused and horrible.

Shouts and battle cries filled the air, howls of anger and pain, the neighing and screaming of frightened and dying horses. The jarring scrape of metal on metal, the thud of swords striking shields. The horrible sound of iron slashing and piercing flesh. The hiss of arrows, the thwack of spearheads driving into living bodies.

The army of General Herewulf Ironfist was attacking the citadel from west, north and south, the savage Saxon warriors raging across the open lands in their multitudes. But this was no rabble – the great general had taught them well the art of slaughter. The bulk of the Saxon warriors were divided into blocks of men who moved with the slow weight of mountains, beating the defenders back and back towards the defensive ditch of the citadel.

Worse still were the arrowhead wedges of soldiers, hemmed all about with shields, barbed with spears and swords, crashing headlong into the Powys lines, ripping them apart and killing without mercy all who stood in their way. Saxon banners cracked in the air, the white dragon on the red field, pressing forward from all sides as the warriors of Powys were beaten back.

Branwen scanned the hideous battlefield, seeking any sign of Ironfist or of the king of Powys. But the mayhem defeated her eyes – there were too many Saxon banners for her to find the general, and what few red dragons still flew were pressed all about by the enemy.

Rather than have their fortress burned around their ears, the defenders of Pengwern must have chosen to meet their enemy on the field. A more noble option, but surely a doomed one against such numbers? Even as she sat stunned and horrified on the hilltop, Branwen saw a standard fall – the red dragon of Powys fluttering to the ground to be trampled and torn under Saxon feet.

'Oh, by the sweet saints!' Iwan's voice at her side was barely audible over the clamour of the battlefield. 'We have come too late!'

Too late.

Too late to do anything other than watch Pengwern burn. The gates were thrown down, the towers ablaze on either side. The causeway to the citadel was clogged with warriors, Saxons hacking and slashing their way forward, the guards and soldiers of King Cynon falling back to the inner ramparts.

Now the others had come to the edge of the hill at her side. Branwen heard their cries of woe and dismay. Too late!

'Pengwern is lost!' shouted Dera. 'Powys is lost!'

Branwen's eyes were drawn from the carnage of the battlefield to the burning towers of Pengwern – and there she saw a sight that crushed her soul. A sight that had come to her as an omen when she had looked into the fire in Merion's cave.

Perched high among the flames was a mighty raven – a huge creature, far larger than the monster that had attacked them before. Vast it was, its black wings outspread, its neck stretched and its head thrown back as it screamed its triumph, its eyes smouldering and its tongue of fire.

Ragnar loomed above the bloody battlefield, encompassed by roaring fire, fanning the flames with his sable wings as the smoke billowed thick and ugly into the sky, shrouding the sun and polluting the air.

'I am no coward, Branwen,' Iwan called to her. 'But it would be madness to throw ourselves into this butchery!'

'What would you have us do, Iwan?' shouted Dera. 'Turn tail and run? Hide ourselves in the mountains until

Ironfist's men dig us out like fox cubs in the den?'

'No, of course not!' spat Iwan. 'But neither would I have us throw our lives away uselessly. Pengwern is lost – but we can spread the word – rally warriors – create a force to harry Ironfist's army every step of their way.' He looked urgently at Branwen. 'We could do this – make them pay for every valley they pass through. Attack them in every forest. Ambush them in every mountain pass. Fortify every citadel against them.' He stared out over the furious and bloody turmoil of the battlefield. 'That, or ride down into the world's end.'

'Rhodri said to come here and deal with what we found,' Branwen replied, slipping her shield on to her arm and drawing her sword.

'I did!' called Rhodri's voice from behind her. 'But I'm in my better senses now!'

Branwen swung around. Aberfa and Rhodri were approaching fast, and now Rhodri was sitting up in the saddle and his eyes were clear.

'And what does wisdom tell you now?' Branwen asked him, searching his face for some sign that he was still the boy she knew.

'To escape this battle, and to live to fight on.' Rhodri rode up to her. 'I am myself again,' he said, looking into her eyes. 'I am changed, but I am not possessed. Say rather, I have grown into something . . . *older*. Deeper. I see many things. I do not understand them. They rush in my head like . . .' He frowned. '. . . like salmon come to spawn in the rivers of their birth . . . like the evening flocking of starlings . . .'

'Can the poetry wait?' interrupted Iwan. 'If we are to go, we should go *now* – before we are seen. I would not wish for a hundred horsemen on our trail!'

'I fear the time for flight is past,' said Dera. She pointed down the hill. A group of Saxon horsemen were gathered there, captains or favoured lords under Ironfist's generalship, clearly holding back from the affray while the men under their command ran headlong into battle.

Branwen saw that one was pointing up towards them and shouting. The other horsemen turned, drawing their swords.

Orders were bellowed. Some of the horsemen rode in among the foot soldiers, howling commands. In no more time than it took to draw three breaths, Branwen saw wedges of horsemen and warriors go streaming around either side of the hill, running fast, their swords and spears and iron helmets glinting.

'They will cut us off from retreat!' shouted Aberfa. 'If we are to depart in safety, we must ride like the wind!'

'It is too late for that,' Branwen called. 'We will be pursued and cut down.'

Even as she spoke, more soldiers and horsemen began to swarm up the hillside towards them. An arrow sang, skidding past Iwan's shoulder.

'Form a circle!' Branwen howled, her eyes filled with the fearsome sight of the onrushing Saxon warriors. 'Back to back! Let them see how the Gwyn Braw meet their end!'

'And let us take as many of them as we can to the halls of Annwn!' shouted Dera, her sword ringing as she drew it.

They pulled their horses back from the brow of the hill, gathering together in a gap between two clusters of trees. Branwen stroked Fain's feathers.

'Fly to the trees, my brave one,' she murmured to him. 'You cannot aid me here – you are too badly hurt.'

The falcon cawed once and then sprang from her shoulder, flying clumsily over their heads. Twice more he cried, as though wishing them well – or wishing them *farewell* – then he sped to the trees and Branwen lost sight of him in among the bare branches.

She looked for the last time into the faces of her companions. Iwan, smiling a little, as though ready to laugh in death's face. Dera, grim and dark, her eyes burning. Banon, testing her bow-string with her thumb, her red hair blowing about her cheeks. Aberfa with her great limbs and her brow like a boulder, hefting a spear in her hand and watching for the first target to come within range.

And Rhodri, at her side now as they formed a defensive circle with their horses' heads facing outwards. At her side, as he had always been since that first day of mist in the mountains when Rhiannon's goraig-goblins had led her to him and she had knocked him off a cliff edge with a tree branch.

'You were a fool ever to ride with me, Rhodri,' she called to him – not for the first time. 'And now your folly reaps its reward.'

'Perhaps so,' he replied. 'But something within me says you are not destined to die here.'

'Is that so?' She could almost have smiled. 'I'm glad to hear it. Although if you knew the doom that Ragnar has planned for me, you might think death less of a burden.'

He frowned, then a look of alarm came into his face, as though he had somehow understood what she meant. 'No,' he said. 'The Shining Ones would never let that happen to you. Ragnar will not take you. Have no fear of that.'

'The Shining Ones?' said Branwen. 'They cannot save us, Rhodri. I know what they said to Blodwedd – they have no power here. Rhiannon said it herself . . . they are bound to the land and can do nothing to alter the course of the battle that is to come. She was speaking of *this* battle, Rhodri.'

'They are upon us!' hissed Aberfa. 'Farewell, friends, we will meet again in Annwn!'

Branwen turned her face outwards, bringing her shield rim up to her eyes, tightening her fist around her sword hilt, gripping hard with her knees around Terrwyn's sturdy body.

They were coming.

Like swarming rats the Saxons flooded in from every direction. They pressed forward, their shields locked together in an onrushing wall, arrows and spears flying as they shouted their dreadful battle cries.

A spear ran quivering through the air. Branwen lifted her shield, angling it so that the spear was deflected. She rocked in the saddle from the impact, her arm tingling. She heard Aberfa roaring.

'Gwyn Braw! Gwyn Braw!'

More arrows hissed. Dera's horse fell screaming. Rhodri's sword arm rose and fell, rose and fell as the Saxons pressed in around him.

But then they were upon her, and she had no more time for fear or grief or guilt as she slashed at the yelling Saxons and lost herself in the red fog of battle madness.

CHAPTER TWENTY-SIX

'You fool! You fool, Warrior Child! Did you not heed the Lady Rhiannon's words? Did you not *listen*?'

The voice came sharp as needles in Branwen's mind through the boil of her blood and the din of battle. Blodwedd's voice? Geraint's? Linette's? It was impossible to tell as she twisted and swung in the saddle, angling her shield to fend off spear and sword, striking down on her attackers with her bloodied blade, kicking at the Saxons to drive them back while Terrwyn reared and struck out with his hooves, cracking skulls and snapping limbs.

I did listen! I did!

'Remember these words! We three are bound to the land and cannot be called upon to hold back the army that is coming! Tell her exactly these words, Messenger of Govannon – and hope that she understands.'

I do understand. We are alone in this.

No! No! Think, Branwen – *think*!

'. . . we three are bound to the land . . .'

We *three*!

But the Shining Ones are four in number.

'Caradoc!' Branwen gasped, a clear light igniting in the blood-red moil of her mind. She filled her lungs and howled to the sky. 'Caradoc! Caradoc! Aid me! I am Destiny's Child! Come to me!'

Hardly had the words left her lips than the world seemed to erupt all about her. She saw the Saxons thrown back in disarray on the crown of the hill. Her companions were driven to the ground, horse and rider both, by a mighty wind that came beating down on them from the sky. Terrwyn stumbled, neighing as he was thrown on to his side.

Branwen braced herself to go crashing to the earth – but did not fall. A fierce wind rushed around her, holding her, snapping her clothes, tugging her hair with its goblin fingers, spitting splinters of cold into her eyes so she had to screw them shut as her sword and shield were ripped from her grasp. Then the wind stilled and she found herself standing on the hilltop, her enemies and companions lying senseless around her and Caradoc of the North Wind before her.

He had the form she had seen before: a golden youth, flaxen-haired, dressed in flowing robes, beautiful and bewitching, his eyes dancing with mischief, his smile captivating, his teeth like glimmering pearls between his full lips.

'Why do you disturb me at my play?' he asked, and his voice was sweet and captivating. 'I was tossing tempests down on to a merchant ship on the open waters.' The alluring smile widened. 'You should have heard their screams as the waves flowed over them!'

'Do you know who I am?' gasped Branwen, finding it hard to concentrate under the beguiling gaze of the beautiful golden boy.

'I do,' said Caradoc. 'Why would I come, else? You are the Chosen One – the Warrior Child, beloved of my brother and sisters.'

'I saved you,' said Branwen, forcing herself to keep focus. 'I let you out of your prison.'

The boy's head tilted. 'Did you?' He gave a dismissive shrug of his shoulders. 'If you say so.'

'I *do* say so,' said Branwen. She pointed to the raging battle and the burning towers of Pengwern, surprised to realize that she could hardly hear the noise now, and puzzled to see that the view was blurred, as though through a haze of mist. 'My destiny is to hold back the Saxons from the land of Brython,' she exclaimed. 'But I cannot do it! There are too many of them. Pengwern will fall, and one by one the citadels of Powys will be destroyed.' She added urgency to her voice, seeing that the boy was looking at her without interest, as though he was eager to be off and away about his cruel games. 'Brython will be lost! All will have been in vain! Do you not care?'

'Why should I care?' he asked petulantly. 'Let the Saxons come, if they desire it; the waxing and waning of these human cattle does not concern me. They come, they go, what of it? The tempest blows. The storm rages. It matters not to me whose heads the rain falls upon.'

For a moment Branwen was lost for words. Had it come to this – all her striving and all her heartache and loss – brought down to this one moment as she stood upon a wind-torn hilltop, pleading for help from an indifferent child-god?

She pointed eastwards again, pouring all her hopes into one final effort. 'Look!' she demanded, thrusting her arm towards where the raven Ragnar perched still on the flaming gate tower of Pengwern. 'Do you not know who he is?'

The boy's eyes narrowed and a sneer curled his lip. 'I know yonder carrion,' he snarled. 'Did I not best him in the mountains, with my sister at my side? Did I not send him fleeing in dread?'

'Yes! You did! But he is returned!' shouted Branwen. 'He mocks you, Caradoc of the North Wind! He mocks the Shining Ones. He laughs in your faces! Do you not see? If you do nothing, he will triumph – for it is by his will that the Saxons have come. If they are not beaten back, they will flow over this land like foul water, Lord Caradoc! And he will come with them, and they will build temples and shrines to him. They will worship him and you will be cast out. You, and your brother and your sisters – you will be thrown into the outer darkness, never to return!' Now she could see the outrage building in the boy's face. 'Can even Caradoc's winds blow over a land ruled by Ragnar? Will you stand by and let this happen?'

'Never!' Caradoc's voice changed beyond all recognition. It was no longer the sweet, mellifluous voice of the golden boy; it was a raging, roaring voice that boomed in Branwen's ears like a hurricane. 'Never! *Never!*'

He was no longer a boy. His shape expanded and grew, flowing like clouds as it rose high above the hill, dark as a storm, edged by lightning, roaring like thunder. Branwen threw her hands up over her ears, as the booming of Caradoc's voice became the crack of a thunderclap loud enough to split the world open. The ground rocked under her feet.

Far, far above her head, she saw a limb of cloud reach beckoning into the north. She turned on teetering legs. Already the far northern horizon had turned dark – as though a range of black mountains had come suddenly into being on the very rim of sight.

Even as she watched, the darkness rose. Like a pack of wolves the storm clouds came racing across the heavens, approaching with an impossible speed, drowning the land under their shadow, devouring the sky.

Branwen heard a harsh croak, distant but strangely loud in her ears. She turned her eyes to the east. The raven monster was still crouched on the burning tower, but staring northwards now, wings unmoving, head down as its red eyes watched the wrath of Caradoc advancing. Then it turned its head to Branwen and she felt Ragnar's evil will beating on her like a great hammer. She flinched as the malice ate into her brain. Even as she reeled, a bright light sped past her, like a golden thunderbolt streaking into the east. The raven took to the air with a wild cry and turned and hurtled away, pursued by the wild and wilful boy-god of the Shining Ones.

Branwen shook her head, clearing it of the evil that had threatened to infest it. The storm was almost upon them, mighty and magnificent and terrible. While she stood numbed by reverence and dread, the racing edge of the storm curled over Pengwern and with a noise like a thousand hissing snakes, the blizzard struck.

The howling snow came down over the battlefield in an obliterating white blanket, drowning everything that lay beneath. And although the violent snowfall did not strike the hilltop itself, the icy wind that brought it almost took Branwen off her feet.

She could see nothing in the valley save for the rolling clouds and the lashing snow. Above the roar of the snowstorm, she could hear men's voices crying out in fear. Closer by, Terrwyn neighed loudly as he struggled to his hooves, flicking his tail and turning his head from side to side as though trying to shake off some enchantment. The other horses were getting up, also, as were Branwen's companions – stumbling and blinking as though ripped from deep sleep to find the world utterly changed about them.

None of the Saxons that lay scattered on the hillside stirred. Caradoc had put a swift end to them, Branwen guessed.

'By the saints, what has happened here?' gasped Dera, staggering to Branwen's side.

'I called on Caradoc, and he came!' Branwen shouted above the storm. 'This is his work.'

'Such a storm!' gasped Aberfa. 'From nowhere, it would seem!'

'I thought the Shining Ones would not help us?' asked Iwan, staring at Branwen in amazement. 'Wasn't that what you were told?'

'Rhiannon said that the three that were bound to the

land could not help us!' called Branwen.

'And Caradoc is *not* bound to the land!' laughed Iwan, taking her by the shoulders. 'Well done, my barbarian princess!'

'But do not the warriors of the king suffer as badly as do the Saxons?' asked Banon. 'Will the blizzard know friend from foe? Who will have the upper hand when Caradoc's storm has passed over the land?'

'I do not know,' said Branwen, holding Iwan's hands for a moment in hers before turning back to stare down into the whirl of the snowstorm. 'Would that I could see! Would that I could find Ironfist in all this chaos and bring him to his end.'

'You shall find him,' said Rhodri, from behind Branwen. She turned and saw that he was holding Terrwyn's reins, and that there was a golden light in his eyes. 'Mount up, Branwen – your destiny lies below – go you and seek it!'

'That is madness,' said Dera. 'She will not be able to keep in the saddle in such weather.'

'She will,' Rhodri said with quiet assurance and command. He rested his hand on Terrwyn's muzzle and murmured some soft words close to the horse's head. 'There – he will not let you fall, and he will guide you true to your enemy, Branwen.'

She stepped forward, but felt Iwan's hand on her arm.

She turned her head to look into his worried face.

'Do not fear for me,' she reassured him. 'All will be well. I shall see you again before this day is done.'

He frowned. 'I hope so with all my heart,' he said. 'If you do not return safely to me, I shall be very angry with you, Branwen. I may never speak to you again!' He looked at Rhodri. 'But if harm befalls her, be warned I'll have harsh words for you, Druid − or whatever it is that you have become.'

'I cannot foresee what will happen between Branwen and Herewulf Ironfist, Iwan,' Rhodri said calmly. 'And it is too soon for me to know *what* I have become.' He turned his head slowly, looking at each of the Gwyn Braw in turn. 'But I do know this. None of you can go with her into the blizzard − it will be the death of you − Branwen must do this alone or not at all.'

'Then go with our blessings on you!' said Dera, resting her hand for a moment on Branwen's shoulder. Aberfa and Banon moved forward and briefly took her hands. Then Rhodri gave her Terrwyn's reins and stepped aside so that she could mount up.

She paused, looking into his face. 'Is it still you, my friend?' she asked him.

'It is,' replied Rhodri. 'But I am no longer half one thing and half another as I have been all my life, Branwen. I am complete − I am whole. I am *one*.' His brows creased. 'Beware the shield, Branwen, it can do great harm.'

She nodded, not quite sure what he meant by that, but determined to remember it.

She climbed into the saddle. Dera handed up her shield and sword.

She took one final look at her friends and companions before flicking the reins.

Terrwyn leaped forward, as though at the sound of battle horns. Branwen saw the faces of the Gwyn Braw blurring as she sped across the hill. She wished for a passing moment that she had thought to kiss Iwan one time before leaving him. Well, it was too late for such regrets, and if she came out alive from the storm, she could easily rectify her omission many times over.

Caradoc's ferocious snowstorm raged below her, filling her vision, drowning out all thought. Fighting against a rising terror, she clung on tightly as Terrwyn cantered over the edge of the world and took her, plunging down at a full gallop, into the devouring white throat of the blizzard.

CHAPTER TWENTY-SEVEN

Branwen was almost blinded by the whirling maelstrom, and it took all her strength to stay in the saddle as Terrwyn forged on, galloping deeper and deeper into the chaotic heart of Caradoc's snowstorm. As she rode, the pelting ice stung her face and hands, and she could feel it gathering in her hair and on her cloak, heavy and clinging, soaking through her clothes, weighing her down.

Above the shriek of the wind, she could hear voices – men crying out in fear, horses whinnying – the frantic tramp of hooves and the sound of running feet. And through the sheets of flying snow she saw blundering shapes – warriors stumbling this way and that, their backs stooped, their arms thrown up as they tried vainly to escape the blizzard's angry bite.

Banon had been right – the storm didn't know friend from foe. The winds bowled over the warriors of the Four

Kingdoms of Brython as readily as it did the Saxon enemy. Branwen saw tattered banners lying on the ground – the red dragon of her own folk wallowing in the slushy mud along with many white Saxon serpents.

Bodies lay scattered in their path, sombre proof of the slaughter that had already taken place. Even at the gallop, Terrwyn avoided treading on the dead, and when the heaps of corpses grew too dense, he slowed, his head nodding as he picked his way forward.

A new sound came to Branwen through the roaring wind, or rather, an *old* sound that she had not expected to hear. It was a single voice shouting defiance, accompanied by the clang of iron on iron. Even in all this madness, someone was still fighting!

'*Aet ic cempas! Aet ic garhéap!*'

She grinned a hard, fierce grin, baring her teeth. She knew that voice.

So, even in the very teeth of Caradoc's rage, Ironfist fought on undaunted!

Good! So much the better!

Terrwyn was moving slowly now, lifting his hooves high over the fallen warriors, searching for some clear space to walk on. Dead faces stared up at Branwen as they waded through the slain, the bearded faces of Saxons and the faces of her own menfolk with their heavy moustaches and shaven chins. Some were hacked about and bloody, others lay with gaping mouths and empty, sky-seeking eyes, pale and peaceful, or ashen and twisted in some final agony. Enemies in life they might have been, but they were comrades now in death as the snow began to drift and heap, mantling them in its chill cerements, hiding for a time the brutal horrors of warfare.

Now she saw movement through the snow – dark shapes darting to and fro around a tall figure that blazed at the centre with a wheel of pure white light.

Terrwyn paused, shaking snow out of his mane. Branwen leaned forward, puzzled by the circle of light, trying to make sense of what she was seeing.

And then it came to her, as though a veil had been drawn aside in her mind. The towering warrior at the heart of the action was Ironfist, and the white light that blossomed on his arm came from her own white shield! The mystic shield that had been gifted to her in the summer! The shield of the Worthy Champion.

Branwen knew from experience the protective powers of the white shield. It had saved her from certain death on Merion's mountain, when rocks had rained down all around her and the ground had broken under her feet. No arrow could hold in it, no sword or axe bite it. And Ironfist had taken it for his own – little wonder then that he was able to stand and fight in Caradoc's storm. The greater mystery to Branwen was how his opponents still had the courage and heart to throw themselves upon him.

But they would not fight on alone! She lifted her shield, gripping Terrwyn's reins in her fist. Tightening her thighs about his broad body, she raised her sword high.

'On!' she shouted. 'Onward to death or glory!'

Terrwyn burst forward, his head down, his great muscles knotting under her as he pounded towards Ironfist.

'The Shining Ones! The Shining Ones!' yelled Branwen as she bore down on her enemy. The warriors who had been surrounding Ironfist, split apart and ran, vanishing into the storm as she came careering through the teeming snow.

She saw Ironfist's lone eye widen in surprise. Then his mouth opened in a roar of anger and delight. 'The waelisc shaman girl!' he shouted. 'Beyond all hope you come to die by my hand!'

Branwen braced herself, her sword arm poised for a powerful downwards slash as she came up level with the great general. A single well-placed sweep of her sword and all would be over. His head would roll in the dirt.

But Ironfist was not so easily bested. He stepped aside as Terrwyn thundered forward, lifting his shield as Branwen brought her sword down.

The impact of her blade on the mystic shield numbed

her to the shoulder. She had feared her blow would be turned aside, but she had not expected such agony to explode up her arm. It was as if she had struck at a block of iron.

She rocked in the saddle, almost falling as Terrwyn galloped on past the general. Gathering herself, she pulled on the reins and Terrwyn slowed, rearing and neighing.

She turned him, trying to ignore the pain in her arm, trying to think of some way of getting through the Saxon general's guard.

He stood facing her, spread-legged, shouting, brandishing his sword while the shield burned on his arm like the winter sun.

Again Branwen urged Terrwyn on. Again she lifted her sword.

'You have something of mine, Thain Herewulf!' she shouted as Terrwyn gathered speed. 'I would have it back!'

He laughed. 'Then come and take it, witch girl! If you are able!'

'I come!' she cried. 'Be patient – I come!'

She was more cautious now, her eyes pinned to the shield as he lifted it. She must get in past it somehow. She must draw blood. Closer and closer, Terrwyn galloped. She would wait for Ironfist's sidestep, then she would lean low over her horse's neck and swing her sword down and around, slashing beneath the shield, opening up his belly and spilling his guts!

But Ironfist did not sidestep this time. He stood unmoving in Terrwyn's path, his feet braced, the white shield up to his ice-blue eye.

Too late, Branwen realized what was happening. At the last moment she yanked on the reins, trying to turn Terrwyn aside. But her brave steed's momentum carried him forward on to the white shield.

Ironfist withstood the charge as a hale old forest oak might withstand the futile butting of a young roe deer. Terrwyn was brought to a halt by the shield's power, and as he tumbled sideways, his hooves flailing and his mouth open wide in a scream of pain, Branwen was flung out of the saddle.

Ironfist slashed upwards at her as she was hurled through the air. The blow went wild, but she felt the point of his blade cut her upper arm, quick and shallow, as she was tossed on the wind.

She came crashing to the ground among a pile of the dead. For a few moments she was too stunned even to draw breath. Pain flooded her like black water. She could hardly close her fingers around her sword hilt. She could hardly move for the agony.

But a warrior's instinct took over. She turned painfully

on to her side and thence to her hands and knees, still holding her shield on her arm, still gripping her sword.

Terrwyn was lying still, maybe killed by the impact. Ironfist was stamping towards her through the ranks of the dead.

'What's this?' he howled. 'Still awake, pretty maiden? Then let me sing you to sleep!' He came at her faster now, the white shield up, his sword spinning in his hand.

Branwen forced herself on to her feet.

She tried to remember what Gavan ap Huw had taught her in the forest outside Doeth Palas when she had been green and impetuous and foolish. She tried to recall all that she had learned since, in a hundred battles, a hundred victories.

She dared not let Ironfist come upon her flat-footed. She had to bring the fight to him. Weight for weight, he could wear her down and crush her, even without the aid of the white shield. She had to rely on speed and agility.

She sprang forward, focused on the coming conflict, blotting out pain and fear, ignoring the snow that flew into her face, paying no attention to the slither of blood and gore under her feet or the congregation of dead eyes that stared up at her.

The white shield came up to Ironfist's eye as she darted forward. She brought her weight down on her left foot, feigning a blow that drew his shield instinctively to block her sword. But she changed her balance, coming in close, striking around his shield to the right, hoping to bite into flesh.

But he was too skilled a fighter to be caught out so easily. He twisted into her blow, cracking down on her sword with his shield and almost cutting her with a sharp swing of his sword to her neck. She sprang back out of danger, her shield to her eyes, the upper rim angled outwards, her sword arm lifted and bent so the sword ran along her back, ready for her to unleash all the power of her arm and shoulder when the moment was right.

'Good! Good!' crowed Ironfist, his single eye glinting. 'There's little to savour in a swift victory! Fight well, witch girl! Fight for your life!'

He threw himself at her, his sword bearing down on to her left shoulder. But she ducked, fending the blow off with her shield and bringing her own blade up to sweep his aside. His weight crashed against her, shield to shield, and she stumbled back. Again his sword flew to her shoulder, again she blocked it, dancing back and to one side, trying to sneak in under his shield arm, her aching leg muscles taut as she bobbed and wove, stabbing and withdrawing, stabbing and withdrawing.

She moved to the left then jinked to the right, bouncing on her feet, drawing him first one way and then the other, waiting for the moment when she could angle her sword in past his defences and score a hit. But always the white shield blocked her, always his sword whistled close to her head and she was forced to leap back to survive.

He loomed over her, swinging his sword in a great arc. She crouched low, so that his blow swept above her head. She stabbed at his feet and he pushed the shield down to keep her sword off. Quick as lightning she sprang up again, leaping into the air and bringing her sword down at an angle into his neck.

Roaring in anger, he thrust the shield up to buffet her sword away, but not before she had drawn blood. She pranced backwards, grinning, drops of blood flying from the edge of her blade.

But it was not a deep wound, and it enraged rather than hurt him.

She heard Gavan ap Huw's voice in her head.

Do not let your emotions rule you. The blood may be hot, but the mind must be always cool.

Branwen smiled grimly as the furious Saxon came at her, swinging wildly in his pain and ire, wasting energy as she skipped away from him, darting to the left and right as he stormed forward like a wounded bull.

But his rage did not last. Ironfist's attack became more measured, more wise. He struck from above and she deflected his sword with a twist of her wrist. Again and again he smote down on her, like a blacksmith forging iron. The power of his blows was gradually bleeding the strength out of her and she knew she could not afford to trade blows for much longer.

She lowered her sword, bringing her shield up instead to protect her shoulder. The edge of his sword bit deep into her shield while she swung her arm in a long low arc and snagged his ankle with her sword. She cursed that she had not struck a better blow – she had hoped to take his feet out from under him.

But now she was in danger – his sword was wedged in the rim of her shield and she could not pull free. She dropped to one knee, aiming for his legs again, but he was ready for her now. He brought his shield down hard, driving her sword into the ground. With a roar, he lifted the shield and hammered it down a second time – and now her sword broke halfway to the hilt.

And as she stumbled to her knees, the hilt slipping from her fingers, the white shield was brought up quick and vicious into her face. She was lifted to her feet by the power of his blow, her neck stretching, her head snapping back, pain filling her skull.

Her feet slipped from under her as her mind spun. She pivoted sideways, her left arm still trapped by the leather grips of her shield and the broken shield still snagged on Ironfist's sword.

She fell heavily, jarring her elbow and hip, spitting

blood from the blow to her face. Her arm slid free of her shield. She saw a flare of white from the corner of her eye as Ironfist hammered the shield down on to her head and shoulder, beating her to the ground.

She could not think for the pain. She could not get up for the fatigue that wracked her body. All she could see was a red fog dotted with fleeting flecks of white snow.

Ironfist's foot came down on her chest, crushing her to the ground. She flailed with her arms, praying to feel a fallen weapon under her scrabbling fingers. Praying for a miracle.

She stared upwards with swimming eyes. Ironfist towered over her. He leaned to the right and beat her shield on the ground until his sword came free. She felt his foot grinding down on her breastbone, making it impossible for her to breathe. She saw him lift his sword above her face, the point aiming down towards her eyes.

A thousand images of her life wheeled in front of her eyes – the good and the bad and the wonderful and the terrible – changing rapidly as the blood pounded in her temples. And echoing the beat of her blood was a word, growing out of the confusion, filling her head.

Caliburn. Caliburn. Caliburn.

Pulsing in her mind, louder and louder as the world began to drift away.

. . . call for Caliburn when all is lost . . .

She had no breath in her body. She could not call – she could not even speak. But her lips formed the word and she let it out silently into the snowbound world.

'. . . Caliburn . . .'

'What's this?' growled Ironfist, leaning closer. 'Do you beg for mercy, witch girl? I cannot hear you.'

'. . . Caliburn . . .'

The pressure lifted a little from her chest and she was able to gulp in air at last.

She stared up into the Saxon general's scarred face. 'Caliburn!' she gasped. 'Caliburn!'

He stared at her for a moment, then he lifted his sword arm again. 'Enough of this,' he said. 'Let's put an end to you!'

But before his blow could fall, a blast of thunder rocked the world, almost shaking him off his feet. And as he tottered and flailed for balance, a shaft of lightning came flashing down with a fearsome scream, striking the ground only a few paces from where Branwen lay, exploding in a ball of blinding light.

When the flare of the lightning bolt was gone, a sword jutted out of the scorched ground. A sword that shone like silver, a sword with a hilt that glittered with gold. A sword that radiated light like the noonday sun.

In a daze, she got to her feet and stepped over to the sword. Its blade was sunken into stone. She took hold of the hilt, vaguely aware of Ironfist's voice shouting behind her.

She tightened her grip on the sword and pulled it out of the stone, the shimmering blade ringing like bells as it came free.

She turned, holding the sword up – holding Caliburn like a blade of pure light. Ironfist threw himself at her, the white shield up, his sword swinging.

Effortlessly, Branwen swung the sword. It clove through Ironfist's descending blade as though through a willow wand, sending sparks flying. Effortlessly, the sword danced over the rim of the white shield. Effortlessly it took Herewulf Ironfist's head from his neck.

The great body crashed down at Branwen's feet, the white shield flying from the limp arm, rising into the air, spinning like a wheel.

She lifted her left arm and the white shield came to her.

And as she stared down at the dead body of her old enemy, the blizzard ceased and the storm clouds lifted and the midday sun shone down on her.

CHAPTER TWENTY-EIGHT

All around Branwen, stunned and frightened warriors were picking themselves up and staggering ankle deep through the impossible snow while horses stood shivering, or galloped away over the battlefield with their reins flying.

The dead and wounded were mantled in the fresh snow, but already blood was staining the whiteness and in places it had become pools of red slush from which jutted broken spears and shield rims and clawing dead fingers.

Above the field of carnage, the sky was blue. To the north a tail of dark cloud flicked for a moment as it fell below the horizon.

Branwen walked forward in a daze, the shield of Cudyll Bach on her left arm, the sword Caliburn in her right fist. She stood over the fallen head of Herewulf Ironfist, one time Thain of Winwaed, commander of

King Oswald's armies.

She heard voices around her. Angry voices.

'*Awyrigende waelisc galdere!*'

'*Astyrfan awyrigende!*'

She glanced around herself, seeing Saxon warriors moving towards her from all sides. She slung her shield over her back and stooped. She grasped Ironfist's head by the hair and raised it high. She turned slowly in a circle, showing the bloody trophy to the advancing warriors – showing them their dead general.

They hesitated, watching her with eyes filled with hate and fear.

'I am Branwen of the Shining Ones!' she howled. 'I am the shaman girl of the waelisc! I am the witch girl of Pengwern! Fly from here if you value your lives!'

She did not know if any of them understood her words – but she knew they would respond to the deadly and ruthless tone in her voice.

The ring of Saxons wavered as she stood defying them. One or two turned and ran. Others followed. Soon they were all running, running hard to the north, throwing down their weapons, slithering and sliding on the snow, trampling the slain in their panic.

And as they ran, Branwen heard war horns blowing from within the walls of Pengwern.

Grimacing with distaste, she released the grisly head,

watching dispassionately as the Saxons fled. Like ripples in a lake, the word was spreading across the battlefield. 'Ironfist is dead! The shaman girl killed him! The witch girl brought the storm down upon us! Run! Run for your lives!'

The whole wide field was alive now with fleeing Saxons. Bands of King Cynon's warriors pursued them, some on foot, others mounted, whooping and shouting and cutting down any who lagged behind. A troop of riders came bursting from the ruined and charred gateway, and Branwen saw the gallant standard of the king being carried along with them.

The blizzard had doused the flames, and of the evil black raven and the golden boy-god there was no sign. Whether Caradoc had brought Ragnar to his doom, or whether the hellion of the Saxons had escaped, Branwen could not know.

She lifted the marvellous sword up in front of her eyes. There was no blood upon its burnished blade, and as she looked closely she saw her reflection staring back at her from the slender strip of metal, as clear as if she was looking into still water. She gazed mesmerized into her own eyes, hardly recognizing herself – hardly able to believe that she was looking into the face of Branwen ap Griffith.

She heard a snort and the thud of hooves close by. She

broke free of the enchantment of the sword and turned as Terrwyn thrust this heavy head against her shoulder. She slipped the sword into her belt and threw her arms around the horse's wide neck, pressing her face into his coat for a moment of comfort.

'I thought you were dead,' she murmured. 'I thought the whole world was dead.'

She was still pressed up against Terrwyn's soft hide when other hoofbeats sounded and joyful voices called out to her.

'You are alive!'

Yes. I am alive. It is strange and I cannot quite believe it – but I am alive!

'Beyond all hopes, Branwen! Beyond *all* hope!'

'And see – the great general is dead!'

Branwen turned, smiling as the Gwyn Braw leaped down from their horses and threw themselves upon her with wild delight. As she embraced them, she saw Rhodri standing slightly apart, smiling, too, but with a deep sadness in his eyes.

'I knew you would not come to harm,' said Iwan, his eyes shining as he looked at her. 'Fate could not be so cruel!'

'Fate can be cruel enough, Iwan,' she said, pushing past her friends and going to stand in front of Rhodri. For a brief time they looked silently into one another's eyes. 'I would give my life if it would restore Blodwedd to you,' she murmured at last, for his ears only. 'You know that, don't you?'

He nodded.

'Can you love me still, Rhodri, after what I did?'

His eyes glimmered with unshed tears. 'Would I lose my dearest friend as well as my true love?' he whispered, his voice cracking. 'No, be sure, Branwen – our lives are bound together a while longer yet.'

'I called on Caliburn, as you said I should – and it came to me,' she told him, sliding the silken sword from her belt and showing it to him. 'Where does it come from, Rhodri? What is it?'

He frowned. 'I cannot tell you,' he said. 'But it is not yours, Branwen. It belongs to another.'

'Ahh. So this is the sword that Blodwedd spoke of. I thought it was so, but I could not be sure. It belongs to the other Chosen One – the boy. Must I take it to him now? Do you know where I might find him?'

'All things in their right time,' said Rhodri, gazing out past her shoulder. 'The king of Powys comes – you should speak with him, I think.'

Branwen narrowed her eyes. 'Oh, I shall do that, Rhodri! I shall certainly do that!' She turned, her face tight with anger. Several riders were approaching. Above them flew the king's standard.

She searched the faces of the mounted warriors, puzzled not to see Cynon among them. Prince Drustan she recognized, and Dagonet ap Wadu, and other captains of Pengwern and warriors of Dyfed, Gwynedd and Gwent. But of the king, she saw no trace.

The horses were reined up and Drustan dismounted. There was blood on his face and his cloak was torn, but he seemed otherwise unhurt.

'My people quailed when the fireball came blazing across the sky towards us,' he called, his eyes bright and eager as he strode towards her through the snow. 'But I saw how it dismayed that great black bird of ill omen. I saw how the demon of the Saxons fled before it! And I knew in my heart that you had returned to us, Princess Branwen.' He glanced around them. 'And this unimaginable snowstorm – that was your doing also, I am sure.' He shook his head. 'A powerful shaman, you are, Princess. You command formidable sorceries, indeed. I understand now why my father feared you, although I think he was wrong to do so.'

'What of the king?' demanded Branwen. 'Is he afraid to face me, after the treachery he worked upon me?'

Drustan looked solemnly at her. 'My father is dead,' he said. 'He led the first charge from the citadel and was cut down by many Saxon warriors as he fought to prevent them crossing the causeway. Prince Llew is also among the slain, as are Captain Angor and many another brave warrior of Doeth Palas.' Drustan looked steadily at her. 'I owe you a blood-debt, Branwen of the Gwyn Braw. You have done nothing but good for us, and we have treated you shamefully.' His eyes flashed. 'Be assured that the new king of Powys will ever be your friend, Branwen of the Shining Ones.'

Branwen gazed at him, not quite able to grasp the reality of what he had told her. King Cynon dead? And Llew ap Gelert too? She had always imagined that she and the prince of Bras Mynydd would face one another at sword's length before the feud between them was ended. But he had been killed, after all, defending the land he had tried to betray. There was at least some strange kind of justice in that.

Her attention was taken from Drustan as Dagonet ap Wadu came forward, bowing his head to her. 'For my part in your betrayal, I offer you my atonement,' he said. 'I was too ready to listen to the whispered words of the prince of Bras Mynydd – as was my king.' He looked into her eyes. 'We were wrong to do so.'

'You were!' said Dera, trembling as she confronted her father, her dark eyes burning with outrage. 'You should throw yourself upon the ground and beg her mercy for your actions! It was base and it was wrong!'

'A warrior cannot question the commands of his

king, Dera,' Drustan said mildly. 'Forgive your father, as you would forgive all those who believed in Prince Llew's twisted counsel.' He looked out over the battlefield, his forehead creased in sorrow. 'Much damage has been done this day, and some can never be put right. But in one thing the new king of Powys will not fail.' He looked at Branwen. 'You will be honoured, Princess, and you will have for ever a high place among my counsellors. I will have my captains search the fallen and see if any can be saved. The rest shall be laid to rest, be they warrior of Brython or of Mercia. In the meantime, I will hold true to the pledge between my father and the prince of Bras Mynydd. I will wed the daughter of Llew ap Gelert and our children will rule in Powys for a hundred generations.' He reached out his hand to her. 'Come, Branwen. Enter the citadel at my side. You and all the Gwyn Braw with you. I promise that you will receive the welcome you deserve – for it is by your hand and the hands of those great ones you follow that we have won this victory today.'

'I will go with you, King Drustan,' said Branwen. 'I will enter Pengwern with my people, because they deserve warmth and rest and comfort after all they have been through. But as for the rest – as for a seat at your right hand – well . . . that is something I cannot promise. My destiny may make other demands on me.' She glanced at Rhodri. He was watching her closely, but his expression was unreadable. 'For I am Destiny's Child,' she continued, 'and my burdens and my duties go beyond the kingdom of Powys!'

'So be it,' said the new king, and they all mounted and with slow, sombre dignity rode together across the battlefield and in through the burned gates of Pengwern.

CHAPTER TWENTY-NINE

Branwen stood upon the ramparts of Pengwern, gazing northwards and thinking of her mother. Of Caradoc's storm, all trace had gone; the snow melted away, the freezing wind abated. But it was bitter cold all the same, and Branwen stared out over a bleak winter landscape of mud and brown earth and bare black trees.

Three days had passed since the battle had been won. Three days filled with hard, bitter toil. Too many had died on the battlefield for the survivors to rejoice in their victory, and the manner of their delivery from the Saxons was too uncanny for them to feel at ease with it. But at least Branwen and the Gwyn Braw were saved the outright hostility of former times. As fearsome as the witch girl might be, and as dreadful were the gods she followed, she had proved herself an invincible enemy of the Saxons.

And so Branwen and the Gwyn Braw had helped the

people of Pengwern to try and put back together the fragments of their shattered lives. There was silence and awe as they passed, but the hatred and rancour were gone.

Riders had been sent out, north, east and south, and they had returned with good news. Not a Saxon could be found west of the River Dee, and those who rode furthest and sought hardest learned that General Ironfist's great army had fallen to pieces. The levies had fled back to their homes and the captains had ridden north to give the grievous news to the king of Northumbria. His general was dead. His dreams of conquest were done.

The burned gate towers of Pengwern had been pulled down and the timber used to make a great pyre upon which King Cynon and Prince Llew had been burned. Lesser fires had taken the rest of the dead, while Rhodri and the physicians of Pengwern worked tirelessly to save those that could be saved, and to give some measure of peace to those who could not.

New towers were already under construction, trees being felled on the western hill and the timbers being shaped and cut while new postholes were dug for the founding piles.

Now a kind of heart-sore quiet had come over the citadel – a storm-wrecked stillness, as though the stunned soul of Pengwern had succumbed at last to a much-needed sleep. In a few days the citadel of the king of

Powys would reawaken for the wedding of Drustan and Meredith, but on this cold and blustery winter's day, all Branwen could do was clutch her cloak close around her body and stare longingly at the northern horizon and wish for home.

'It's a cold morning to be admiring the view, Branwen.' Startled from her daydreams, Branwen turned at the sound of Meredith's voice. The young princess stood swathed in a long, thick ermine cloak with a deep hood that left only her pale face visible.

'How is your sister?' Branwen asked. She had not seen the two girls since the funeral of their father. Romney had been inconsolable as the consuming flames had leaped, clinging to Meredith and weeping as though her tears had no end.

'She is as you would expect,' sighed Meredith, stepping up to stand at Branwen's side. 'She loved our father with all her heart.' She glanced sidelong at Branwen. 'They were very similar,' she said. 'Stubborn, proud and headstrong.' She paused as though weighing her words. 'Not always wise in their choices. Not always fair.'

Branwen looked at her, not sure how to respond.

'I have had long talks with Drustan these past days,' Meredith continued. 'We are both the children of great fathers, but we are not like them.' Her eyes burned into Branwen's face. 'I am not like my father, and Drustan is not like his father. I wanted you to know that.'

Branwen nodded.

Meredith's voice softened. 'My father was not a traitor, Branwen,' she said. 'I will never believe he was a traitor. He died fighting for Powys.'

'He did,' Branwen agreed, although she could have said a great deal more.

'Drustan would like you to stay here,' Meredith said. 'Will you stay?'

'I don't think so.'

Meredith bit her lip, her hand slipping from her cloak to touch Branwen's arm. 'Stay,' she said. 'If not for our sakes, then for your own. The gods you worship will destroy you, Branwen, I am sure of it.'

'I do not *worship* them,' Branwen murmured. 'And do you forget how you were saved by one of those gods?'

'No, I don't forget,' Meredith replied. 'But fire is a friend when tamed and a great foe when set loose. You do not control these powers, Branwen, and I fear you will be burned to death by them.'

'Perhaps,' said Branwen.

'The Saxon menace is gone,' Meredith persisted. 'Be at peace now with us. What more could the Old Powers ask of you?'

Branwen thought of the white shield and the silvery sword that lay together on her bed in the long house of the Gwyn Braw. She said nothing.

Meredith frowned. 'I know you follow a great destiny, Branwen,' she said. 'But if you cannot stay, where will it take you next? Do you know?'

'I'm waiting,' Branwen said quietly.

'Waiting? Waiting for what?'

A bleak smile curled Branwen's lips. 'For a sign,' she said. 'Rhodri is sure it will come soon. He has told me as much.'

'What sign?'

'The young bear,' whispered Branwen. 'I'm waiting to follow the young bear.'

It was in the deep dark of the night before the wedding day of King Drustan and Princess Meredith that Branwen was awoken by a hand on her shoulder.

Rhodri leaned over her, a rushlight illuminating his face. 'Come,' he said softly. 'I have something to show you. Bring your sword and shield.'

She dressed in warm clothes, slinging the shield over her shoulder and sliding the glowing sword into her belt. Following Rhodri, she studied for a moment each of her sleeping companions. Fearless Dera with her mass of black hair half covering her face. Banon, lying on her front with her long limbs sprawling and her red hair glowing like fire. Iwan. He looked so innocent, lying there asleep. Too handsome for his own good. Too clever. And Aberfa, lying on her back, snoring like a boar. She loved them all.

She slipped silently out the door in Rhodri's wake.

The moon was full and round in the sky, so bright that it cast shadows on the ground. Rhodri took her to the southern ramparts, putting his arm around her shoulders and pointing over the walls of the citadel.

'What do you see?' he asked.

'Nothing,' she said, shivering a little in the chill. 'Shadows, that's all.'

'Look more closely.'

Now she saw it. A small dark shape that she had taken to be no more than a boulder, some fifty or sixty paces from the walls, close by a bend in the River Hefren. She leaned forward, narrowing her eyes. The shape moved, lifting a blunt head, the long snout turning from side to side. Then it rose clumsily on to its haunches and she knew for certain that it was a young bear.

A sudden sense of fear and loss pierced her. She gripped Rhodri's hand. 'Must I?' she asked, her voice thick with misery. 'Do I have no choice?'

'You always have a choice, Branwen,' Rhodri replied.

'Then I choose to throw this shield and this sword into the river,' she said bitterly. 'I choose to go north. I choose to return to Garth Milain and be with my mother.

There! It is done – I have made my choice.'

Rhodri nodded. 'Very well,' he said.

She frowned at him. 'As easily as that?'

'I am not your keeper, Branwen. I will guide you if you wish it, and I will stand aside if not.'

'Then stand aside! I'm going back to bed, and tomorrow I will attend the wedding of the king, and when that is done I will take Terrwyn and ride north and be free of destiny for ever.'

Rhodri said nothing.

'This is no jest, my friend!' she insisted. 'I am done with hardship and strife.' She turned from the walls and walked steadily away from him.

After a few paces, she halted and turned back. 'What will you do?' she called softly.

'I don't know.' His eyes seemed very large as she looked into his face. 'You still have the sword and shield, Branwen. Weren't you going to throw them into the river?'

She ran back to him and stood quivering in front of him. 'I hate this!' she cried.

'I know.'

'I want to go home.'

'Who's to say you won't?' Rhodri asked gently.

'But first I must follow my destiny, is that it?'

'If you choose.'

She frowned at him, holding back her anger. 'Who is this boy?' she asked. 'This other Chosen One? Is he like me? Does *he* have a choice?'

'The same choice given to you,' said Rhodri. 'Except that your choices will touch him, whether he wills it or not.' He nodded at the sword glimmering in her belt. 'This belongs to him, Branwen.'

'And if I do not give it to him?'

'No one is told what would have happened at the end of a path not taken,' said Rhodri.

'But will he do great things if I give him the sword?'

'Yes. You both will.'

'And will he be able to do them if not?'

Rhodri didn't answer.

'Then I have the same choice as I have always had,' said Branwen. 'The choice between doing good and doing as I would wish.'

'We all must make that choice,' said Rhodri.

She rested her hand on the sword hilt. It felt warm under her fingers. She had noticed that about it before – even in the worst cold, the silvery sword was always warm.

'Will you come with me?' she asked.

'If you wish it.'

'The others deserve to be spared this quest,' she said. 'They would come willingly if I asked, and I think they might follow me even if I told them to stay behind.'

'Terrwyn and another horse are saddled and ready,' said Rhodri.

She arched an eyebrow. 'Are they, indeed? Am I so predictable then, Rhodri?'

'The moon is high and there are no gates to bar our exit from Pengwern,' Rhodri said. 'The young bear is waiting. If you wish it, we can leave now.'

'The two of us together alone as it was in the beginning?' said Branwen.

'The two of us together alone.'

'Shall I ever see any of them again?' she asked with a deep pang of sadness and loss. 'Shall I ever see Iwan again?'

'I cannot say.'

Branwen linked her arm with his as they turned and walked away from the walls. 'I hope I shall see him again,' she said, barely above a whisper. 'There is something I need to tell him – something I want him to know.'

Silent as ghosts, the two friends slipped into the stable and led their horses out across the deserted courtyards of Pengwern. They took the path down from the ramparts and into the bailey where the half-rebuilt gate towers stood stark and white under the moon.

Branwen ached with the weight of her destiny. To

have done so much only to be given another task seemed cruel beyond belief. And to know that she was leaving Iwan to awake and find her gone was perhaps hardest of all to endure. If he felt about her the way she believed he did. As she felt about him.

They mounted and rode around to the southern palisade of the citadel.

The young bear stood on a low mound, its eyes shining green with moonlight as it stared towards them.

It turned, ambling away, and they rode after it, side by side in the still night.

But they had not gone far when a sound behind them made Branwen turn in the saddle.

It was the rapid pulse of hoofbeats.

She frowned as she saw a rider chasing after them at speed.

'I had the feeling I would not be rid of him so easily!' sighed Rhodri.

'Who?' asked Branwen, trying to make out the face of the approaching horseman. And then she did see his face, and her heart leaped. He was grinning as he came alongside them, reining his horse up sharply.

'Praise the saints that I am a light sleeper!' he said. 'You'd have got away from me else!'

'Iwan, don't try to stop me,' pleaded Branwen. 'I must go. I *have* to.'

'Of course you do,' Iwan replied. 'But I cannot leave you all alone with this dull-witted and gloomy Druid!' He leaned forward over his horse's neck, smiling at her with shining eyes. 'Where you go, barbarian princess, I must go, too. If you will have me.'

'I will,' said Branwen, her heart filling with gladness. 'Yes, Iwan, I will have you.'

A haunting yowling cry sounded from ahead of them. 'The young bear becomes impatient,' said Rhodri.

'Then let's not keep him waiting!' said Branwen, flicking the reins so that Terrwyn broke into a canter. 'Let's follow destiny's path together and see where it leads.'

And so, with the night wind rushing in her ears and the moon shining down on her and with her two fond companions riding at her side, Branwen ap Griffith, Branwen the shaman girl, Branwen of the Shining Ones went flying southwards to new and unknown adventures.